LOVE BLOOMS AT MERMAIDS POINT

SARAH BENNETT

Boldwood

For M, who is the inspiration behind every hero x

CHARACTER LIST

Alex Nelson. Tom's half-brother, Emily and Max's uncle, son of Archie and Philippa Nelson. Former accountant, secret author of the bestselling novel *The Marriage Roller Coaster*. Hero of *Love Blooms at Mermaids Point*.

Alun Wise. Local estate agent.

Andrew Morgan. Married to Sylvia, Laurie and Nick's father. Owner of The Mermaids Cave, a large gift shop on the seafront.

Anna Nelson. Tom's late wife and mother to Emily and Max.

Archie Nelson. Tom and Alex's father. Married to Philippa, grandfather of Emily and Max. Known in the family as 'Pop'.

Aurora Storm. Pop star who staged a number of mermaid sightings around the Point as part of a viral campaign for her comeback album. Had a very brief fling with Nick Morgan while she was in the village.

Barbara Mitchell. Part of the local knitting circle. Lives with Malcolm Gadd.

Ben. Married to Tracy who works in the local solicitor's office.

Bev. Part of the local knitting circle, known to have a sharp tongue.

Carlotta. Barbara Mitchell's cat.

Danny. A P.R. rep who works at Alex Nelson's publisher.

Emily Nelson. Tom and Anna's 15 year-old daughter.

Henry 'Harry' Davenport Jnr. The village's local solicitor and an old school friend of Ivy, Laurie and Nick.

Henry Davenport Snr. Harry's uncle, now retired and living in Portugal.

Immy. Alex Nelson's editor.

Ivy Fisher. Runs a small business from home where she does repairs and alterations. Like a one-woman version of *The Repair Shop*. Laurie's best friend. Heroine of *Love Blooms at Mermaids Point*.

Jake Smith. Investigative journalist currently working on a non-fiction book about county lines drug smuggling. Hero of *Summer Kisses at Mermaids Point*.

Jen Fisher. Ivy's mother, recently deceased after a long illness.

Jo Nelson. Alex's ex-wife.

Keith. Works on a fishing trawler. Patient at the surgery.

Kevin Fisher. Ivy's father and Jen's ex-husband. Lives in the village, though he and Ivy are long estranged.

Kitty Duke. Part of the local knitting circle. A darling.

Leonard Cavendish. Owner of the local bookshop who is hoping to retire.

Linda Smith. Jake's mother and a close friend of Nerissa's. Recently widowed.

Lindsey. Member of the marketing team at Alex Nelson's publisher.

Lorelai 'Laurie' Morgan. Runs a café next door to her parent's gift shop. Heroine of *Summer Kisses at Mermaids Point*.

Luca. Owns and runs the local delicatessen. Married to Maria.

Lucy aka Lucifer. Mr Cavendish's cat. Hangs around the bookshop. Alex's nemesis.

Malcolm Gadd. Mermaids Point's former doctor, known to everyone as 'Doc'. Mostly retired. Lives with Barbara Mitchell.

Maria. Runs the local delicatessen with her husband, Luca.

Maureen Wise. Married to Alun, the local estate agent.

Max Nelson. Tom and Anna's 12 year-old son.

Nerissa Morgan. Andrew's younger sister, paternal aunt of Laurie and Nick. Heroine of *Second Chances at Mermaids Point*.

Nick Morgan. Runs a tourist boat business from the Point's commercial harbour with his and Laurie's uncle, Tony. Still pining for Aurora Storm.

Pete Bray. Landlord of The Sailor's Rest, a popular pub on the seafront. Owns the Penny Arcade a few doors down from the pub.

Philippa Nelson. Archie's wife, Alex's mother and Tom's stepmother. Step-grandmother to Emily and Max. Known in the family as 'Mimi'.

Reverend Steele. Mermaids Point's vicar.

Shaun. Alex Nelson's former friend. Had an affair with Jo, which led to the break-up of Alex and Jo's marriage.

Sylvia Morgan. Married to Andrew, Laurie and Nick's mother. Runs The Mermaids Cave with her husband as well as working part-time at the village school as a classroom assistant.

Toby. Tom and Nerissa's golden retriever.

Tom Nelson. Widower of Anna, and father to Emily and Max. The village doctor. Hero of *Second Chances at Mermaids Point*.

Tony Evans. Sylvia's brother and maternal uncle of Laurie and Nick. Owner of Mermaid Boat Tours, a pleasure boat business, which takes tourists on trips around the area and out to the Seven Sisters, a group of nearby islands.

Tracy. Harry Davenport's secretary at the solicitor's office. Married to Ben.

Wendy Hancock. Kevin Fisher's long-term girlfriend. Works in the local greengrocer's.

1

One step at a time, darling. Ivy Fisher touched her fingers to the pretty cameo brooch pinned to the collar of her bottle-green velvet jacket as her mother's words came back to her. They'd planned today down to the last detail, Jen Fisher determined to shoulder as much of the burden of her own funeral as possible in the final weeks of her life. She'd chosen everything from the simple wicker coffin to the flowers, and even the readings she wanted. It had been almost unbearable for Ivy at first, until she'd realised her mother's motivation had come from a place of love, as well as a need to control something – anything – while her body failed her more with every passing day. Ivy had been grateful for it in the immediate aftermath once Jen slipped away into her final long sleep. There'd been no demands on Ivy to make decisions because everything had already been settled. The undertaker was able to take control and leave her largely in peace while he notified the florist and liaised with Reverend Steele about a suitable date for the funeral. She patted the brooch again – it was another one of her mother's choices – and managed a wan smile towards her reflection before turning away. One of the things she'd promised her mum was that she would wear a piece from Jen's extensive jewellery collection every day, and smile when she put it on.

The doorbell rang. *What now?* Ivy closed her eyes for a second as she drew in a deep breath and braced herself for yet another well-wisher. The fridge and freezer were already stuffed full of meals friends of her mother's had dropped around, as though Ivy were a child incapable of taking care of herself. It had all been meant with kindness, so she'd set aside the mild aggravation and accepted everything with grateful thanks. As she descended the narrow stairs of the little cottage, the competing scents of a dozen or more different bouquets hit her like a sickly-sweet cloud. She'd run out of vases, even the borrowed ones that Sylvia Morgan had dropped round, and the last couple of bunches she'd received rested inelegantly in a plastic bucket next to the little hall table. Condolence cards covered every surface, and dangled, perhaps inappropriately, from a wall hanger her mum had usually used for Christmas cards. It was that or leave them stacked on the mantelpiece, which felt disrespectful.

Taking one more deep breath, Ivy fixed a smile she didn't feel to her lips and pulled open the front door. 'Hell...oh!' She froze in surprise at the sight of the man on her doorstep as much as from the frigid blast of the cold, January wind.

'Hello, yourself,' Alex Nelson said with a smile. He looked almost unrecognisable in a smart pinstripe suit complete with a waistcoat and a dark woollen overcoat. Like so many others he'd sent a card and some flowers after her mum passed. It was a thoughtful gesture given their brief acquaintance, and she'd been touched by it. He'd started growing his beard again, she noticed, although it was neat and cropped close to his skin rather than the wild bush he'd cultivated for a while. It gave his face a sober, more serious air that was only enhanced by his formal clothing. He looked older, much more of a man than the overgrown boyishness she was familiar with.

'What are you doing here?' Ivy raised a hand to cover her mouth, but it was too late to stop the blurted question.

Alex smiled then, looking much more like himself as he extended his arms at his sides. 'I'm your designated shoulder for the day.'

'My what?' Another gust of freezing air chose to make itself felt at that moment, ruffling the short strands of Alex's neat brown hair and cutting through the heavy material of Ivy's ankle-length black skirt as though it were thin as silk.

'Get inside, before you freeze to death.' Not sure she liked his proprietorial tone, Ivy nevertheless found herself stepping back as Alex all but shooed her inside then followed her into the hall. 'That's better,' he said, as he pushed the door closed behind him. 'First things first, where's the kettle?'

Speechless, Ivy gestured behind her in the general direction of the kitchen. She watched in silence as Alex shrugged out of his winter coat and hung it on the hook beside the black cape and matching cloche hat she'd put there ready for the short walk to the village church. She'd told the undertaker she didn't need a car. Her mum had left the cottage they'd shared all of Ivy's life with a smile and that was how she wanted to think of her, not cold and silent in the back of a hearse. Laurie and Jake were due in a bit to walk with her up the hill, but everyone else was going directly to the church. Thinking of them, she automatically checked her watch, even though she could feel every slow minute counting down in her heart.

'There's plenty of time,' Alex assured her in a gentle voice. 'You can leave everything to me.'

'What are you doing here?' She couldn't help asking again.

He shrugged. 'I felt so bloody bad when Tom broke the news

about your mum the other week. I haven't been able to stop thinking about you having to face today on your own, so I decided to do something about it. I know you've got Laurie and everyone else, but they all knew your mum and will be struggling with their own feelings today. I don't have that same connection to her, that same sense of loss...' He frowned as his words trailed off, the first sign of uncertainty he'd shown since she opened the door. 'I should've asked you, shouldn't I? Rather than just pitching up here. I'm sorry.'

He'd come all the way from London just to stand by her side? A hot rush of tears burned behind her eyes, and she raised a hand to fan her face, trying to chase them away.

Alex's expression shifted from doubtful to pained. 'Oh, bloody hell, now I've made you cry, which was the last thing I wanted. I'm sorry, I've totally screwed this up, I'll go.'

He'd already unhooked his coat before Ivy managed to gather herself enough to reach for his arm. 'Stay.' It came out a croak around the lump in her throat, but it was enough to stop him.

White-faced, Alex stared down at her. 'Are you sure?'

She gulped, swallowed, then nodded. 'Yes.'

Colour flooded back into his face together with a look of relief. 'Okay, let's start again.' He opened his arms. 'I'm so sorry about your mum, and I want to do everything I can to help you through today.'

Without a moment's hesitation, Ivy stepped into his offered embrace, her hands rising to grip the lapels of his suit jacket as she rested her cheek over the strong, steady beat of his heart. Tension drained from her, like water from an overfilled bath when the plug was pulled out just in time. Alex closed his arms around her, cradling her close, but there was a gentleness in his hold that told her he'd let her go at the slightest indication. She closed her eyes, feeling at peace for the first time in days. No, it was more like months, if not years. Since her father had walked away when she'd been barely a teen, Ivy hadn't felt able to lean on anyone like this, wanting only to be strong for her mum. 'Thank you.'

There was a fleeting brush of his lips against the hair that she'd tried to tame into something less flamboyant than her usual cap of riotous red curls before his arms dropped away. 'Fancy a cuppa?'

Still gripping the front of his jacket, Ivy tipped her face up and met his hazel eyes. As intimate as it was to be standing so close to this man who was still more of a stranger than a friend, there was nothing in his gaze beyond a tender concern. 'That sounds good.' Willing her fingers to unclench, she took a step back before reaching out to try and brush the wrinkles she'd made in the fabric of his jacket. 'Oh, I'm sorry.'

'Leave it, it's fine.' Alex clasped her hands between his own, forcing her to stop. 'You don't need to apologise for anything – not today. I'm braced and ready for whatever the day brings. Tears, snot, make-up smears, the lot.'

A flash of white teeth in the darkness of his beard had her own lips tugging up at the corners. 'Snot?' She laughed. 'Are you sure?'

Releasing her hands, he raised a finger and tapped the tip of her nose. 'How bad can it be coming from something so small?' He reached into both of his trouser pockets and pulled out a pair of neatly folded white handkerchiefs. 'I've got a spare one in the inside pocket of my coat, too. I am fully snot-proofed.'

She shook her head at his antics, amazed at the lightness he'd managed to conjure in her heart on this, the heaviest of days. 'Idiot.'

'So harsh.' He gave her a look that was all sad puppy-dog eyes as he tucked the handkerchiefs away once more and she couldn't stifle another laugh. His expression flashed back to a cheeky grin. 'Right, let's get that cup of tea sorted, shall we?'

* * *

Still a little shell-shocked, Ivy found herself perched on a stool at the little breakfast bar Andrew Morgan had installed for them the summer after her father had moved out. He'd just shown up one day, toolbox in hand, and told her mum he was there to sort out whatever jobs needed doing. Married to Sylvia, her mother's best friend, he'd known both her parents all his life, and had been friends with her father, Kevin, since their school days. Nothing had ever been said, well, not in Ivy's presence at any rate, but both Andrew and Sylvia had made it clear where their loyalties lay and had stepped in where they felt they were needed.

Alex moved around the kitchen with that same sense of self-assurance she always got from him, though this was a much-muted version of the man who'd flirted with her at their first meeting, and teased her at their second over pre-Christmas drinks. He filled the kettle then started opening and closing cupboards as he hunted out what he was looking for. Two mugs were soon joined by a teaspoon from the cutlery drawer and the floral caddy that her mum used to store the teabags. *Had used.* God, she was never going to get used to thinking of her in the past tense. She pinched the fleshy pad of her palm until the threatening rush of tears was stemmed.

'Sugar?' Alex asked, his eyes thankfully still fixed on the contents of the cupboard where Ivy kept all her baking ingredients.

Clearing her throat a touch, Ivy was relieved her voice sounded relatively normal when she replied: 'Just a splash of milk, please.' Maybe she should've been more concerned about the way he was rooting around without asking, but it was just nice to have someone taking care of her, even for a few minutes. Grateful for the momentary distraction, she held her peace and watched with a growing sense of amusement as he continued to explore even after accumulating everything he needed to make the tea.

'Did you manage anything for breakfast?' It was asked without judgement, just a tone of understanding so warm Ivy wanted to wrap it around herself like a cosy quilt.

'I had a couple of digestives with a cup of tea,' she admitted.

'Do you think you could manage a few mouthfuls of this if I make it?' Alex turned towards her, holding an instant porridge pot in his hand. 'It's bitter out, and you'll be glad of the energy later.'

Though she wasn't the least bit hungry, Ivy knew he was right, so she nodded. 'I'll try.'

Beaming as though she'd agreed to wolf down a full English breakfast, Alex turned his attentions back to the kettle. A couple of minutes later he set down a steaming mug of tea, the porridge and a little pot of runny honey. Rather than crowding onto the stool next to hers at the narrow breakfast bar, he stayed on the other side, propping his back against the wall. Ivy glanced from his expectant expression to the porridge before taking a deep breath and reaching for the honey and adding a small dribble to the top of the pot. Another deep breath and she scooped out a mouthful of porridge. It was better than she'd expected, the warmth of it a balm to her tear-roughened throat and before she knew it she'd eaten almost half the pot. Deciding not to overdo it, Ivy pushed the pot to one side and reached instead for her tea.

'All done?' Alex straightened up and, once she'd nodded her thanks, took the discarded porridge and spooned the rest into his mouth in a few swift bites. Ivy watched in disbelief as he licked the back of the spoon. 'What?' he asked, all twinkling innocence.

'What if I had some terrible communicable disease?'

'I'd count myself lucky that my big brother is a very skilled doctor.' He eyed her, then the spoon, with a look of mock trepidation. 'You don't, do you?'

She shook her head, unable to stop a giggle. 'No.'

'Well, that's all right, then.' He gave her a grin full of mischief before heading to the sink to rinse out the pot and wash the spoon.

Ivy glanced at the clock on the wall, all humour fleeing as the porridge in her belly seemed to congeal into a rock-hard lump. Alex turned and must've caught her expression because he followed her eyeline to the clock. 'You've got time to finish your tea,' he said, all calm and no-nonsense once again.

'I'm not sure I can drink it.'

Without a word, he swept away her mug and poured the contents down the sink, rinsed it and set it on the draining board. 'Do you mind if I use the bathroom before we leave?'

Ivy shook her head. 'Of course not. There's one down here. You can use that, and I'll nip upstairs.' She touched the door to indicate where he could go. They'd converted the dining room to a bedroom with a small wet room area and toilet thanks to a grant from the council when her mum found getting up and down stairs too challenging. It still held too many memories, and Ivy hadn't entered it since Alex's brother, Tom, and his partner, Nerissa Morgan, had helped Ivy strip the bed and tidy up when her mum had moved to the hospice. It was silly to leave the room empty, especially when she was trying to run her workshop from the cramped confines of the back bedroom, but she hadn't had the wherewithal to start transferring her equipment as yet. It definitely wasn't something she needed to think about today.

Leading the way back into the hall, she indicated the correct door to Alex then paused at the foot of the stairs. 'In case I forget to say so later, I'm so grateful you came today.'

He flashed her a quick smile. 'It's no problem.'

* * *

Ivy didn't need to use the bathroom, but decided to bank an emergency wee just in case. She washed her hands then spent the next few minutes fiddling around in front of the mirror. She hadn't bothered with any make-up, but one look at her ghostly pallor had her reaching for her tinted moisturiser. She washed her hands again, then rifled through the basket she kept on the counter beside the sink for some hand cream.

'Everything all right?' Alex called from below. Ivy dropped the tube of hand cream back in the basket with a sigh. Her hands were fine. Just as her face had been fine a few moments earlier. She'd just been looking for excuses to not go back downstairs and face what the rest of the day had in store.

'One minute.'

She'd barely got the words out before the bell rang, calling time on her procrastination. It would be Laurie and Jake, come to walk with her to church. Ivy closed her eyes, counted to five and blew out a long, slow breath, ignoring the slight shakiness of her exhalation. As she stepped out onto the landing, she heard many more voices than she would've expected and shook her head as she smiled to herself and headed down the stairs and straight into the loving arms of Sylvia Morgan.

'There you are, darling! Oh, I know we said we'd meet you at the church, but honestly we couldn't bear the thought of it, could we, Andrew?'

'No, we couldn't, my love.' Leaning past his wife's shoulder, Andrew bussed a kiss on Ivy's temple. 'How are you coping, sweetheart? Yes, yes, it's a stupid question, Sylvia, don't give me that look! What on earth else am I supposed to say on such a bloody awful day?'

Extricating herself from Sylvia's hug, Ivy met Laurie's eyes and exchanged a familiar look. Though they'd been estranged for several years, once reunited it hadn't taken long to fall into the old patterns of their long-established friendship. Jake gave her a quick wave from just outside the front door, unable to make it into the crowded hall. Ivy waved back then patted Andrew's broad chest over his big heart. 'It's fine. I've already decided that nobody can say the wrong thing today.'

'Wise beyond your years, and always have been.' Andrew beamed down at her, before a frown creased his brow. 'Now, where's your coat?'

Alex stepped in, one hand braced on the open door. 'Why don't you wait outside with the others and give Ivy a bit of space?'

'Yes, good idea. Everybody out!' Sylvia declared, shifting into mother-hen mode as she shooed her daughter and husband before her.

To Ivy's surprise, Alex swung the door closed on them all, enveloping the hall in a moment of blessed silence. 'They'll wait,' he said when she opened her mouth to protest at his high-handed behaviour. 'I told you before that my only concern today is you. I don't want you feeling rushed and then finding you've forgotten something.'

She thought about her friends huddled outside in the cold and knew he was right and that they would understand. 'Thank you.'

She let Alex help her into her cloak, turning obediently when he gestured and standing passively as he tugged and straightened the back of the garment until he was satisfied. Her gloves and hat were next. Only once she'd picked up the vintage patent leather handbag she'd found a couple of years ago when she'd been scouring eBay for bargains did he reach for his own coat and scarf. 'Ready?' When she nodded, he opened the door and offered her his arm as they stepped out. No one seemed the slightest bit put out about Alex shutting the door on them, their faces all bearing smiles of affection and sympathy. It wasn't only Laurie, Jake, and Laurie's parents who were waiting. Alex's brother, Tom, was there too. Though he'd been around for much of the time during the past difficult days, she'd never noticed the striking similarity between the brothers until they stood side by side in their matching dark suits. Ivy gave him a grateful smile as she accepted a hug from Nerissa, who completed the little group.

'We left the children at home,' Nerissa said as she stepped back. 'But Emily wanted you to know she's thinking about you. She sent this in case you get cold in the church.' Nerissa raised her arm to indicate a folded cream blanket that Ivy knew well. It had been made by the children's late mother when she'd been expecting Emily, and Ivy had managed to repair it after it had been damaged in an accident.

A lump formed in Ivy's throat at the significance of the gesture from Emily. 'Thank her for me, won't you?'

Nerissa smiled. 'You can thank her yourself. I told them they can join us at The Sailor's Rest later.' Though she'd hadn't wanted a wake, Ivy knew people would expect it. Laurie and Sylvia had handled all the arrangements, liaising with Pete Bray, the landlord, who'd offered them the bar for as long as they needed it.

'Shall we make a move?' It was Andrew who spoke, one eye on the watch at his wrist. As though they'd discussed it beforehand – and knowing the Morgans they probably had – they formed a protective cordon around Ivy. Andrew and Sylvia took the lead, with Laurie and Jake to her right, Alex to her left and Tom and Nerissa at the rear. The only one missing from the Morgan clan was Nick, Laurie's brother. When Ivy asked about him, her best friend smiled. 'Him and Uncle Tony went ahead to the church to act as ushers.' Because, of course, they'd thought of that too. Though her feet felt as though her shoes were made of lead, her heart was lightened by the consideration and care from the people who meant the most to her in the world.

As they started along the street, doors on both sides opened and Ivy's neighbours appeared. They waited for the little group to pass then joined the back of it until by the time they'd neared the end of the road their numbers had swelled well into double figures. More people waited on the junction. Ivy sent them all a grateful smile, letting her eyes scan over the gathered faces until she locked onto the couple standing to one side. *Not today...*

'What the bloody hell does he think he's playing at?' Sylvia hissed as she too spotted Ivy's father and his girlfriend, Wendy. Before Ivy could lie and tell her it was okay, Sylvia was marching across the road, Andrew following swiftly on her heels.

'Come on,' Laurie said, tucking her arm through Ivy's so she was nestled between her and Alex. 'Let them sort it out.'

'But what is he doing here?' Ivy muttered to her in disbelief.

'Making a prize tit of himself, as per usual.' The acid comment from Nerissa behind them was so out of character that neither Ivy nor Laurie could help a gasp of shocked laughter. When Ivy glanced back over her shoulder, Nerissa looked entirely unrepentant. She flashed Ivy a wicked smile, which helped as much as the rudeness of her earlier remark to relieve some of the initial shock, and Ivy found herself returning the smile with a little grin of her own.

When she turned back and glanced up at Alex, thinking she should perhaps explain, he shook his head as though reading her thoughts. 'Nothing and nobody else matters today. Only you, remember?'

She nodded, shoving the anger and resentment of too many years into the little mental box where she hid all the things she didn't want to think about. 'Only me.'

Jake stepped in front, taking the space vacated by Sylvia and Andrew, and they set off once more. Ivy spared one glance across the street to where they were still talking to her father and her eyes widened. The villagers who'd been waiting on the corner had stepped into the road, leaving a much larger gap than necessary to get past the foursome. The gesture said more than any angry words might have done and it gave Ivy the strength she needed to walk on.

2

The service went about as well as could be expected and, true to his word, Alex hadn't minded in the slightest when she'd sobbed into his jacket. By the time she'd allowed him to settle her at a table in the corner of the pub, she'd worked her way through two of his three handkerchiefs and a packet of tissues. Her face felt raw, her eyes bloated, but the funeral had served its purpose and drawn the worst of her choking grief out. She could breathe easily for the first time since she'd awoken – even with the horrible stuffiness of her nose. An ice bucket sat on the table with a bottle of white wine from which she'd accepted half a glass. Laurie, Sylvia and Nerissa shared her table while the men remained standing, forming an unconscious phalanx between them and the rest of the mourners. 'Are you sure you won't eat something?' Sylvia coaxed, sliding the plate she'd filled from the buffet table towards Ivy.

'I'm not hungry.' When Sylvia said nothing, only inched the plate closer, Ivy gave in to the inevitable and helped herself to a mini quiche.

'She's nothing if not persistent,' Laurie leaned in to whisper as she helped herself to a sandwich. 'Besides, it'll help to soak up the wine.'

Ivy managed a weak smile as she eyed Laurie's almost full glass. She wasn't the only one not in much of a drinking mood. The same couldn't be said for most of the rest of the people gathered around them. There'd been a steady flow back and forth to the bar and as the pints and glasses of wine had gone down, the volume in the room had gone up. Ivy had to admit she preferred it now to the almost embarrassed hush when she'd first entered the bar. In ones and twos those people who hadn't spoken to her at the church had wandered over to offer their condolences or share a nice memory of her mum. There'd been no sign of her dad – whatever Andrew and Sylvia had said to him, he hadn't shown his face at the service, nor here afterwards. And that was fine as far as Ivy was concerned. He'd made his choice to leave a long time ago, it was too late to try and get back on Ivy's good side – not that she had a good side when it came to him. Oh, she knew she'd have to speak to him at some point. One of her mother's final requests had been for Ivy to make peace with him. Not for his sake, but for Ivy's own. Jen Fisher hadn't wanted her daughter to go on into the future burdened with the resentment and anger she'd already carried for too many years. For now though, he could stay stuffed down in the depths of the box in her head, along with all the other crap she didn't have the energy to deal with.

'Penny for them.' Laurie nudged her shoulder gently.

Ivy snorted. 'They're not worth a penny.' Giving herself a shake, she reached for her wine, took a sip and winced. She'd left it too long and it was starting to go warm. Reaching out, she fished a couple of ice cubes from the bucket and dropped them into her glass. Watering it down a bit wouldn't be the worst idea.

'I can get you something else if you prefer? I'm on my way to the bar.'

Ivy glanced up at Alex, who was clutching an empty beer bottle. 'No, I'm fine, thank you. You don't have to watch over me all day, you know. I've got plenty of minders here.' She cast a quick grin to her right and left at Laurie and Sylvia.

'If I can just squeeze past, young man?' Ivy recognised the speaker even as Alex glanced behind him before quickly stepping to one side. Mr Cavendish's voice might not be as strong as it had been, nor was there any hiding the stoop to his shoulders, but he still looked sprightly enough. How many Saturday mornings had she and the other children from the Point spent perched on cushions around his chair in the bookshop as he transported them to far-off lands of fantasy and adventure during story hour? Now he'd decided to sell up and retire it would be the end of an era for so many of the local residents. 'Ah, it's you, Alex. I thought I'd spotted you earlier. Down for another recce?'

The fond memories Mr Cavendish's arrival had conjured vanished in an instant and the small sip of wine soured in her stomach. The sense of betrayal as she stared up at Alex was so strong it stole the breath from her lungs. What an idiot she was to believe all that rubbish he'd spun her earlier about coming to the Point expressly to see to her welfare today. He'd been trying to charm his way into her knickers from the moment they'd met and probably thought a couple of clean handkerchiefs and a few pats on the arm would have her tumbling straight into bed with him, given her heightened emotional state.

'Not this time, Mr C. I'm here to offer Ivy a bit of moral support, that's all. I'll be in touch soon, though.' He sent her a quick smile before turning his attention back to the older man.

Reaching for her glass, Ivy took a large mouthful and forced her racing mind to slow down. Nothing in the way Alex had behaved today justified such an extreme reaction. He'd been kind and solicitous, an absolute gentleman. Watching him exchange pleasantries

with Mr Cavendish, Ivy understood the reason for her sudden
suspicion of Alex, and it had nothing to do with him flirting with
her a couple of times. When they'd all met up for a pre-Christmas
drink he'd picked up the estate agent's particulars for the bookshop
– the ones she'd left on the table after showing them to Laurie.
Buying the bookshop had been little more than a fantasy, an idea
put into her head by her mum, who had been determined Ivy
should get on with her life. Part of her had hoped the interest Alex
had shown in the business was nothing more than a passing fancy,
but, from the way Mr Cavendish had greeted him just now, it looked
as though he was seriously pursuing the idea.

Perhaps if she'd said something at the time he wouldn't have
even entertained the notion, but she'd been feeling too raw about
her mum so she'd told a white lie and said the leaflet had been on
the table when they'd sat down. Alex couldn't be blamed for
seeking a new business opportunity and if he wanted to move to the
Point to be closer to his brother, niece and nephew that was entirely
understandable. And yet... The lid on the box in her head where
she stuffed all the bad things creaked ominously.

Ivy went to place her glass on the table, almost missed and
would've spilled the contents in her lap had Laurie not reached out
to steady it. 'Everything all right?' her friend asked, a frown of
concern etched between her brows.

'What? Oh yes, I'm fine.' Ivy tried to laugh it off, but didn't like
the shaky way it came out. When she glanced down, she realised it
wasn't just her voice that was shaking and knew she'd reached her
limit. Bracing her hands on the table, she stood. 'I think I need a bit
of fresh air so I'm going for a walk on the beach.'

Laurie rose and let her out from behind the table. 'Do you want
me to come with you?' She was still frowning.

Ivy shook her head. She was so close to the edge now she feared
what might spill out if she opened her mouth. Scrabbling at the pile

where they'd all put their coats, she managed to extricate her cloak and swing it around her shoulders before slipping past Mr Cavendish. She vaguely heard Alex call out to her, but she didn't dare stop, her eyes fixed on the door, her only thought now to escape. By the time she burst out onto the pavement her breath was coming in sharp little pants, the ache in her chest making it hard to draw any deeper. She managed a quick glance over her shoulder, expecting to see Alex or Laurie on her heels, but the door remained shut. Not sure how long the reprieve would last, she turned and ran for the steps that would take her down to the beach, grateful the sun had come out enough to melt any lingering ice from the stones. Her feet hit the pebbles, slid a little before she found purchase and then she picked up speed, heading for the thin strip of sand above the waterline where she knew she'd find a firmer footing. A lone seagull screamed overhead and she felt the urge to join in, to expel the pain and ugliness inside in one raucous cry. Holding a hand to her lips, she kept moving, ignoring the wet flick of sand hitting the backs of her legs. She ran until her muscles felt weak, until she ran out of space and found herself up against the fence that had been erected to keep unwary explorers away from the caves at the base of the Point. Threading her fingers into the links of the fence, Ivy closed her eyes as her knees gave way and the lid on the box in her mind flew open, drowning her in a wave of emotions.

* * *

Why did her fingers hurt? It was the first coherent thought she'd been capable of forming and it was swiftly followed by a cold, wet sensation in her legs. Blinking the last of her tears from her lashes, Ivy eased the claw-like grip she had on the fence and flexed her stiff knuckles. The rush of cold came again and she scrambled to her feet, almost toppling over when her numb legs wouldn't work, and ended up crab-walking away from the tide, which was starting to come in. Sea water had soaked into the bottom of her skirt and the material had absorbed it like a sponge. She untangled the soggy mass from around her legs and did her best to hold it away.

'There you are! I've been looking for you everywhere. Are you all right?'

Clutching her ruined skirt, Ivy turned to face Alex. 'I'm fine,' she lied. 'Go back to the pub and finish your drink.'

'"Fine", she says, through lips almost blue with cold and a wet patch on her arse,' Alex muttered as he shrugged out of his coat and hooked it around her shoulders. 'Come on, let's get you somewhere warm.'

She resisted his attempt to get her moving. She would not be paraded through the streets like a pathetic waif. 'I don't want anyone seeing me like this.'

'Point taken.' Keeping one arm clamped around her shoulders, Alex pulled his mobile out of his suit-jacket pocket and used his thumb to access his contacts. 'Jake? Yeah, I've got her. We're up at the top of the beach by the fence. Your place is closest, can you meet us on the path?' He paused, obviously listening to Jake's reply, then spoke again: 'Yeah. Cheers, mate. See you in a minute.'

'What the hell did you do, call out a search party for me?' Ivy gasped, horrified at the idea of half the village scouring the streets for her.

'Don't be daft,' Alex replied, his voice still low and gruff. 'Most people didn't even notice you leaving. Laurie said you wanted a bit of air, but when you didn't come back we started to get worried so we slipped out to try and find you.'

'I wasn't gone that long,' Ivy huffed, still embarrassed that he'd been the one to find her in such a state.

'Three quarters of a bloody hour and a storm rolling in is more than long enough.'

She stiffened at the anger in his tone as much as the shock at how much time she'd lost track of. A quick glance to her right showed her the bank of ominous cloud building on the horizon. 'I didn't mean to worry anyone. I just—'

'You needed to be on your own. Hey, I get it, okay?' Alex's voice was much softer now. 'You held it together for much longer than I could've done in the same situation. Come on, let's get you up to the cottage and out of these damp things. I'm sure Laurie will have something she can lend you.'

As though her brain had finally caught up with the reality of her body, Ivy realised how badly she was shivering. With a nod she allowed Alex to guide her back along the deserted beach towards the nearest set of steps. To her relief, the only people in sight were Laurie and Jake. She hadn't even thought about the rest of her things until that moment, but was relieved to see her handbag hooked over Laurie's arm. When Ivy stumbled, Jake hurried down to take her arm on the opposite side of Alex and the pair of them all but carried her up the steps. 'Oh, you poor thing,' Laurie exclaimed, grabbing her in a quick, tight hug. 'Are you sure you can manage it up the hill?'

Ivy wasn't altogether sure that she could, but as the other alternative was trekking through the village she forced her shoulders to straighten and nodded. 'I'm okay. I just sat for too long and my legs are stiff.'

Laurie gave her an appraising look, but let it go. 'Okay. I'll go on ahead and get a bath running.' She spun on her heel and started determinedly up the steep path.

Ivy couldn't hope to match her pace, but the going was easier than expected once she got the blood flowing and the lingering pins and needles in her feet passed. It might have had something to do with the fact Jake had one arm slung around her shoulders and Alex one around her waist from the opposite side. Either way, they were soon in sight of the little cottage in the grounds of the Walkers' farm.

* * *

A wall of warmth hit her as Jake abandoned his post at her side just long enough to open the door, followed swiftly by the herb and tomato scents of something rich and comforting wafting from the oven. 'That smells good,' Alex said with a deep, appreciative sniff.

'I made lasagne this morning,' Jake said, ushering them in and securing the door behind them with a click of the key. 'You're welcome to stay for supper.'

'Oh, I wasn't hinting, or anything.' Alex looked abashed.

'Don't be daft,' Jake retorted with a shake of his head. 'I made enough to feed the five thousand. You'd be doing us a favour.'

Just then Laurie bustled in. She'd swapped her navy dress for a pair of jeans and a pink striped jumper with matching cosy socks on her feet. 'Come on,' she said, gesturing to Ivy. 'Your bath's ready. I've laid out some spare clothes on the bed in the guest room and we've loads of toiletries in the cupboard under the sink so you'll have everything you need tonight.'

It was Ivy's turn to feel nonplussed. 'I'll be fine once I've warmed up a bit and my clothes have dried out. No need to go to any trouble.'

Jake laughed. 'If you think you're getting out of here before the morning, you've got another thing coming. It was all I could do to stop Laurie swooping down on you last night and dragging you up here. Resign yourself to your fate and things will go much easier... on all of us.' Though he was teasing, there was a clear hint of worry behind his smile, a look echoed on Laurie's face.

'Yes, stay. I don't want you to be alone tonight.' It was an odd sentiment, given Ivy had been living in the cottage on her own for the past few weeks, but she understood her friend's concern.

Not at all sure she would be fit company, Ivy nevertheless relented. 'That lasagne *does* smell good.'

'That's settled, then.' There was no mistaking the relief in Laurie's voice as she turned towards Alex. 'You're welcome to stay, too, if you like. The sofa's pretty comfy and we've plenty of spare bedding.'

Alex held up his hands. 'Dinner will be more than fine.' A loud rattle of rain struck the glass of the kitchen window like a burst of gunfire, making them all jump. Alex's expression turned doubtful. 'On second thoughts...'

'Well, see how the weather is later, but the offer's there.' Jake opened the fridge and pulled out a couple of beers. 'Let's leave the ladies to sort themselves out and then I'll get changed and sort you out some joggers and a T-shirt.'

They left them to their drinks and Ivy was grateful, if a little embarrassed, when Laurie had to help her unbutton her clothing because her hands were shaking from the cold. 'I didn't make it too hot,' she said, turning to gather Ivy's discarded clothing and giving her privacy to slip into the soothing balm of the bubble-topped water.

'It's perfect,' Ivy said on a sigh as she laid her head back against the tub. 'I'm sorry for all the fuss.'

'It's no fuss. Now, you stay in here as long as you like, okay? I flipped the immersion heater on so there'll be loads of hot water if you want to top it up in a bit. Do you want a drink?'

Ivy rolled her neck so she could turn sleepy eyes towards her friend. She felt... okay. The crying fit on the beach might not have been her finest hour, but it had released a valve on everything she'd been holding onto for far too long. She still hadn't addressed any of the things she'd been avoiding, but acknowledging their existence felt like a step in the right direction. Ivy's eyes stung from the salt of too many tears and her throat was parched, but she felt at peace. 'A glass of water, please.'

'To fight the dehydration?' Laurie grinned.

'Something like that.' Ivy managed a laugh before raising a bubble-clad arm to shield her face. 'How terrible do I look?'

'You look fine.' Setting the bundle of clothes on top of the toilet lid, Laurie crouched and began to rifle through a basket of tubes and bottles she'd pulled out from the cupboard. 'I've got some cucumber eye gel in here somewhere,' she muttered before holding up a small tube with a triumphant smile. 'It's an absolute miracle. I'll pop it in the fridge for a few minutes then bring it back when I fetch your water.'

'Thank you.' Ivy watched the door to the bathroom close behind Laurie before leaning her head back once more and closing her eyes.

She must've drifted off almost immediately because Laurie's gentle knock startled her. Forcing herself to sit up, she accepted the glass of cold water and took a few sips before tilting her head back so Laurie could dab some of the cool gel beneath her eyes. 'Oh, that's wonderful.' When Laurie continued to frown, Ivy laughed. 'I don't look *that* bad, do I?'

'Hmm?' Laurie made a distracted noise before shaking her head and laughing too. 'No, you look fine, it's just...' She trailed off, that deep furrow knotting her brows once more. 'Never mind.'

Well, that wasn't going to work, and the break of several years in their friendship wasn't enough for Laurie to have forgotten she couldn't keep anything from Ivy for long. 'Spit it out, whatever it is.'

Laurie sighed. 'I probably got the wrong end of the stick just now, but it sounded an awful lot like Alex was talking to Jake about buying Mr Cavendish's bookshop.'

Ivy sank back into the water with a groan. 'No, you didn't get it wrong.'

Shifting from her knees to a more comfortable position, Laurie rested her arm along the top of the tub. 'But how on earth did he even find out it was up for sale?' Ivy sank a little lower until the water covered her almost to her nose. 'Ivy?'

Huffing out a breath that formed a circle of bubbles on the surface, Ivy sat upright. 'I might have given him the details when we had that drink at Christmas,' she muttered.

'What? How? I thought *you* were going to try and buy it yourself?' Laurie's expression was a perfect mixture of confusion and exasperation.

'I didn't want to go into all the stuff about Mum so I told him someone must have left the estate agent's flyer on the table before we got there. I didn't think he was seriously interested in it.' Which wasn't strictly true, because Alex's eyes had glowed as if he'd found a treasure as he'd tucked the leaflet into his pocket.

'Have you even spoken to Mr Cavendish about it?' Laurie's gentle question was full of sympathy and understanding and Ivy didn't need to do more than shake her head. Laurie sighed. 'Is it a done deal?'

Ivy blinked. 'What do you mean?'

'I mean if they haven't exchanged contracts – or whatever it is when you buy a business rather than a house – then you might still be in with a chance to buy it.'

'I don't even know if I want it.' Even as the words came out of her mouth, Ivy knew the truth of it. She did want the shop. In the dark lonely nights of the past few weeks she'd spent hours mentally rearranging the interior layout, stripping out the heavy old shelves to create bright cosy reading spots using furniture she'd reclaimed and reupholstered. She'd pictured bright bean bags and squishy cushions scattered on the floor in the children's section and Mr

Cavendish's old rocking chair brought back to life with a coating of beeswax and lots of elbow grease. A splash of bathwater hit her face, jolting Ivy out of her musings. 'What was that for?' she spluttered.

'For telling an absolute whopper of a lie!' Laurie retorted as she dried her hand on the edge of a towel. Folding the towel in a neat square, she set it aside with a sigh. 'Look, I can understand you being hesitant at taking on something so big, especially when everything is still so raw, but have you ever considered it might be exactly what you need?'

Ivy blinked away the last of the bathwater from her lashes as she drew up her knees and hooked her arms around her legs. 'It would mean selling the cottage.'

Laurie rested her chin on the edge of the bath and met her gaze. 'I know, but it would also be a fresh start. You'll always have your memories of your mum, no matter where you are, you know that.'

'But what if Alex has really set his heart on buying the book-shop?' A tiny voice inside Ivy said it would serve him right for stealing it out from under her nose, but she quickly hushed it. She wasn't the sort of person to spite another and, besides, Alex still had no clue she was even interested in the shop – and she had no one but herself to blame for that.

'What if he has?'

The hard note in Laurie's response surprised Ivy. 'I thought you liked him?'

Laurie blew out an exasperated breath. 'Of course I do. He's one of the good ones, to be sure, and he and Jake get on great, which isn't something to be ignored...' Jake was a lot more insular than bubbly, outgoing Laurie and he didn't find it as easy to make friends. Ivy could understand how much it meant to Laurie that Jake was forging his own roots and connections in the village, beyond his bond with her. 'But you are my main concern,' Laurie continued. 'If Alex doesn't buy the bookshop he's not going to stop visiting the Point, given how close he and Tom are. As far as I'm concerned, if he hasn't signed on the dotted line then there's no reason that you shouldn't go for it.'

'I don't even know if I can afford it.' Ivy had a meeting lined up in a few days with their solicitor to start the ball rolling on probate for her mum's estate. There was a box file full of paperwork in the bottom of her mother's wardrobe she needed to go through with him. Mum had wanted to review it all with her, but Ivy had refused, wanting her last few weeks in the hospice to be as stress-free and relaxed as possible. 'I'm seeing Harry Davenport to sort everything out. I can ask him for some advice.' As the only solicitor in the village, Harry was something of a jack of all trades so he'd know the ins and outs of buying and selling a property.

'That's settled, then.' Laurie braced her hands on the side of the bath and climbed to her feet. 'I'll leave you in peace to finish your bath.'

The hot water had already done the trick and Ivy was feeling a lot better. 'I won't be long. Hey, Laurie?' When her friend paused at the door to glance back at her, Ivy held out a hand towards her. 'Don't say anything to Alex, okay? None of this is his fault, and, if I don't decide to go through with it, I'd hate to be the one who put any tarnish on things for him.'

Laurie frowned. 'Even if that means you end up losing out to him because he can move quicker than you?'

Ivy nodded. 'Even then.'

3

'I'm sorry, Alex, but I think I must've misheard you because I'm sure you couldn't possibly have just told me you're buying a bookshop!' Immy's tinkling laugh was edged with shattered glass, and Alex winced at the harshness of it. Thank god he'd called rather than accepting her offer of a FaceTime chat, using the flimsy excuse of poor reception. It was the morning after the funeral and he was still in the Point so it was easy to claim the broadband wasn't up to scratch. The fact that he was sprawled on the bed in his brother's spare room with a film paused on his laptop and a full reception signal on his phone was none of his editor's business.

'I need to get out of town, to get out of the house and away from all the memories of Jo. Surely you can understand that?' Alex mentally braced himself for a bolt from above at such an outrageous lie. The ghosts that still lingered from his failed marriage didn't have anything to do with the bricks and mortar of the home he and Jo had shared together. It had always been Alex's place more than his ex-wife's anyway. Whether he'd had a sixth sense about the future of his younger son's relationship, or it'd been purely pragmatic, his father, Archie, had insisted Alex buy and keep the house in his own name. He and Jo had split the rest of the living expenses, but the mortgage had been his responsibility alone. It had made untangling their lives that bit easier after Jo had betrayed him with someone Alex had thought of as a friend. Though both Jo and Shaun had sworn they'd never been together in the house, he hadn't trusted either of them enough to believe them, so the bed and all the bedding had been junked, but that was it. He had enough of his father's practical streak to see the house for what it was – a roof over his head and a sound investment. The valuation he'd had before putting it on the market had proven that point.

Immy sighed. 'Oh, Alex, I'm sure it can't be easy for you, but I can't countenance the disruption such a huge step is going to cause.' There was a lengthy silence and Alex's gut lurched because he knew what was coming next. 'Not when you're so behind with, well, everything.'

It was said with such kindness, such sympathy that Alex almost fell for it. Immy was nothing if not a ruthless operator – even in her ballet flats and Boden skirts. She'd given him more than enough rope already when it came to delivering his follow-up book that she wasn't going to let him hang himself with it. Though she'd told anyone who asked that she'd *always* believed in him as a writer, they'd all been blown away by the runaway success of his semi-autobiographical debut, *The Marriage Roller Coaster*.

He'd written the book in an attempt to purge his anger and bitterness over Jo's betrayal. It hadn't started out that way. Not liking how much Alex had been drinking, Tom had gone into full big-brother mode and hooked him up with a counsellor he knew through his work as a GP, and she'd suggested he try writing down his thoughts – regardless of how dark and ugly they were – rather than suppressing everything. Though he'd enjoyed writing stories as a kid, it was never anything he'd considered as a career. Ever-practical Archie had steered his son towards the financial sector, where he'd made his own fortune, and, not feeling a passion for anything else, Alex had been happy for a bit of direction.

Once he'd started scribbling in the notebook he'd picked up in a supermarket for a couple of quid, he'd found he couldn't stop. He'd rapidly progressed from paper to keyboard, unable to keep up with the rush and tumble of thoughts any other way. Somehow he'd ended up with the bones of story, a tale of a love turned sour. Nothing new perhaps, other than the fact it was a man confessing all. Tom had a connection to Immy through a partner at his practice, and, though Alex was sure she'd promised to take a look out of nothing more than politeness, he'd unknowingly tapped into the zeitgeist. Men talking about their emotions, their mental health, their vulnerabilities was one of the next big things and before he knew it he had a three-book deal and 'The Heartbreak Kid' – a terrible pseudonym but he'd had nothing better to suggest – was born.

The book had moved further from the truth as the editing process had progressed, until the male protagonist had been nothing more than the innocent victim of a cruel, heartless bitch. What did it matter? It wasn't as if anyone was ever going to be able to connect the book back to him, or Jo, and he'd been well into the bitterness stage of his recovery by that point.

* * *

Alex had known from the moment they'd met at university that Jo was the kind of woman who drew her confidence from without rather than from within. She craved attention and, madly in love, he'd been more than happy to lavish it upon her. The warning signs had been there – when he'd had a frank sit-down with his tutor and been told he needed to stop pissing around if he wanted to graduate with a decent degree, Alex had toned down the partying and thrown himself into his studies. Jo had stewed and sulked at what she'd seen as him neglecting her and, rather than address her sometimes suffocating need, he'd twisted the silver foil from a discarded KitKat wrapper into a ring and presented her with it. Mollified with the promise of a big wedding where she would be the centre of attention, she'd knuckled down as well and they'd both graduated with honours.

Happy to surrender the wedding plans entirely to Jo and her mother, and grateful her parents were footing the bill for what had soon become a three-ring circus, Alex had continued to ignore the warning signs. All brides got stressed out before the big day, didn't they? As he'd waited for her at the altar trussed up in full morning gear, including a bloody top hat, the only thing he'd felt was relief that the madness would be over, and they could get things back to normal.

Only there'd never been anything resembling normal. They'd found jobs at the same company, one of the big four accountancy firms, though working in departments that had no dealings with each other. The hours had been crazy, the workloads ridiculous and most of his energy had gone into getting through each day. Alex got on well with most people, because as the youngest child and the product of a second marriage he'd always been the one to smooth things over. Jo had never had quite the same success with people and their journeys to and from work had soon become a one-way examination of the perceived slights and jealousies she'd encountered. Alex had soothed her ruffled feathers, fed her ego and tried to ignore the fact it was only ever *other women* Jo had problems with.

But then it had started leaking into their social life. He'd laughed too hard at a female friend's joke, or lingered too long in conversation with their hostess at the endless round of dinner parties and pub nights out that were the staples of a young couple living in the capital. So he'd drunk a little more than he should to insulate himself from the hissed rows in the back of black cabs or, when they'd needed to tighten their belts, interminable Tube journeys to the almost-end-of-the-line station closest to home. The less he'd responded to her attempts to start an argument, the harder she'd tried to compete for the attention that had already been hers, because even on the worst days he'd never looked at another woman, never thought they wouldn't find a way to muddle through. She'd just needed a bit more time to mature than him, would grow to understand there was no competition, because no one could hold a candle to her.

'Earth to Alex!' Immy's laughing exasperation dragged him from the past.

'Sorry, I zoned out there for a minute. I was thinking about Jo, and, well, everything.' He sighed, hating his inability to focus on anything for more than a few minutes. Even as he tried to give Immy the attention she deserved his eyes were already straying to the clock on his computer screen. They'd stayed up far too late the night before keeping Ivy distracted from the awfulness of the day with a rowdy game of Monopoly. Jake had dug the board out from a stack of games Mrs Walker had left in the cottage for holiday-makers before she'd allowed Jake – and then Laurie – to rent it on a long-term basis.

Even after Ivy had staggered to bed just before midnight, with Laurie a few minutes later on her heels, he and Jake had stayed up into the early hours, nursing a couple of beers while they'd chatted quietly about the events of the day and what the future might hold for Ivy. The conversation had inevitably wound back to Alex's potential purchase of Mr Cavendish's bookshop and Jake had been honest about the pros and cons of moving to a community as tight-knit as Mermaids Point. Though the rain had let up by the time they'd swallowed down a cup of coffee and a glass of water each around 2 a.m. Alex had accepted the offer of the sofa rather than trying to negotiate his way down the hill with only the moon to guide him. Besides, if he'd rolled into the surgery at that time of the morning it would only have reinforced all Tom's not-very-well-hidden worries that Alex was backsliding into bad habits. Truth be told, Alex hadn't touched a drop since after Christmas, but yesterday had been too bloody grim to get through without a beer or two and he hadn't even known the woman they'd been mourning. He didn't know how Ivy had managed it.

'And then I stripped naked and danced the hokey-cokey on the boardroom table.'

'*You did what?*' Alex blurted before realising he'd fallen hook, line and sinker for Immy's verbal trap. Focus! Giving himself a mental slap, Alex pushed off the bed and began pacing in circles around the small area between the bed and the door. The movement was enough to fill up the bit of his brain intent on mischief and he apologised profusely for once again allowing himself to become distracted. 'I'm listening, I promise.'

'If you really are struggling to concentrate this badly, maybe a change of scenery would help.' Immy still sounded sceptical. 'It just seems like an awful lot to take on. I don't wish to sound rude, but what do you know about running a *shop*?'

The emphasis she put on the word shop made it sound as if he'd said he was training to be an Olympian or fancied being an astronaut. 'I'm a fully qualified accountant with extensive business auditing experience. I'm sure I can handle the financial challenge of selling a few books.' His response came out stiff, and more than a bit pompous, but he was fed up of trying to justify his decision to all and sundry.

'Well, I didn't mean to suggest otherwise, and, of course, it's none of my business.'

Great, now he felt like even more of a dickhead. 'You didn't. I mean, it's okay. Everyone in my family thinks I've lost the plot so you're not alone in wondering if I'm taking on more than I can handle. I don't know what to say other than it feels right. It's the first thing that's felt anything remotely like that in a very long time.' Now that wasn't strictly true, but he'd already sworn off Ivy. Even if she wasn't trying to cope with the most traumatic thing he could imagine, Alex was still enough of a gentleman that he wouldn't try and impose himself on her when he was such a complete shambles.

Immy sighed. 'Then I wish you every success with it. Now, shall we get back to the purpose of our call? How are you feeling about your writing now you've had a few weeks' break?'

'It's good,' Alex said, crossing his fingers behind his back like a naughty five-year-old. 'Giving myself permission not to worry about it really helped. I've managed about a thousand words this morning.' Which wasn't a lie. The walk down from Jake and Laurie's with a strong black coffee in one hand and a bacon butty in the other had seen off the cobwebs lingering from his late night. Though he'd wanted to stay and see how Ivy was, he'd been persuaded to let her sleep and he hadn't wanted to outstay his welcome. In trying to rediscover his enthusiasm for writing he'd joined a few online author groups over Christmas, one of which posted a photo as a weekly idea prompt. The idea was to write two thousand words of whatever came into one's head after seeing the image. The first had been a couple kissing and he'd skipped over that. The second had been of a dog, grey around the whiskers but still bright of eye, and he'd ended up sobbing over a story written from the point of view of the dog as he waited patiently in a cage at a rescue centre to be adopted. It was the most maudlin nonsense he'd ever written, but the words had flowed and that was all he cared about.

The latest photo had been posted a couple of days ago. He'd spotted it on the drive down to the Point when he'd stopped for a break and been browsing through Facebook while he chewed his way through a disappointing panini in one of those soulless service rest centres. The image had been of an average-looking man dressed in a serviceable suit. The kind of person he'd passed every day in the corridors at work. The same sort of office drone he'd been himself not so long ago. There'd been something about him though, a look of determination, a hint of hardness beneath the bland shell. Jake had mused over the photo for the rest of the drive, his brain chasing an idea but not quite able to grasp hold of it. He'd forgotten about it in the flurry of activity his arrival at Tom's had inevitably generated and there'd been no time to think of anything yesterday other than Ivy.

As he'd munched his breakfast on the go that morning after leaving Jake and Laurie's, however, a story had started to form about the kind of double life the man might be leading. Maybe he was an undercover police officer, or a spook working for the security services. By the time he'd got back to the surgery, his mind had been racing with possibilities and he'd all but brushed off his poor nephew, Max, in his haste to get up to his room and scribble some ideas down.

He glanced over at his laptop where the screen was still frozen on an image of Jason Statham captured mid-leap in some daring stunt. He'd been watching the film with the sound down, interested more in the body language than the formulaic script. Although the leading man had the physicality of a modern-day action hero, there was a quiet grace and confidence about the way he moved that Alex hoped he could capture on the page. It wasn't what he was supposed to be writing, but Immy didn't need to worry about that. He just needed a few sessions under his belt to get his confidence back and then he'd be able to turn his mind back to the book he was meant to be working on. Which reminded him...

'You didn't happen to pick up my notebook when we had lunch before Christmas, did you?' He was sure he hadn't left it in the restaurant because he remembered sitting in a pub before he'd headed back home on the Tube and making notes in it, but he'd turned the house upside down trying to find it so it was time to grasp at straws.

'Not that I recall. Hang on a sec and I'll check my bag.' He heard the faint rustlings as she did just that before she came back on the line a minute or so later. 'Nope. No notebook, I'm afraid, but I did find my favourite pen that I accused my husband of stealing, so I owe him an apology.' She laughed before continuing in a more serious tone. 'Did you lose a lot of work?'

Alex sighed. 'Yes, and no. I felt really inspired after our chat over lunch about "The Heartbreak Kid's" popularity on social media.' The publicity team had agreed to run the account on his behalf, and he hadn't so much as looked at it until Immy had mentioned how many followers 'he' had. 'I had an idea about what it would be like if the cyber version of me struck up a relationship with one of the followers, so I'd made a note of some of the more flirtatious posts that the Kid's account had received. It felt like something really interesting at the time and I scribbled down several pages of notes, but I've lost the thread of where I wanted the story to go.' He'd never been much of a planner, preferring to write with his gut, and now he'd lost his notes, he couldn't seem to recapture the momentum he'd felt. His brain had moved on, convinced it had already done the hard work on it and refusing to get enthused about it again. It was a hard feeling to describe, and he worried about saying stuff like that out loud in case people thought he'd lost the plot completely.

'How very frustrating. It sounds like an interesting direction for the book, though we'd have to be careful how we played it because we wouldn't want it to look like you'd taken advantage of anyone in a vulnerable situation.' Immy hmmed to herself as though musing over the issue. 'I haven't looked deeply into the comments the account gets. Did you come across anything you found troubling in the interactions?'

'Oh no,' Alex replied at once, not wanting her to misunderstand and get anyone on the publicity team in any trouble. 'The posts from the account were all very professional and polite, thanking people who said they'd enjoyed the book and that kind of thing. I have to say I was impressed with the links for mental health services and promoting organisations like Relate. I thought it was a nice touch.'

'That's good.' There was no mistaking the relief in Immy's voice. 'Social media can be something of a minefield. I swear we have a crisis meeting every couple of weeks at the moment because of something one of our authors has said.'

'I feel like I dodged a bullet, there,' Alex confessed, sure he'd be one of the ones to say something without thinking. He'd deactivated most of his socials after Jo left him, unable to bear the constant memory reminders of when they'd been happy. He'd never been a prolific poster, but she had and had tagged him in so many posts and photos that they'd kept popping up. He hadn't missed being online. 'It'd been so long since I was on Twitter, I had to reset my password.' A twinge of guilt at the additional burden he'd placed on the publicity team by refusing to participate struck. 'Please let everyone involved with the account know that I appreciate their hard work. It can't be easy on top of everything else they have to do.'

'That's kind of you, I'll let them know. They're all trying to get to grips with TikTok at the moment.'

'Isn't that for kids?' He'd seen his niece, Emily, spend hours practising some ridiculous dance routine that was all the rage.

'That's where it started, but there's a burgeoning book scene on there now and we have to try and keep on top of these things. Social media is a great way to connect with new readers, but there never seem to be enough hours in the day.' She sounded weary for a moment, then must have caught herself because her next sentence was voiced in a much brighter, more positive tone. 'Anyway, it's an interesting premise, but, as I said, we'd have to tread carefully. I know it's an absolute pain trying to redo your notes, but can you maybe jot an outline down for me so I can have a look? I've got a few other ideas of where you might go, which I'll send over after we finish. If you've gone off the social media thing then something there might spark an interest. And, if you are going to go ahead with this move to the back of beyond, that might make an interesting angle too. A bit of a fish-out-of-water story, the trials of a city boy making a fresh start in the country. There are loads of books like that in the women's fiction market and, from the research we've done, women are your predominant readership. It'd be a nice hook.'

Alex rolled his eyes at the dreaded word. Every story had to have 'a hook', had to be the same as what was popular and yet still be new. Immy also sounded a bit too keen on the idea for his liking. 'Don't forget we've agreed that the next book will be entirely fictional.' He'd bared far too much of his soul the first time around and wasn't in any hurry to repeat the experience. The worst time of his life had been permanently committed to paper, and he'd never be able to take it back. How much worse would it be if he'd not used a pseudonym? Thank god the only people who could connect the book to him had already had a ringside seat to the action and knew the truth of it. What if he met someone new who'd read it and believed *The Marriage Roller Coaster* to contain a realistic portrayal of him? He shuddered at what his new friends in the Point would think of him; what Ivy would think of the level of self-indulgent pity, the exaggerated cruelties he'd attributed to his fictional version of Jo. He wasn't proud of who he'd been in those dark days.

He thought again of his brother and how he and the kids seemed to be making a fresh start here in the Point and he wanted that for himself more than anything. A new home, a new career where he would succeed or fail entirely under his own steam, a chance to take the lessons of the past and move forward as the best version of himself it was possible to be. The possibilities called to him like a siren's song. And unlike the sailors of legend, he was aware of the dangers and was certain he could guard himself against them. The last thing he wanted was to taint his new experiences by sharing them with the world – even behind the safety of a pseudonym.

'Oh, I'm not suggesting you draw directly from life this time,' Immy assured him quickly. 'But there's nothing wrong with using your fresh start as inspiration.'

Alex wasn't convinced, but he decided to leave it for now. 'Send me over those ideas you mentioned, and I'll try and work up an outline.' Nothing would be happening with the move until he'd found himself a buyer and the house had only just gone on the market. He might as well use the time productively rather than worrying about another buyer beating him to the punch when it came to the bookshop. It wasn't as if Mermaids Point was on the map much these days. The people who'd been excited by the staged mermaid sightings of the summer had moved on to whatever the latest news trend was, and, with the Point in the grips of the winter weather, the odds on some tourist stumbling across it the way he had was unlikely. Fate had put that estate agent's leaflet on the pub table for him to find, he was sure of it.

4

A little over a week after the funeral, Ivy sat in the waiting room of the solicitor's office trying to ignore the sympathetic glances Tracy, Harry Davenport's receptionist/secretary/and all the other essential things that kept a small village business running smoothly, kept shooting her way. While she appreciated that people were trying to be nice, she was starting to feel like an exotic zoo animal the way everyone stared every time she stuck her nose outside the front door. It didn't help Ivy's mood that she'd dressed for the weather, rather than the subtropical heating of the three-room suite of offices situated upstairs in a building they conveniently shared with one of the local estate agents. Setting aside the expanding cardboard folder she'd been clutching in her lap, Ivy tugged at the neck of her rust-coloured polo neck and cast a baleful glare at the door curtain blasting out hot air. Her fingers touched the edge of the silver brooch she'd pinned on one side of the folded-over neck of her jumper, and she felt instantly calmer. The little ladybird had been a favourite piece of her mother's and she stroked it like a talisman. She could get through this.

The door to Harry Davenport's office opened and he arrived on a wave of lemon-tinged aftershave. He looked tanned and sickeningly healthy after a Christmas spent in Spain. He might have filled out since their days at the little village school, but his glasses still looked wonky as he shoved them up his nose with one hand and extended the other towards her. 'Ivy. So sorry to keep you waiting. What can we get for you – tea, coffee, a glass of water, perhaps?' He looked at the empty table beside her before glancing over his shoulder at Tracy.

'I've already asked.' Tracy sounded highly put out, as though Ivy had thwarted her hosting efforts.

'I'm fine, Harry, really,' Ivy assured him. He'd taken over the business from his uncle, the original Henry Davenport, who'd chucked it all in out of the blue about a year ago and retired to a villa in Spain overlooking the Mar Menor to live with a very tanned, very handsome waiter he'd met on holiday. Poor Harry had been left somewhat in the lurch, having expected to have a few years working under Henry Senior's guidance, but seemed to be coping with the unexpected responsibility. They were still on good personal terms, at least, what with Harry spending Christmas over there on a visit.

He frowned at her through the smudged lenses of his glasses. 'Well, if you're sure then pop on through and I'll be right with you.' He ushered her towards his office with one hand before heading into the little kitchenette.

Taking the chair closest to the blessedly open window, Ivy indulged in a good old visual nose around Harry's office as she listened to him clattering around making a cup of coffee and answering a rapid-fire list of questions Tracy was flinging at him. The desk was an imposing mahogany monster with a dark-green leather inset and an equally over-sized chair that looked to have seen better days from the strip of masking tape wrapped around one arm. The usual office equipment covered most of the desk, and a printer and what looked like a fax machine jostled for space on top of a pair of ugly grey filing cabinets. Ivy couldn't remember the last time she'd seen a fax machine, not since the times when she'd had to go into the school office and discuss her latest absences and collect whatever work she'd needed to catch up on. The head teacher at the big secondary school they'd all been bused to had always been very understanding of the situation at home, but sitting in one of the hard chairs waiting to speak to him had always made Ivy feel as if she'd done something wrong. Not wanting to head down that particular memory lane, Ivy switched her attention to the row of Funko POP! characters lining the windowsill and couldn't suppress a smile. Harry had always been a bit of a comic-book geek at school, and from the impressive collection of Marvel characters, it looked as though he still was.

'Sorry, again, for keeping you waiting,' Harry said as he kicked the door shut behind him with his heel before rounding the enormous desk and placing a large mug with an image of Wonder Woman on it on the leather blotter. When he caught her looking at it, he pushed it to one side with a laugh. 'A present from Nick,' he said, referring to Laurie's older brother and another one of their little gang of friends. 'I think it was supposed to be a joke, but I love it. Tracy keeps trying to force proper cups and saucers on me, but what's the point in them? They might look nice for clients, but they're so bloody fiddly and half the time my coffee goes cold before I've had a chance to drink it.'

'I like it,' Ivy agreed with a reassuring smile. 'It's a nice reminder of the man behind the suit.'

Harry tugged at the bottom of his waistcoat, a hint of colour highlighting his sharp cheekbones. 'Henry always insisted on a proper dress code, and I guess I got used to it.' He shoved his glasses up with one finger and gave her a gentle, lopsided smile. 'Let's get the awful stuff out of the way, shall we?'

Taking a deep breath, Ivy nodded. 'No point in putting it off any longer.' She lifted the expanding file onto the desk. 'I wasn't sure what I might need, so I've brought everything Mum had.' She'd tried sorting through it all the previous evening, but she'd come across a large envelope with a copy of every school photo documenting Ivy's progress from a shy little thing in a too-large gingham dress and wonky ponytails, to the rather sullen final one at secondary school where she'd developed an enormous spot on her forehead and had tried – unsuccessfully – to hide it with a massive splodge of concealer. Thinking about her mum going through them, reliving the past and maybe thinking about the photos of things she'd never see had undone Ivy and she'd dumped the whole file on the table by the front door. 'I'm not sure you'll need my exam certificates, though,' she said with a wobbly laugh.

Harry smiled. 'Better too much information than not enough.' He settled back in his chair and opened the much thinner file in front of him. 'Well, the good news is that we have a properly certified will in which your mum names you as her sole beneficiary, so that makes things a bit less sticky when it comes to your dad.'

'My dad?' Ivy frowned. 'What's he got to do with any of this? He's been out of the picture for years.'

Sitting forward, Harry folded his hands on top of the open file and stared at her over the rims of his glasses, which had once more slid down to perch on the end of his nose. 'Well, as her legal spouse he would inherit everything without a will to state otherwise.'

What on earth was he talking about? Her mum and dad had split up years ago – everyone in the village knew that, just as they knew every other bit of scandal that happened in their small community. 'They've been divorced for years...'

Harry shook his head. 'Not according to the paperwork we have on file. It seems as if your mum started proceedings, but for one reason and another, it looks like they never formally ended their marriage.' He held out his hand for the expanding file. 'It may be that we've mislaid our copy of the decree absolute, but I can't find any record of the application. There's only details of the application for a decree nisi.'

Trying not to panic, Ivy shoved the file across towards him. 'Help yourself.' She watched for a few moments as Harry examined the contents of the various sections, pulling out each clump of paperwork and shuffling through it before tucking it away and moving to the next one. With each bundle he discarded, the apprehension inside Ivy grew bigger. 'What does it mean, though, if they're not properly divorced?'

He paused to glance up at her. 'Well, worst-case scenario he could dispute the will, but I'm sure it won't come to that.'

Ivy flashed back to that moment when Andrew and Sylvia had confronted Kevin and his girlfriend, Wendy, on the way to her mum's funeral. Though she'd tried to ignore them, she'd not missed the flush of embarrassment on her father's face as the other villagers had given them an obvious wide berth on the pavement. Perhaps she should've done as her mum had urged and tried to patch things up with him before she'd died. 'And if he does?' She hated the way her voice sounded so small and forced herself to sit up straight. 'What can he actually do to me that's any worse than what he's already done?'

Laying his stack of papers aside, Harry removed his glasses to rub the bridge of his nose before settling them back and giving her what she guessed was supposed to be an encouraging smile. 'I'm sure he won't want to get tangled up in any legal dramas any more than you do. Let's not panic until we've got our facts straight.' He turned his attention back to the large cardboard file. 'Okay, this looks like it all relates to the cottage...' Frowning, he pulled out a thick wedge of papers and flicked through them before setting them to one side.

'What's that?' Ivy was already reaching out to turn the papers towards her before he'd had time to answer.

'It's a copy of the deeds to the cottage. I'll have to check the land registry, but it looks like it's still in joint names.'

'He still owns the cottage?' Ivy raised a hand to her chest, willing the sudden tightness to ease. 'There must be some mistake.' Why else had her mother put the idea in her head to sell up and try and buy the bookshop?

'Well, technically, he owns 50 per cent of it as your mother willed her share to you. Do you mind me asking whether he continued to provide financial support after he left? There could be grounds to argue something there – morally at least, even if it's rather sticky in legal terms.'

'He pays every month. There's a standing order that comes into Mum's account.'

'He's still paying?' Harry raised his eyebrows at that. 'Well, then he'll be able to argue that's to cover his share of the mortgage. There is still a mortgage?'

Ivy nodded. 'I don't think it's very much, though. Mum had an insurance policy, which she said would cover the outstanding balance once it pays out.'

'Ah yes, I've got it here.' Harry set a slightly yellowed sheaf of papers on the desk next to the deeds.

Feeling a bit sick, Ivy picked it up and read the first few lines. It was dated a few weeks after her parents had got married and named them as joint policy holders for the mortgage. 'I still don't understand any of this. Mum promised me she'd sorted everything out.'

'Hopefully these are old documents, and we'll find the newer stuff. As you said, your mum seems to have kept a copy of every-thing.' Harry was doing his best to sound cheerful, but Ivy couldn't escape the nagging ache in her stomach. The cocktail of medications Jen had been taking in the last few months had been pretty powerful, maybe she'd got confused. A thought occurred to her. 'When was the decree nisi applied for?'

'Hmm?' Henry gave her a distracted look before he set her file aside so he could look through his own records. 'Here you go.'

Ivy tried to ignore the slight shake in her fingers as she accepted the document. Her eyes scanned over the page, looking for a date and finding it next to a rough-looking version of her mother's signature. *July 2011*, a couple of weeks before Ivy's fifteenth birthday. Things had been settled at home. Her dad had been gone the best part of two years and her mum had been almost back to her normal self after all the chemo and radiotherapy. They'd been making plans for what they would do during the summer holidays, had even talked about jetting off to the Canaries for a week or two in an all-inclusive hotel. A treat for them both to celebrate Jen's recovery and a last chance to relax for Ivy before she'd have to knuckle down in her final year of GCSEs. The check-up had been meant to be routine... 'That was the summer Mum got ill for the second time,' she said to Harry as she passed the paperwork back to him.

'Ah.' The small noise said it all. Understanding, sympathy, a touch of disappointing realisation. It was looking less and less likely they were going to find anything to prove Jen had finalised the divorce.

'I don't understand why she told me she'd sorted everything out though,' Ivy repeated, shivering suddenly from more than the cold draught blowing through the open window. Had she been feeling the heat only minutes ago? Now she felt frozen to the marrow.

Harry must've noticed her distress because he jumped up to wrestle with the old-fashioned sash window, slamming it closed with a thump that made her jump. A knock at the door followed a few seconds later and Tracy poked her nose around the edge. 'Everything all right?'

'Fine,' Harry assured her. 'Just that window sticking again.'

Ivy rearranged her lips into what might have been a grimace as much as it was a smile. 'I got a bit chilly.'

Tracy eyed her with concern. 'You look a bit pale around the edges. I'll get you a cup of tea, that'll warm you up.'

Even if Ivy had had the strength to protest, it was too late as the efficient Tracy had already swept up Harry's mug and bustled out, though she'd left the door ajar behind her. Ivy's gaze swept around the room, settling again on the funny superhero characters lining the windowsill because anything was better than the look of quiet sympathy on Harry's face. The vibration of the window closing had toppled poor Thor onto his side and left Iron Man in a precarious position a bit too close to the edge. As an excuse to do something, anything, other than have to think about the implications of every-thing she and Harry had discussed, Ivy got up and started rear-ranging the figures, concentrating on spacing them out at a precise distance from each other until she heard the rattle of Tracy putting cups and saucers on Harry's desk and closing the door behind her.

Risking a peek over her shoulder, she saw Harry was – thank-fully! – buried nose-deep in another document so she left him to it and turned her attention to the view beyond the window. The familiar shops lined the high street as far as she could see. Leaning forward until her forehead almost touched the glass, she could just make out the white lines of the pedestrian crossing beyond which was the junction to Farriers Way and home to Mr Cavendish's book-shop. Whatever blacksmith's workshop might have once graced the cobbled street had long since vanished, leaving only the name as a clue. Not wide enough for more than one car, it had been part of the old one-way system before the council had redesigned the layout of the village to draw the holiday traffic away to the car parks they'd built at the top of the hill and on an open bit of land close to the old harbour. The high street still got choked up in the height of the summer, but Farriers Way was a rat run used mainly by the locals, so it didn't get the same flow of traffic. Ivy wondered what effect rerouting the traffic had had on Mr Cavendish's business, before dismissing the thought. It didn't matter to her, now, because her chances of buying the shop were diminishing at a rapid rate. Even if her father decided to be reasonable there'd still be a whole lot more legal wrangling to do than Ivy had anticipated. And even if she could sort things out, it sounded as if he owned half of every-thing... With a soft groan she bumped her forehead against the window and wished she'd stayed in bed.

'Ah.'

It was a different noise from the one Harry had made earlier, a bit more positive, and Ivy swung around, unable to keep her heart from leaping in hope. 'You've found something?'

'Not what we were looking for, I'm afraid, but it might explain why your mother thought everything would be okay.' Harry held out what looked like a handwritten letter.

Recognising the black scrawl from the birthday and Christmas cards that had turned up like clockwork every year, she shook her head as she resumed her seat. 'Just tell me what it says.'

Harry cast her an uncomfortable look before clearing his throat. 'It's, umm, well, it's from your dad, obviously.' He squirmed a bit in his seat, then reached for the delicate china cup nestled on an equally dainty saucer on the desk in front of him and took a mouthful that all but emptied it. Setting it back, he adjusted his glasses and began to scan over the letter once more. 'He basically says he doesn't want a divorce because he's worried about what people will think of him.' Harry cast her a look over the tops of his glasses. 'Bit bloody late for that, but there you have it.' The acid scorn in his words made Ivy laugh even though she'd never felt less like it in her life. Harry's grin turned impish before he turned his attention back to the letter. 'Lots of woe-is-me bollocks, he didn't mean to hurt anyone, blah, blah, bloody blah, and then lots of reassurance that your mum doesn't have to worry about anything, and she just needs to focus on her recovery.' Harry's expression turned serious once more. 'In the last line he promises that she never has to worry about the future because he'll always do right by you.'

Ivy's eyes stung with salty tears, and she raised a furious hand to dash them away. 'Like he's ever done right by anyone but himself in his whole miserable, bloody life,' she muttered before snatching up her teacup and draining it down. 'And that's it, is it?'

'Seems so,' Harry said, folding the letter carefully and tucking it back in its envelope. 'Your mum had it tucked away in the same section as the deeds and the mortgage stuff. I guess she must've believed his word was good enough.'

'And will a court see it that way?' Ivy knew the answer even before Harry started shaking his head.

'I'm sorry, Ivy, but I think you're going to have to talk to him and try and sort things out that way.'

* * *

It took a little while for Ivy to pluck up the, well, not so much courage as the emotional will to go and see her father. Following her disastrous meeting with Harry, she had gone straight home and shoved the expanding folder in the bottom of her wardrobe and tried to forget about everything while she threw herself into a whirlwind of cleaning that lasted several days. Down came all the condolence cards and the drooping vases of flowers. She hoovered and dusted every room in the cottage, including her mother's, but still couldn't settle to anything. The curtains came down next, the nets going into the washing machine on a gentle cycle, the rest bagged up and taken to the little 8 'til late convenience store, which also served as the post office and a hub for a dry-cleaning service.

She'd then spent a sleepless night cursing the full moon, which lit up her bedroom like a spotlight. After the third time of turning over a pillow that felt suddenly made of rocks, she threw back her quilt, switched on her bedside light and ended up on her hands and knees in front of the wardrobe hunting for her father's letter. She got as far as setting it down on the bed before deciding she was thirsty, which meant traipsing downstairs to make a cup of tea. Climbing back under her covers, she stared at the envelope for a few more moments before snatching it up and almost ripping the letter in her haste to remove it. Taking a deep breath, she unfolded the two sheets of paper and began to read.

She wasn't sure what she'd been hoping for: a clue, perhaps, as to why he'd chosen to abandon his wife and child at the worst possible moment; a reason to do as her mother had wished and forgive him, or something that would help the adult she was now look past those childish hurt feelings and empathise. It was, as Harry had observed, nothing more than a litany of excuses, however, and when Ivy set the letter aside with a sigh, she had learned nothing new about Kevin Fisher. Ivy picked up her tea, turned off the bedside light and mused long into the early hours about how she might approach him.

After her busy weekend of cleaning, she decided she was too tired to face it and took herself off for a long walk on the beach instead. Though the wind had a bite to it, she didn't mind and by the time she turned back for home she felt calmer and clearer. She passed a few people she knew and returned their greetings and polite enquiries after her with a genuine smile. Her footsteps took her to the door of Laurie's café, but when she peered through the window and spotted the knitting circle holding court in the corner, she decided against going in and asking her friend for advice. Though she knew there was no malice in Barbara, Kitty and the rest of them, they had noses as long as their knitting needles and didn't mind where they poked them. She beat a hasty retreat before anyone spotted her and headed back home.

Home. Just the thought of the word sent nerves dancing in her belly. What should have been a sanctuary was now little more than an empty shell. In time, perhaps, that would change and Ivy would be able to claim the space for herself, but it seemed that fate might deny her the chance. Until she sorted things out with her father, she didn't know where she stood. The ground once solid beneath her feet now felt like quicksand. She'd stopped taking commissions to focus on her mother, but that would have to change. Even if Kevin did agree to sign over the cottage to her, she'd have to speak to the bank about how she might take over the mortgage until all the probate stuff came through. There was no guarantee the insurance policy would pay off the outstanding balance, and, even if it did, she would still have bills to pay, food to buy and what have you.

Feet quickening, she hurried home and started making a list of all the questions whirling in her head. The more things she transferred from her brain to her notepad, the more new worries rose up to fill the gap until she wanted to lay her head down on the table and sob. She tossed her pen down, thinking she might just go ahead and have a pity cry when her phone beeped. Eager for any distraction, she snatched it up, only to feel winded again when she realised it was a message from Alex.

Hey. Just checking in. A x

It should have lifted her spirits, the way his surprise arrival had on the morning of the funeral, but it somehow only made things worse. She couldn't think about him now, without thinking about the bookshop, which meant thinking about the mess with the cottage, and round and round and round. Chucking her phone back on the table, she stomped off upstairs to have a sulk, which could only be done properly in a nice hot bath.

The bath not only helped to alleviate her bad mood, but made her sleepy enough to have a decent nap. Thankfully, it was overcast all night and she was able to sleep without her curtains and she awoke the next morning determined to wrestle back a little bit of control. Sitting around fretting about what might or might not be, wasn't helping so there was really nothing for it but to put on her best pair of big girl pants and get on with it.

Ivy had decided to wait until the following weekend so that she wouldn't have to navigate her father's working hours. And though she'd woken early this Saturday morning, she made herself wait until after ten, not wanting to risk catching him and Wendy still in their dressing gowns. Given what Wendy wore when she was out and about in public, Ivy really didn't want to know what her choice of nightwear might be. Trying to ward off images of leopard print and lace, Ivy did a couple of laps of the high street to kill a few more minutes then set her steps resolutely towards the top of the village. Her father still shared Wendy's little flat situated in one of the small, squat blocks the council had erected back in the seventies to try and alleviate the demand for housing. They weren't at all in keeping with the traditional stone cottages that spilled out in a higgledy-piggledy fashion from the seafront, nor the more stylish town houses nearby where Laurie's parents lived. The flats and small terraces formed a square around a scrubby bit of grass with a climbing frame and a set of swings that gave local children some-where to play. Both had been given a recent lick of paint since the last time Ivy had been up this way, and, though they wouldn't win any prizes for their looks, the majority of the houses looked neat and clean. Pots out the front might be looking a bit barren for now, but come the spring they'd be full of sunny daffodil bulbs and bright tulips.

As she walked down the path leading to the side entrance, Ivy wondered why they'd never moved on to somewhere bigger than the little flat. From what she knew of his work, Kevin had a decent job with plenty of opportunity to work overtime, so she didn't think he was short of money even with the bit he'd been paying her mum every month. Mind you, given his behaviour, perhaps his claims of working extra hours had mostly been a cover for sneaking around behind their backs. Before she had time to think better of it, she pressed the button next to the label that read *Hancock/Fisher* and listened to the buzz echoing through the intercom.

'Hello?' Ivy's stomach sank at the sound of Wendy's voice.

'Hi, Wendy!' she said, with more enthusiasm than she felt. 'It's Ivy. I was just wondering if Kevin was around.' She hadn't called him 'Dad' since the day he'd walked out, and she'd be damned if she was going to start now. A long silence stretched out and Ivy was just reaching for the intercom button to try again when the deeper buzz of the security lock sounded, followed by a heavy click. Feeling apprehensive at the less than warm welcome, Ivy shoved open the door and made her way up the echoey staircase to the second floor. Wendy waited in the entrance to the flat, and Ivy noted she'd been spot on with the leopard print, though thankfully, it was a low-cut sweater over a pair of black leggings rather than a negligee.

'He's in there,' Wendy said in a flat tone, stepping away from the door and gesturing towards the lounge with a tilt of her head. 'I'll put the kettle on.' She walked away without giving Ivy a chance to respond.

Taking care to remove her shoes before stepping over the threshold and onto the fluffy cream carpet, Ivy shut the door and set them down on the mat before shrugging out of her coat and hanging it on an empty hook on the wall. She didn't know how long it would take, and she didn't want to appear rude by keeping it on. On stocking feet, she padded into the lounge where her father occupied one of a pair of matching leather recliners before an over-sized TV suspended from the wall. He barely glanced away from *Sky Sports News* to acknowledge her arrival.

'Just let me listen to this bit,' he said, waving the remote towards the screen. Not sure what else she could do, Ivy retreated to the small two-seater sofa wedged between a wall unit covered in Dalton-style figurines and a large cheese plant. Trying to stave off her rising irritation – she was the one who'd shown up unan-nounced after all – Ivy half watched the pundits on the TV give a rundown of the latest Premiership team news. 'Right, then,' Kevin said at last, turning the volume down, but not off, and turning to face her. 'To what do we owe this pleasure?'

His voice was full of false bonhomie, as if Ivy were in the habit of dropping by, when she'd set foot in the flat not more than once or twice in the past ten years. Trying to ignore the twinge of guilt – she had nothing to feel guilty about, for heaven's sake – she gave him the brightest smile she could manage. 'I had an appointment with Harry Davenport the other day, to talk about...' Her throat was suddenly dry, and she found herself swal-lowing around an unwelcome lump. 'Well, you know,' she finished wanly.

'What do we know?' Wendy's voice was arch as she bustled in with a tray set with mugs and a small plate of biscuits. She plonked the tray on the coffee table, handed Kevin a mug then took one for herself together with the plate of biscuits, which she rested on the arm of her recliner where only Kevin would be able to reach them.

Like that, is it? Ignoring the mug still sitting on the tray, Ivy did her best to look past Wendy and catch her father's eye, but he was already half turned back towards the TV. 'There's a few things we need to sort out. With the cottage, and that.'

'Ah. I might have known it,' Wendy muttered into the top of her mug before taking a sip of tea.

Refusing to rise to the bait, Ivy ignored her. 'Things are more complicated than Mum had led me to believe.'

'And whose fault is that?'

'Well, it's not mine!' Ivy snapped at Wendy. 'I appreciate you and Kevin have been together a long time, but *this* is none of your business.'

'"Kevin!"' Wendy snorted. 'You don't even have the good grace to acknowledge your father properly and now you show up on our doorstep and think you can throw your weight around. Well, I'm not having it!'

Ivy rose, knowing she needed to get out of there before she said something she would regret later. Not because she was bothered about upsetting either of them, but because she didn't want them to know they could get to her. 'This was a mistake. I had hoped we could resolve things between us, but I suppose we'll have to rely on our solicitors to sort it out.' She looked over the top of Wendy's head and met Kevin's miserable-looking gaze. 'If you could let me know in due course who is acting for you, I'll get Harry to contact them.'

The threat of legal action was enough to finally spur Kevin into action. He jumped to his feet, a placating hand extended towards her. 'Ah, now then, love, there's no need for us to go wasting money on legal stuff. Sit yourself down and we can talk things through, like you said. Wendy won't say anything else, now, will you?' Wendy's lips tightened, her bright-pink lipstick emphasising the lines around her mouth. She'd always been a head-turner, but there was a hardness to her appearance, which Ivy thought detracted rather than emphasised her beauty.

Not wanting things to drag out as they inevitably would if they did have to get their solicitors involved this early, Ivy ignored the urge to tell Kevin she wasn't his *anything*, never mind his love, and resumed her seat. Taking a deep breath, she plunged ahead with the thing she hadn't been able to get out of her head since finding it out. 'The most surprising bit of news was to find out that you and Mum were still married. I thought that had all been settled long ago.'

Wendy opened her mouth, but Kevin reached out and touched her arm, shaking his head when she looked his way. Ivy watched as Wendy battled with herself and was relieved when she stood up and walked out. A red-faced Kevin watched her leave before turning back to Ivy with an apologetic shrug. 'Bit of a touchy subject,' he said, speaking much more quietly than he had before.

Ivy glanced towards the still-open door and wondered whether Wendy was lurking – more than likely, but as long as she kept quiet, Ivy could say her piece and go. 'Anyway, it makes things more complicated with the cottage because that's still in joint names. Mum's will leaves everything to me and from the most recent conversations we had before Christmas, I think she assumed that the cottage would be mine.'

Kevin frowned. 'Well, I've no objection to you having her share of it, and the personal stuff, that goes without saying, but I've kept up the payments all this time, even after you were done with school and I wasn't legally obliged.' He sounded disgruntled, as though he'd done them some huge favour.

'So, you do intend to claim your half of the cottage?' Ivy's stomach sank. It wasn't anything worse than she'd been expecting since she'd found out the truth from Harry, but there'd been a small kernel of hope.

Scratching at the back of his neck, Kevin glanced towards the still chattering commentators on the TV. 'I was going to give you another week to sort yourself out before we started with estate agents and what have you.'

Another week? The implication of those words hit her like a ton of bricks and she had to press a hand to her chest to try and stem the flutter of panic building there. In the back of her mind, she'd understood the implication of him owning half the cottage, but she'd thought there would be more time to get to grips with everything. 'So soon?'

'I'm not made of money, love. You can't expect us to stay cooped up in this little flat forever, now, can you?' He sounded like what he was saying was so bloody reasonable, when, in reality, he was telling her he was kicking her out of the only home she'd ever known. Beyond words, she slumped back in her chair and simply stared at him. His cheeks flushed, an ugly creep of colour that told her he knew exactly how devastating this was, and that he was going to do it anyway. 'I thought your mother would've made things clear to you. I can't be blamed if she's led you to believe that the place would be yours to keep.'

Ivy bit the inside of her cheek. Kevin had always looked to blame everyone else – was it really any surprise that he'd stoop so low? 'I don't understand why you just didn't let her sort the divorce out when she wanted to. Surely that would've been the best for everyone in the long run? Rather than this bloody mess.' She gestured helplessly.

'Your mum had enough on her plate,' Kevin protested.

'And you didn't want to look like an even bigger shit than you already did when word got out that she was ill again and we were forced to sell the cottage, because that's what you would've done, isn't it?' Ivy clutched her stomach, sick at the thought of it. Kevin opened his mouth, but she cut him off, too furious now to pretend to be rational about anything. 'That letter you wrote at the time wasn't worth the paper it was written on! Mum clung to those promises you made to do the right thing and all the time you were just putting off the inevitable because of the coward you are.' She shoved herself up from the squashy sofa, needing to get out of there. She was done with letting this pathetic man hurt her. 'Send the details of your solicitor to Harry and he can deal with you. I never want to see or speak to you again.'

Ivy fled from the room, ignoring Kevin's protests. To her surprise, the hall was empty, and she grabbed for her coat with one hand while forcing her feet into her shoes as quickly as she could. She thought she'd made a clean getaway as she clattered down the stairs and wrenched open the communal entrance door for the flats. As she stepped out, a cloud of cigarette smoke wafted towards her. She dodged to the side, trying to avoid the stink of it getting in her hair and clothes.

Wendy was leaning against the wall, one arm folded across her middle, the other dangling a cigarette. 'I want a word with you,' she said, grinding the butt out on the wall before tossing it into a rusty can full of dirty rainwater and mouldering cigarette ends.

'Mind your own business, Wendy,' Ivy snapped, close to tears though she'd be damned if she let one single drop leak in front of this woman. She spun away, but Wendy grabbed her arm and stopped her.

'You think this isn't my business?' She gave a bitter laugh. 'Ten bloody years I've been disrespected by the people in this village because of you and your mother! Ten years of dirty looks and people not giving me the time of day because she wouldn't let my Kev go. Do you know what that's like? Do you?' Her voice rose to something close to a shout.

The shock of the verbal attack was enough to dry Ivy's looming tears and she took a step back, worried for a moment that Wendy might lash out. Ivy cast a quick glance around to make sure they hadn't drawn attention from anyone passing by before saying in as calm a voice as she could manage, 'No one asked you to get involved with a married man, but that's all water under the bridge now. Everything is in the hands of the solicitors, so I suggest we do our best to stay out of each other's way from now on.'

Expecting more abuse, Ivy was shocked when Wendy's face crumpled, and her eyes filled with tears. 'I never meant to hurt anyone. He told me things were over a long time ago between him and Jen. I had no idea she was ill.'

Ivy felt a pang of what might have been pity for the other woman. She had no doubt that Wendy had taken the brunt of things. Small villages like the Point weren't very progressive in their outlook and many would have painted Wendy as the homewrecker. She looked at Wendy now, and noticed how slight she was. She'd always seemed like such an imposing figure, but maybe she'd only seen her through the eyes of a bewildered child. With her make-up streaked down her face and her arms wrapped around herself, Wendy looked as if a strong breeze would blow her over. Whatever lingering animosity Ivy might have felt melted away. 'It doesn't really matter any more, does it?'

Wendy sniffed, a thick wet sound that made Ivy's stomach turn. 'If she'd just let him go with a bit of dignity then Kev and I could at least have got married and I wouldn't still be treated like his bit on the side. All I did was fall in love – how is that my fault?'

God, what an ugly mess everything was. From the sounds of things, Kevin hadn't been honest with Wendy any more than he had been with anyone else. 'Mum filed for divorce years ago.' Ivy said it as gently as she could. Perhaps it would've been best to leave it, nothing could hurt her mum any longer, but she was just sick to death of Kevin and his refusal to take responsibility for anything.

Wendy's head snapped up. 'That's not true! Kev only stayed married to her because she was sick, and he didn't want to make things worse. She poisoned you against him, ruined any chance of the two of you having a proper father-daughter relationship. Do you know how much it hurt him when you turned away from him at the funeral?'

Ivy bristled at that. 'No one poisoned me against Kevin, he managed that all on his own. I was barely thirteen and he left me to cope with Mum's illness. Sending a tacky card every birthday and Christmas wasn't going to fix that.'

When she saw Wendy flinch, Ivy realised it was likely her who'd bought those cards and forced Kevin to sign them and wished she could snatch the words back. They hadn't been tacky, they'd just been a bit over the top with all their '*To my Darling Daughter*' messages. Though Wendy had probably meant well with them, it'd felt like a slap in the face each time one popped through the letter-box. 'Whatever Kevin might have told you, he was the one who didn't want the divorce, not Mum.' With something bordering on sympathy, Ivy dug her hand in her pocket and fished out the letter Harry had found tucked away with the deeds. 'It's here in black and white, Wendy. See for yourself what kind of man you've wasted all these years on.'

5

Alex picked up his phone for the twentieth time on Saturday evening before tossing it back on the coffee table with a sigh. He turned his attention back to his laptop, the screen of which was as blank as the phone's notification screen. It was the first time he'd had to write all day and his mind was as blank as both devices. He'd been up at the crack of dawn, hoovering and polishing – and hiding stuff in cupboards – in anticipation of half a dozen viewings on the house. Hiding stuff rather than actually tidying up had proven a mistake when one particularly intrusive woman had opened the wardrobe in his bedroom and been confronted with the pile of dirty washing he'd chucked in the bottom of it. Though the house had only been on the market a short while, there'd been a flurry of interest but no offers. A couple of the appointments had been obvious time-wasters. Alex couldn't imagine anything more boring than traipsing around houses you had no intention of buying but the agent had told him it was apparently a thing. He had recognised one couple who lived about a dozen doors down from him who were either being nosey or trying to work out what their own place might be worth in comparison. *Bloody Rightmove had a lot to answer for.* He glanced at his watch and saw it was exactly two minutes later than the last time he'd checked it and turned back to his keyboard with a sigh. *Give it until eight o'clock and then you can knock it on the head.*

The promise lasted for all of thirty seconds until something in the kitchen beeped and he tossed his laptop onto the sofa beside him and leapt up. He regretted giving in to the distraction when he yanked open the door to the dishwasher and a cloud of hot steam blasted him in the face. Having hidden all his dirty cups and plates in it that morning, he'd decided he might as well switch the bloody thing on. Abandoning it to cool down, he opened the fridge and reached for a bottle of beer before stopping himself. He'd promised Tom he would take better care of himself, starting with no more drinking for the rest of the month. His eyes strayed to the stack of leftover cartons from last night's Chinese and he promised himself he'd get straight on that healthy living kick... tomorrow.

Ten minutes later he was scrolling through Netflix with a steaming bowl of microwaved chow mein and spicy beef resting in his lap and the open bottle of beer in his other hand. *Nope. Nope. Nope.* What on earth had possessed him to add such dross to his watchlist? His phone beeped and he quickly swapped it for the remote.

Sorry I haven't replied before, it's been a rough few days. Thank you again for coming down for Mum's funeral, you don't know how much you helped me that day. Hope all is well with you, Ivy x

He tapped out a quick reply.

Need to talk? You'd be saving me from myself as I'm just about to watch The Da Vinci Code.

He added the little emoji of a monkey covering its eyes to the end of the message.

He could tell from the app that she'd read it, but when there was nothing else forthcoming he set his phone on the armrest of the sofa with a sigh. Though she'd been polite about him showing up unannounced he still worried he'd been too pushy and here he was again trying to barge his way into her business even when he told himself he was going to back off. He flicked play on the remote control and settled back into the cushion. The film had only got as far as Tom Hanks delivering his lecture on symbolism through the ages when his phone started ringing. He snatched it up and accepted the video request. Ivy's pretty pale face popped up on the screen and he noted immediately the deep black-purple shadows beneath her eyes. 'Hello!' he said. 'I was worried for a minute you were going to leave me to suffer through this terrible movie alone.'

Ivy laughed. 'I was just sorting myself out. I decided that misery loves company so I thought I'd join you. Have you started watching?'

'I'm only a few minutes in, hang on, I'll pause it.' He juggled the phone, the remote and the bowl in his lap as he tried to stop the film.

'Ooh, what have you got there?'

He glanced down at his dinner. 'Just some leftover takeaway from last night.'

'Well, that sounds better than my dinner,' Ivy replied, holding up a bag of crisps and a large bar of Dairy Milk to show him. 'There's a freezer full of stuff, but I can't be bothered.'

He swallowed the urge to chide her for not taking better care of herself because he was hardly in any position to talk. Grabbing a couple of cushions, Alex propped his phone up so he could see the screen without having to hold it. 'That's better. Can you see me okay?'

'Yes. That's a good idea, let me do that.' The screen bobbed and dipped, giving Alex a view of Ivy's ear, a quick flash of the ceiling and then it settled into a sideways image of her sitting cross-legged on her bed. She was dressed in what looked like a pair of pale grey leggings and an oversized black cardigan. Her feet were burrowed in the ugliest pair of slipper boots he'd ever seen and he thought that for all his best intentions he might be the tiniest bit in love with her. 'Does that work?'

'What? Oh yes, that's great.' Though he'd much rather if she were curled up here on the sofa beside him, or better yet if they were snuggled side by side on her bed together... He squashed the unruly thought deep down inside and tried to get his mind back on track. 'You don't really intend to watch this silly film with me, do you?'

Ivy nestled deeper into her pillows, her eyes fixed on what he assumed was her TV. 'Why not? I've never actually seen it before and I love Tom Hanks.'

He started laughing. 'Do you at least know the story?'

'Something about the Holy Grail? I must be one of the few people in the country who've never read the book.' She glanced at him through the screen, a bleakness in her eyes. 'I was a bit too young when the film came out and then, well, a lot of pop culture stuff has kind of passed me by.'

He thought for a moment about his own carefree upbringing. There'd been some tension between their father and Tom, who was his half-brother, but that was something he'd only come to understand in later years. When he'd been growing up, his parents had doted on him almost to the point of spoiling him. His father had taken early retirement so he'd been around all the time and when Tom had visited on his designated weekends and in the holidays it had been as if the sun had come out. Alex had hero-worshipped the older boy, and Tom had been unendingly patient with him toddling around after him. He wondered when things had changed for Ivy. Had she at least known some times of joy, or had her mother always been sick? He didn't know how to ask.

'When it comes to the literary works of Dan Brown, you haven't missed much.' Alex caught himself falling into the easy trap of snobbery and shook his head. 'That's not fair. *The Da Vinci Code* was an absolute page-turner. I think he's one of those authors people like to mock because it makes them feel superior somehow. He's sold millions of copies so he must be doing something right.'

Ivy smiled then. 'I'll see how the movie goes, but I might check the books out. Lord knows I could do with something that's fun and easy right now.'

'I can't imagine how hard things must be for you,' he said, wishing there were something he could offer her other than platitudes. 'It'll take time to get used to things, but you've got plenty of people there who you can lean on.'

'Yeah, I know, but it's not missing Mum that's the problem.' She raised a hand to her mouth, a stricken look in her eyes. 'God, that sounded awful, and that's not what I mean at all.'

'Hey, hey, it's fine.' Alex set his food aside and turned so he could look more directly into the camera. 'You don't have to apologise for anything or worry about how anything sounds. Just talk to me.'

Ivy heaved a sigh so huge it raised her whole upper body. 'I'm not sure I know where to start.' For the next few minutes he listened as between mouthfuls of the chocolate bar she stumbled through an explanation about confusion over ownership of the cottage and how, although they'd been separated for years, her parents had never finalised their divorce. When she raised a finger and pressed it to the corner of her eye as though trying to stem tears, he wanted to punch something and settled for gripping his beer bottle between both hands. 'And then he said he'll give me a week before we need to put the place up for sale as he's not made of money, the bastard!' Ivy shoved another chunk of Dairy Milk in her mouth to underline her disgust.

'But he can't force you to sell, can he?' Alex couldn't believe anyone would stoop so low, especially with everything that Ivy had been through. Mind you, from what she'd said, her father had left her to cope when her mum had first become ill so Alex supposed he couldn't put anything past him.

'When I first found out, Harry said we could take it to court, but it's an expensive process and it would only be postponing the inevitable. I can't afford to buy him out. I was hoping to be able to expand my business and boost my income to something halfway decent, but I don't have any savings or collateral other than my share of the cottage.' She scrubbed her face with her hands. 'I don't think Kevin can do anything until we get the probate sorted, but as soon as it's granted, I can't see any way to stop him.'

'The thing I can't understand is if he was so worried about what people would think before, why doesn't he care now? Once the rest of the village finds out he's planning to turf you out, he'll be a pariah.'

Ivy shrugged. 'I'm not sure he ever cared that much, he just said that to avoid the hassle. It's not just Mum he lied to, he's been stringing Wendy along all these years, telling her he couldn't marry her because Mum wouldn't agree to the divorce. I almost felt sorry for her. She's hung all her hopes on a coward and a liar all these years. I doubt he'd recognise the truth if it jumped up and bit him on the arse.'

Alex laughed, liking the bite in her tone as she said those last words. He didn't want her to sound defeated, he wanted her feisty and fiery and ready to stick up for herself. What he really wanted was to jump in his car and race down to the Point, find Kevin bloody Fisher and knock him for six. *Nice hero complex, Alex.* He wasn't in any position to try and play the white knight, and, besides, the last thing Ivy needed was another man muscling in and trying to complicate her life. The best thing he could do was get his own affairs in order and get himself relocated to the Point so he could offer her proper moral support while she sorted things out for herself.

'It's not like I hadn't thought about selling the cottage. It was something Mum talked to me about before she died, after all, but with only half the profit I was expecting, I doubt I'll be able to find anywhere big enough to live and work out of.'

Alex hadn't even thought about that. 'How much room do you need?'

'Not masses, I mean, I've been managing out of the back bedroom here for years, but I wanted to try and grow the business into something more than doing mostly repairs and alterations. I've refurbished a few bits of furniture and really enjoyed doing that, but I'd need some decent outside space for varnishing and painting, especially if I wanted to tackle some bigger pieces.' She glanced at the screen before looking away. 'Andrew and Sylvia have let me display a few things in The Mermaid's Cave, but I'd kind of hoped to expand into a bit of retail space of my own one day.'

And just like that the pieces clicked into place and he knew what he could do. 'Just a shame you don't know anyone who's in the process of buying a shop, isn't it?' He kept his tone ultra-casual as he continued. 'A shop that happens to have a back room full of junk the current owner doesn't want to take with him and a large yard out the back...'

Ivy leaned closer to her phone screen. 'What are you saying?'

'I'm saying,' Alex said as he picked up his own phone and brought it close to his face, 'there's a way we can help each other out and both get what we want. Do you remember that flyer I picked up in the pub at Christmas?' He shook his head, because why would she? 'To cut a long story short, Mr Cavendish is selling the bookshop and I'm planning to buy it.' When Ivy gave him a blank look, he realised he was making a hash of explaining the idea still forming in his head. He tried again. 'It's very dark and old-fashioned inside and I was planning on completely overhauling the place.' He hadn't said anything to Mr Cavendish as he hadn't wanted to hurt his feelings, but he intended to rip out everything and start from scratch.

It was one of the reasons Alex had agreed to buy the shop with all its contents – including the room full of bits and pieces of old furniture and miscellaneous junk. The old man was leaving the village to move in with his widowed sister down in Cornwall, so it wasn't likely he'd see what Alex did to the place. He was still musing over exactly what he wanted to do other than get rid of all the gloomy brown. He pictured pale walls, neutral shelving and lots of nooks and crannies where people could sit and browse.

With Ivy's input, there was a real chance of transforming the shop into something special. 'You've got an amazing eye for things so, if you wanted to, you could help me with the redesign and in return, I could give you somewhere you could work from. I'm sure with a bit of imagination we can find the perfect balance between books and some displays to sell your clothes and furniture and whatever.' He waved a hand vaguely as he still wasn't altogether sure what it was that Ivy did – or planned to do.

Wide green eyes stared out at him from the screen. 'Are you serious?'

It was Alex's turn to shrug. 'It's only just occurred to me but, yeah, why not? Buying the bookshop is all still a bit up in the air at the moment, until I can get the house sold and what have you. The proceeds should mostly cover the purchase as London property prices are so inflated, and I've got plenty of savings, which would cover the refurbishment works.' The royalties he'd earned from *The*

Marriage Roller Coaster were supposed to be locked away for his future retirement, and he tried not to think about what his father would say about him throwing all his proverbial eggs into one basket. The shop would work – he would make it work.

Ivy shook her head. 'I've never met anyone like you before.'

'I hope that's a compliment, though somehow I fear otherwise,' Alex said before taking a swig of his beer.

She laughed then. 'A bit of both perhaps. You seem far too relaxed for someone who is contemplating changing their whole life. Do you even have any experience in retail?'

Alex shrugged. 'Not as such, but I know my way around a spreadsheet and I—' Realising he was about to blurt out that he also had experience of the publishing industry, he caught himself and wound up saying, '—I like books.'

'I like food, but I'm not about to try and buy a restaurant.' Ivy snorted.

'So, you think I'm making a big mistake?' Alex was surprised at how much her opinion meant to him.

'Not necessarily, you just seem a bit light on details.' Ivy held up a hand. 'Not that it's any of my business.'

'But I thought we'd just agreed that it *would* be your business, or at least you're going to be a big part of it,' he countered. 'Don't tell me you're getting cold feet already.'

'I don't remember agreeing to anything,' she protested with another laugh. 'All you've offered me is a room full of junk and a bit of outside space!'

'One person's junk is another person's treasure!' He liked the sound of that. 'Hey, that could be the name of the shop – The Mermaid's Treasure.'

'You're going to change the name?' Ivy asked, looking sad. 'I hadn't considered that.'

Alex frowned. 'Well, Cavendish's Books and Ephemera doesn't

exactly trip off the tongue. I wanted something that will appeal to tourists and didn't think the locals would mind much one way or the other. I thought I'd cash in on what's left of the mermaid hype, you know?' A mad idea occurred to him. 'Hey, I wonder if Nick still has Aurora Storm's phone number – maybe we could rope her in to do the grand opening.'

'That would certainly be a coup if you could pull it off. And I'm sure you are right about changing the name, I'm just being senti-mental, but don't you think you should keep some reference to it being a bookshop?'

'Good point.' Alex tapped his beer bottle against his lip as he considered the possibilities. 'Mermaid Books and Treasures?' He muttered it to himself a few times, testing it on the tongue, but it didn't feel quite right. 'Mermaid Stories and Treasures?'

'Tales and Treasures? Alliteration works well with names,' Ivy suggested.

She was a flipping genius. 'That's it! And the pun is an added bonus.' He could already picture the sign over the door: a mermaid with flowing locks and a long, sinuous tail with the name painted in gold across her aquamarine scales.

'Pun?' Ivy's nose scrunched in an endearingly thoughtful expression before she raised a hand and slapped her forehead. 'Mermaid Tales, a mermaid's tail. Oh, goodness, that never even occurred to me!' She started to laugh. 'It's a bit cheesy, but also adorable – I love it.'

'Cheesy but adorable is totally my brand.' Alex waggled his eyebrows at her.

Though she rolled her eyes, he couldn't miss the sweet smile that lit up her whole face. She still looked tired, but the defeated look had been banished and he intended to keep it that way. Having Ivy around all the time might not be the most sensible idea when he'd sworn off women, and particularly her, but he would find a way to deal with his attraction to her. Moving to Mermaids Point offered him a chance to really turn his life around, to stop going through the motions and finally start living again. It wasn't just that Tom and the kids were there, although that was a huge part of the pull. He was starting to make friends of his own there as well. He'd clicked with both Jake and Nick from the moment they'd been introduced, and it had made him realise how much Jo and Shaun's affair had been a double betrayal. There were a few mates from university that he still kept in touch with, but most of those relationships were intrinsically bound with memories of Jo. He hoped that time would address that, and he'd feel better able to reconnect, but for now he was all about the promise of a fresh start.

'Well,' Ivy said, drawing him back out of his thoughts, 'that's the work side of things sorted out, now all I have to do is try and find somewhere to live.'

The housing situation in the Point hadn't really occurred to him before – the shop came with a spacious two-bedroom flat on the upper floor, which was liveable if a bit old-fashioned. As long as the plumbing worked he would be happy to move in and focus on the shop. And it hadn't been an issue for Tom either as the doctor's surgery had a large family home incorporated into the sprawling white building. Speaking of which... 'There's always the flat above the surgery. I could have a word with Tom and see if he and Nerissa have any plans for the place.'

'Oh, I don't know about that. I'm sure they wouldn't want me gatecrashing when they have so much else going on. It doesn't even have its own access, so I'd be traipsing through their living space every time I went in and out.' Ivy's dubious expression said she didn't really like the idea of that.

'Fair enough, but it might be worth at least asking the question, even if it's only as a back-up plan. It could take months to sell the cottage.' He tried to sound hopeful, not wanting her to get all stressed out about it again.

'Or it could get snapped up in a day.' Ivy shook her head. 'I can't just cross my fingers and hope it doesn't happen. I have to prepare for the worst and be ready to move sooner rather than later.'

Alex sighed. 'I get what you're saying. I don't suppose one of Nick's flats would be an option?' His friend was working on his own big refurbishment project, converting an old warehouse overlooking the village harbour into four apartments. One was for Nick, the other three he planned to sell to local couples looking to get a foot on the ladder. Alex wasn't sure, but he didn't think Nick had even secured planning permission yet so it could be months, if not a year, before they'd be ready.

'In the longer term, it might be.' Ivy disappeared from the screen for a moment. When she resumed her seat on the bed he could see a notebook and pen in her lap. 'I'll start a list of prospects.' She made a couple of notes before casting him a sheepish grin. 'I always feel better when I've written things down. I feel more in control when I have a list, even if I haven't done anything about the items on it. Does that make sense?'

Alex nodded. 'Better to have a point of focus rather than everything swirling about in your brain.' Which was what he usually did these days. It had been easier when he'd worked in an office, with a defined list of tasks and targets and a diary to keep him on track. Maybe he needed to start doing that again. As he couldn't use his phone while they were chatting, he grabbed his abandoned laptop and clicked on the Amazon shortcut on his toolbar.

'What are you doing?' Ivy had tilted her head as though she could somehow see through the screen and over his shoulder.

'I'm ordering myself a desk diary. If I'm going to be a small-business owner soon, I need to be a responsible small-business owner.' He scrolled through the listings until he spotted an A4-sized diary similar to the one he'd had on his desk at work and added it to his basket. Ever eager to maximise an upsell, Amazon immediately suggested a whole range of other stationery items and before he knew it Alex had thirty quid's worth of stuff ready to checkout. 'I need to start working on a budget,' he muttered to himself as he completed the sale before the website's blasted algorithms persuaded him to buy anything else.

'Oh, do you know how to do that? I might have to pick your brain.' Ivy gave him that adorable scrunched-up-nose look again. 'I've tended to work on a piece-by-piece basis, but if I'm going to try and scale up so I have enough stock to sell to people browsing in the shop then I need to get my head around the numbers much better.'

'I can knock you up a basic set of P & L accounts and show you how to use them,' Alex assured her. 'You'll want to think about an accountant in the longer term though.' He made a mental note to ask Mr Cavendish who he was using as it might be advantageous to employ someone already familiar with the business. 'But I can get you going without you spending anything up front while you work out some costings. Once things are up and running there's loads of user-friendly accounting packages and, again, I'll help you find one that works best for what you'll need.'

Ivy held up a hand. 'Slow down, slow down! I need to get these things on my list. First question, what's a P & L account?'

'Profit and loss.' He grinned. 'Sorry, I went full accountancy nerd on you, didn't I?'

She smiled. 'I'm just grateful one of us knows what they're talking about.' She hesitated, then asked, 'Is that what you do for a living at the moment?'

Should he just go ahead and tell her about the book? Part of him wanted to be completely honest with her, but, then again, he'd been in full woe-is-me mode when he'd written it and there were parts he wasn't proud of. What if she was curious enough to read it? The Alex who'd written those words felt more and more like a stranger these days, and he didn't want any of his new friends, Ivy least of all, judging him based on that phase in his life. No, he decided, best to leave that behind him. 'It was what I did until quite recently,' was all he said in the end. 'Tom making a big change in his life helped me realise I've been stuck in a bit of a rut. I studied accountancy because I was good with numbers and my dad wanted me to do something with sensible career prospects. He made his money working in the City, and I never felt drawn to anything else enough to go against it. After my divorce—'

'You've been married?' Ivy blurted out. 'How did I not know that?'

Alex felt his cheeks heat and he scrubbed at the two-day-old stubble on his jaw. 'Well, the marriage didn't end well, hence the divorce. And although I haven't been deliberately hiding it, it's not something I've wanted to talk about.'

'I'm so sorry.' She sounded so warm and sincere her words were as comforting as if she'd given him a hug.

'Thanks. I was sorry too for a while, but now it feels more like a lucky escape.' Not wanting to say much more in case he spilled the whole pitiful tale out, he steered his thoughts back in a more positive direction. 'I'm thirty in a few months, and it feels like a bit of a crossroads. I don't have any financial or emotional ties so now is the right time to take a risk and try something different. I didn't want to stay in the house Jo and I shared, but it didn't make sense to move for the sake of it. Now it would be a positive step to take because Mermaids Point feels like it could be home – if that doesn't sound too soppy and sentimental.'

'It's the community.' Ivy drew her knees up and propped her chin on them, her expression thoughtful. 'There's been times over the years when it's chafed to know I can't do anything without the whole world – or at least the *whole* village – knowing about it. Since Mum first got sick, they've been a godsend. I've never had to ask for support, never worried that there was no one I could turn to – even with Dad taking off like he did. I had Laurie to hold my hand when I didn't want to go to school. Nick was there for big-brother hugs and Andrew and Sylvia were like surrogate parents. Teachers, neighbours, Luca and his family at the deli giving us extra credit when finances were tight. They all held me up when I didn't have the strength to stand on my own.'

Alex thought about the way Tom and his children had been embraced by the residents of the Point since their arrival at the end of last August. There'd been a few teething problems at the surgery, for sure, with Tom's predecessor finding it harder to retire than perhaps he'd expected. But with a bit of clever thinking on his brother's part, he'd resolved that problem and put Doc Gadd in charge of a men's health programme that both kept him occupied and improved the service Tom was able to offer to the more reluctant members of the community. They bred them hardy in the Point, but that had its drawbacks too.

The kids were thriving at college and secondary school, respectively, and the heavy blanket of grief that had lain over the three of them after the tragedy of Anna's death had finally lifted. Nerissa was a huge part of that, of course, but the villagers were owed a debt of gratitude Alex wasn't sure he'd ever be able to repay. Turning the local bookshop back into a thriving hub for the community might be a good place to start.

6

Ivy opened the front door and cast a baleful eye at the dark clouds lurking on the horizon. Being this close to the sea, it wasn't always easy to predict the course of a storm and it might just as easily blow itself out as descend on them. Knowing her luck right now, it would be the second option, so although she was bundled up with several warm layers beneath her waterproof wax jacket, Ivy removed her umbrella from the hooks by the door and tucked it under her arm. It had originally been designed for a child, edged as it was with bright red and black ladybirds, but the see-through dome meant she could pull it right down over her face and shoulders and the depth of it meant it was less likely to be turned inside out by a sharp gust of wind. It also made her smile, and on a grim March day that wasn't something to be taken for granted. The old saying about the month coming in like a lion was certainly proving true.

Though it took her out of the way of her lunchtime destination, Laurie's café being one of the many premises lining the seafront, Ivy headed deeper into the village so she could walk along the high street instead. It had been a month since her showdown with her father and Ivy hadn't heard so much as a peep from him. Harry had let her know he'd been in touch with details of a solicitor and the probate wheels were grinding away. Ivy had left as much to Harry as possible, although, as she was the executor of her mother's will, there was plenty of form-filling to be done. Luckily, he was happy to drop her a message when the next round of paperwork was ready and explain things as and when necessary, rather than overwhelming her. An initial certificate of probate had been granted so they'd been able to formally notify the bank and the mortgage company as well as apply for the insurance policy her mum had taken out.

Unable to face the appointment herself, Ivy had cleaned the cottage from top to bottom and made herself scarce when Alun Wise, the estate agent, had needed to come and do the valuation. Like everyone else in the Point, he understood the circumstances and was happy to collect the spare key from Harry and look around on his own. The price Alun had quoted had been higher than she'd expected, and put paid to any lingering notion she would ever be able to afford to buy her father's share of the property. He seemed hopeful of achieving close to the valuation and had a list of people who'd previously registered an interest in the area to get in touch with. Harry had calculated a rough figure of the assets and liabilities, so Ivy had something to work with when it came to looking for somewhere to live.

Alan had had less positive news on that front. Flats and starter homes were rarer than hen's teeth and there was nothing currently on the market unless she was willing to move out of the Point, which was an absolute last resort. There were a few holiday places she might be able to rent on a short-term basis until the season started up, but she was still holding out hope of finding somewhere she could move into on a medium-to-long-term basis. Though she'd made a list of all her current options, it hadn't done the usual trick of stopping her brain from fixating on the problem, which was why she'd chosen to escape the cottage for an hour and pay Laurie a visit.

* * *

Ivy's first stop was a furtive browse in the estate agent's window, more out of hope than expectation. A quick scan over the properties on display was enough to assure her that nothing new had come onto the market. She was turning away when a knock came behind her and she glanced over her shoulder to see Alun with his hand raised and an awkward smile on his face. He pointed towards the front door and Ivy walked to meet him there. 'Hi, Alun, everything okay with the cottage?' she asked, immediately concerned Kevin might have thrown a spanner in the works.

'Oh yes, everything is fine on that front. I've sent out the particulars to quite a few folk, so fingers crossed for a nibble soon.' A hearty beam stretched his round face wide in what she guessed was supposed to be encouragement.

'That's a relief. If it's not the cottage, then what is it? I can't stay long as I'm meeting Laurie for lunch.'

Alun's brows lowered and he cast a quick look up and down the deserted high street as though he expected a horde of people to appear. Most of the residents had better weather sense than Ivy and were sticking close to home. 'It's a bit of a delicate matter,' he said in a hushed tone. 'Could you step inside for one minute?'

The moment she stepped inside, he slipped the bolt on the door to lock it before tugging down the shade for good measure. The heat of the office hit her like a brick and she unzipped her coat, even though she had no intention of staying long. 'Blimey, Alun, what's with all the cloak and dagger stuff?'

'Sorry.'

When she glanced up at him after shrugging her coat off and

draping it over the nearest chair, she was concerned to see he was rubbing his hands together in a nervous gesture. He was an ebullient and outgoing man as befitted his trade, and this strange body language worried Ivy. She decided she'd better sit down. 'What is it?' A horrible thought suddenly occurred to her. 'Are *you* okay?'

'What? Oh, yes, I'm right as rain! Goodness, I'm making a proper three-course meal of this, aren't I?' With a sigh he pulled a chair over and sat opposite her. 'It's nothing awful, just... a bit awkward. I wasn't even going to mention it but then I saw you looking in the window and decided I should let you know all potential options.'

'Oka-a-ay.' She still had no idea what he was going on about.

Alun took a deep breath and a torrent of words poured out. 'A new property has come onto the market. It's actually ideal for what you are looking for, a one-bed flat that's been kept to the highest standards. There's just one thing that might be an issue for you – it's Wendy Hancock's place.'

A burst of hysterical laughter escaped from Ivy. 'You can't be serious!'

The estate agent hung his head. 'I know, I know, it's a terrible idea, but I felt I had to let you know on the off chance.'

'On the off chance I want to move into the place my father's been holed up in with his girlfriend for the past ten years?' Ivy didn't know whether to laugh or cry at the absurdity of it.

Alun clapped his hands over his rosy, red face. 'Stop it. It sounds even worse when you say it out loud. I should never have said anything.'

His distress was comical enough to put paid to any idea she might have had of crying. 'Oh, Alun. How long have you been tying yourself in knots over this?'

He dropped his hands into his lap. 'Three days. She came in on Monday and declared they were selling up and would be leaving as soon as everything was settled.' He shot her a horrified look. 'Oh god, I can't believe I broke it to you like that. Honestly, if my Maureen was here she'd give me a clip round the ear and tell me to take my foot out of my mouth.'

Ivy chuckled because she could imagine petite Maureen Wise doing exactly that. 'It's fine, Alun, honestly. No doubt I would've heard about their plans sooner or later and at least you had the kindness to do it behind closed doors.' Though the vast majority of residents were wonderful, the Point still had its share of gossips who would delight in being the bearer of such news to her door just so they could further gossip about Ivy's reaction to it.

Reaching out, Alun laid a beefy hand on top of hers. The contact jolted her. Not because there was anything untoward about it – Alun was a sweetheart and absolutely devoted to his wife. It was the fact she couldn't remember the last time anyone had touched her – not since the funeral, perhaps? A wave of sadness threatened to engulf her and she might have let it had Alun not leaned forward to catch her eye as he said, 'I have thoughts about the whole sorry situation, Ivy. I can't tell you what they are, but I. Have. Thoughts.'

The deliberate pause he put between each word as much as the purse of his lips told Ivy exactly what those thoughts were. She wanted to throw her arms around him and hug him for his loyalty but settled instead for patting the back of his hand with her free one. 'I have thoughts, too.'

Alun pulled his hand back with a relieved laugh. 'So, that's a pass on the flat, I take it?'

'A very hard one.' Rising to her feet, Ivy reached for her coat. 'I can't wait to see Laurie's face when I tell her about this.'

Alun jumped up to unlock the door. 'Just don't tell her in earshot of her mother or Sylvia will be round here to clip my ear!'

'And then she'll tell Maureen and you'll get one again when you get home.' Ivy grinned. 'Honestly, you've done me a favour because

I didn't think I'd be able to laugh about anything to do with this whole awful situation, but you've proven me wrong.'

'Don't let the bastards grind you down.' Alun patted her back as she slipped past him and out of the door.

Ivy was still grinning to herself over poor Alun's discomfort five minutes later when she entered the café, the jangling bell over the door announcing her arrival. Laurie glanced up from behind the counter where she was serving someone to give her a quick wave, which Ivy returned, before beginning the laborious process of de-layering. The rain had thankfully held off, but the way the sky was darkening, it wouldn't be long before it made its presence felt. Oh well, getting rained in and spending the afternoon with her best friend wasn't the worst thing that could happen. Ivy did a quick survey of the room, noting with an inward sigh the presence of the knitting circle in the corner. Her eyes met the appraising glance of Bev, one of the worst gossips, and she gave her a bright smile because she'd be damned if she'd let her start carrying tales of 'poor Ivy' to all and sundry. She added a little wave and a mental 'up yours' for good measure.

'You beat the rain, then,' Laurie said as she opened the door for the departing customer then swept Ivy into a quick, tight hug.

'Just about,' Ivy replied before pecking a kiss on her friend's cheek. One of the worst things – and, god, there were so bloody many – about losing her mum was the lack of physical contact. She flashed back to the melancholy she'd felt when Alun had patted her hand and knew she hadn't shaken it off.

'Hey, you okay?' Laurie had positioned herself so she was blocking Ivy off from the rest of the room and Ivy wanted to hug her all over again.

'I'm fine. Just a silly case of the blues.' Ivy took a deep breath and tucked the sadness away. Not forever, as she'd tried to do before with everything, but for later when she could acknowledge it properly in private and then hopefully be able to let it go. She couldn't let herself get back to the point after the funeral when she'd lost control. Not just couldn't – wouldn't. It wasn't healthy to keep hiding from her feelings. Knowing her comedy run-in with Alun would be the perfect thing to distract them both, she gave Laurie a conspiratorial grin. 'Let's go out the back. I've got something I must tell you but I don't want old elephant ears over there trying to listen in.'

Laurie's eyes lit up. 'Ooh, sounds juicy. Come on, then.'

Ivy followed her back around the counter and couldn't resist the urge to glance over at the knitting circle again. Kitty blew her a kiss, bless her lovely, kind heart, and Ivy made a mental note to go and collect it in a minute. Bev, on the other hand, had a face like a smacked arse at the prospect of missing out on something and not for the first time, Ivy wondered why the others tolerated her. The moment she stepped into the kitchen, all thoughts of the odd dynamic of the knitting circle fled and Ivy simply closed her eyes and breathed in. 'Something smells heavenly,' she said with an appreciative sigh.

'Chocolate cherry brownies,' Laurie said as she whipped a tea towel off a cooling rack covered in Ivy's favourite treat. 'But you can't have one until you eat a bowl of soup and the side salad I've prepared for you.'

'Worried I'm not eating properly?' Ivy raised a guilty finger to cover the uncharacteristic spot that had broken out on her chin the day before. Though she was trying harder since her all-time low of crisps and chocolate for dinner the night she'd chatted to Alex, it was still hard to garner much enthusiasm for eating.

'Indulge me.' Laurie gave her a helpless smile. 'You know I'm a feeder, just like my dad. I can't help it.'

Ivy thought about the enormous Sunday spreads Andrew Morgan was famous for and her stomach rumbled. 'Tell your dad to add an extra plate for Sunday, will you?'

Laurie beamed. 'He'll be over the moon. It's all I can do to stop him and Mum popping around to see you. They were both relieved to hear you were coming for lunch today.'

'Ah, I haven't meant to do a disappearing act, I promise,' Ivy said, with more than a pang of guilt. 'The weather's been so filthy it hasn't been fit to set foot out and I've been so busy working on building my stock up.'

'I get it, don't worry, but that's not going to stop me making a fuss of you today.'

Thinking how lucky she was to have people as wonderful as the Morgans on her side, Ivy put her arms around Laurie for another hug. 'You're the best, and I am very up for being made a fuss of. I'll stop in and see your folks on the way out and wangle that Sunday invitation myself.' The building that housed The Mermaid's Cave and Laurie's café had been a family-run business for several generations, morphing over time from a general provisions store to a gift shop as the village shifted from a traditional fishing port to a tourist hot spot. When Laurie had approached them about opening the café, her parents had redesigned the sprawling building to accommodate her dream and an archway connected both businesses to encourage customers to move from one to the other.

'They'll like that.' Laurie gave her a squeeze then stepped back. 'Now, come on, what did you want to tell me?'

They were still laughing like a couple of hyenas about the prospect of Ivy buying Wendy's flat when a voice called through from the café. 'Hello? Is there any chance of getting a fresh pot of tea at some point this morning?' It was Bev, in all her spiky glory.

'Be right there, Bev!' Laurie shouted back before sticking her tongue out, which sent Ivy back off into hysterics. Leaning close with an evil grin on her face, Laurie whispered to her. 'She just can't bear to be out of the loop for a second, can she?'

Ivy shook her head. 'Come on, I'll give you a hand to smooth those ruffled feathers and then we can have our lunch.'

* * *

As they approached the table with a fresh pot of tea and a set of clean mugs, Bev was speaking in a voice designed to carry. 'She couldn't wait to tell everyone, not that anyone is interested in anything she gets up to. I only went in for a cauliflower for our dinner and she kept rabbiting on about it.'

Ivy knew she had to be talking about Wendy, who worked in the local greengrocer's, and was glad Alun had given her the heads up about the flat being on the market. Steeling herself, she waited while Laurie put down the pot and began swapping the dirty mugs for the clean ones on the tray Ivy was holding.

'Flashing it around, she was, like she was conducting an orchestra,' Bev continued, sounding two parts outraged and one part thrilled at having a gossip bomb to drop. 'Huge bloody stone, which she claimed was a diamond, but I'll bet it's nothing more than that Rubik's zirconia that's just as cheap as she is! No shame at all, and Jen barely cold in her grave.' Ivy felt understanding land like a blow, but she stiffened herself against it. Wendy had run out of patience, it seemed, or perhaps Kev had bought her a ring to try and wiggle out of being the one who'd not wanted a divorce from her mother. It was a shock that it had come so soon after her mother's death, but the only disappointment Ivy felt was that Wendy had let herself be talked around. Whatever. They were nothing to do with her, no matter how much spiteful cows like Bev might want them to be.

'Shh, Bev, not now!' Kitty snapped, her face growing bright red as she met Ivy's gaze before letting her eyes slide quickly away.

'Don't stop on my account,' Ivy said, unable to keep the acid from her voice. 'Although I'm sure this is *all* for my account, isn't it, Bev?'

'Well, it's not like it's a secret,' the woman spluttered, not used to being called out for her behaviour. 'You would've heard about it sooner or later.'

'And I might have heard it from someone other than you, and where's the fun in that, hey?' Spitting mad, Ivy slammed down the tray of mugs and rounded on Bev. 'I really hate to disappoint you, but nothing that Kevin or Wendy choose to do has any effect on me. They are free to live their lives as they please, and I wish them both well.' She didn't, of course. Kevin could get in the sea, as her mother had once memorably remarked, but she held no real ill will towards Wendy.

'Come away, Ivy,' Laurie pleaded, tugging on her arm when Ivy refused to move. 'It's not worth it.'

Ivy didn't budge, her eyes locked onto Bev's until the woman finally dropped her gaze. 'Next time you see me, best cross the street, eh?' Ivy looked around at the other women at the table to see a mixture of embarrassment, upset and outright anger in the case of Barbara, their nominal leader, all of it aimed at Bev. 'Enjoy your tea, ladies.'

Ivy let Laurie shoo her away to a seat by the window about as far away from the knitting circle as possible. 'Are you all right?' Laurie murmured. 'Do you want me to get her to leave?'

Ivy shook her head. 'I wouldn't give her the satisfaction.' As quickly as it had flared up, her anger evaporated. 'I'm sorry for making a scene.'

Laurie snorted. 'I'm not. It's about time someone put Bev back in her box and you not only did that, you locked it and threw away the key.' She flashed Ivy a wicked grin. 'Mum's going to be livid that she wasn't here to witness it.'

Ivy bit her lip, trying not to giggle. 'Oh god, don't tell her, no one else needs to know about it.'

'Ha! If you think this isn't going to be round the village faster than the news of Wendy and her *Rubik's* zirconia engagement ring, you haven't lived in Mermaids Point all your life.' Laurie emphasised the error Bev had made in naming the manufactured gemstone. 'Right, if you can behave yourself for five minutes, I'll go and sort out our lunch.'

Though she was dying to look in the direction of the furious whispers coming from the corner, Ivy made a point of taking her phone out of her pocket instead and followed the link saved in her favourites for a material wholesaler she liked. Though she still preferred hunting around local charity shops for clothing she could revamp and give a new lease of life to, she'd also been working on some individual designs for simple sundresses, beach wraps, bandanas and other things she hoped would be popular with summer tourists. She didn't even look up when the bell over the door jangled a few minutes later, the row with Bev already at the back of her mind as she bookmarked several new patterns for closer inspection on the bigger screen of her laptop. She was just admiring some funky canvas prints she thought might be good for beach bags when there was a soft touch on her shoulder. Bracing herself for another round with Bev, she looked up instead into Kitty's kind, smiling face. 'We're going to leave you and Laurie in peace, darling.'

Ivy cast a quick glance to where the other women were in various stages of putting on their coats and tying headscarves on to protect their hair from the impending storm. Bev was noticeable by her absence, and Ivy recalled the bell, which must have signalled her departure. 'You don't have to leave on my account,' she assured Kitty, returning her smile. 'I'm absolutely fine.'

Kitty patted her shoulder. 'Of course you are, but poor Bev may never recover from that first-class scolding you gave her. Not that she didn't deserve it.'

'I shouldn't have lost my temper like that,' Ivy conceded.

'And we should have spoken to her before about her behaviour. We've let it slide for too long because it just seemed easier to ignore her and try and keep the peace within the group. Her actions today were unforgivable, and we've let her know that.'

Much as she disliked Bev, the past weeks had proved to her how important friends were. 'Please don't fall out with her on my account. I said my bit and now I'd like to forget about it.'

Kitty pursed her lips for a moment before giving Ivy a nod. 'I'll pop in and see her in the morning. Now, how are you getting on? Is there anything you need? I'm making a steak and ale casserole for dinner this evening, I could drop you off a portion when I'm out and about tomorrow, if you'd like?'

It was on the tip of Ivy's tongue to refuse, but she knew how much it would mean to Kitty to feel as if she'd been able to help Ivy in some small way. 'That would be lovely, thank you. Cooking for one isn't much fun.'

Kitty petted her hair the way she had when Ivy had been a small child and Ivy leaned into it for a moment, accepting the small comfort. 'It'll probably be around ten o'clock, if that suits you?'

'Ten will be fine. I'll probably be at my sewing machine so give the knocker a good thump to make sure I hear you.'

'Oh, are you back working again?' Kitty raised her brows. 'I didn't like to bother you, but if you're taking on jobs again I've managed to rip the lining in my coat sleeve, right under the armpit. I've no idea how I did it, but every time I put it on now, I end up sticking my arm between the lining and the sleeve and making it worse.'

'I'll fix it for you when you come round if you like?' She held up her hand when it was obvious Kitty was going to protest. 'I'm just working on some things I'm hoping to sell at a later date so it won't be any bother to do it there and then. We can call it payment for the casserole.'

'Well, that's a deal, then. I'll see you in the morning.' With another quick brush over Ivy's curls, she went and joined the rest of her friends, who were waiting by the door.

* * *

Laurie came out of the kitchen bearing two steaming bowls just in time to catch the chorus of goodbyes. She set the bowls down, then headed to the door to wave the knitting circle off. As soon as their backs were turned, she flipped the lock and turned the sign to 'closed'. 'Now we can have some peace and quiet,' she said as she rejoined Ivy at the table. She cast a look at the lowering sky. 'I doubt I'll get many more customers today.' Right on cue a smattering of raindrops hit the glass next to them. 'That settles it,' she said with a rueful laugh.

'I'm not in any hurry to get home so I'll wait it out here, if you don't mind?' Ivy asked as she lifted her spoon and dipped it into the rich, tomatoey depths of the soup.

'That would be lovely,' Laurie assured her. 'I'll probably potter around and do a bit of batch baking. I don't fancy walking up the hill in this.' She side-eyed the rain, which had started coming down in sheets. 'Besides, Jake won't thank me for disrupting him if I go home early. He's got a deadline for a follow-up piece on some of those county lines investigations he wrote about and he's an absolute grump when he's up against it.'

'We can have a nice girly afternoon, then. I've been working on some designs for things I think might sell well in the shop if you've got time to check them out?'

'Sure thing, I'd love to.' Laurie rested her spoon in her bowl. 'How's that all going, then? You've decided to take Alex up on his offer, I take it?'

Ivy nodded. 'It seemed pointless to cut my nose off to spite my face, so to speak. I can't afford to buy the bookshop and he can. Besides, it's the most logical way to try and expand my own business. I haven't had an update from him recently, but I assume it's all going to plan. I'll find out on Saturday – it's movie night.' Having giggled their way through *The Da Vinci Code*, Ivy had decided she was a glutton for punishment and a fortnight later she and Alex had watched the follow up, *Angels & Demons*. She quite fancied Ewan McGregor, but even his presence hadn't been enough to redeem what was an absolutely preposterous film. It had been fun, though, and they'd made arrangements to watch *Inferno*, the last of the Robert Langdon trilogy, this weekend.

'You two are getting on well,' Laurie observed with an arch to her brow that Ivy didn't like the look of at all.

'What's that supposed to mean?' she huffed, spooning up a mouthful of soup before she said any more.

'Just an observation. If the two of you are going to be working *closely* together, it's important that you get on with each other.' Laurie scooped up her own soup, unable to hide a grin.

'We're friends.' Ivy knew she shouldn't rise to the bait, but it was impossible to keep the exasperation out of her voice.

'Of course you are. It's nice to have friends. Jake and I are friends.' Laurie barely managed to get the last sentence out before she broke into a fit of giggles. 'Oh my god! The look on your face. Ivy Fisher, do you have a crush on him?'

'What? No!' Feeling horribly flustered by the conversation, she balled up her napkin and threw it at her friend, who batted it away, still laughing.

'You do! Oh, Ivy, how delicious. I'm not a fan of the beard, but other than that he's absolutely gorgeous.' Laurie raised a hand to her brow and fell back in her seat as if overcome by the mere thought of Alex and his gorgeousness.

'It's not like that!' Ivy protested, feeling as if she was fighting a losing battle and not just with her friend's assumptions. A teeny, tiny part of her might also think that Alex was indeed gorgeous, but she wasn't ready to admit it to herself, never mind anybody else. 'We're friends. Hopefully business partners of a sort, nothing more.'

Laurie pouted. 'Are you sure?'

Ivy nodded, though she was not at all sure of anything right then. 'Apart from anything else, it would be foolish to get involved with him. I need somewhere to work, somewhere I can grow my business and hopefully start making enough money to get myself properly established. It's not worth the risk.'

Laurie gave her a steady look. 'I said the same about Jake and look where that got me.'

'You're not helping!' But Ivy couldn't help but laugh as she ducked her face over her bowl to try and hide a blush. 'He is very good-looking though, isn't he?'

Laurie reached out to pat her shoulder. 'Very. Look, I'm sorry for teasing you, but I think it would be nice if you had a little fun in your life.'

Ivy raised her head to meet her friend's knowing gaze. 'Fun. Is that what the cool kids call it these days?' They giggled like a couple of naughty schoolgirls before Ivy set her spoon down with a sigh. 'It's been so long since I had any... fun, I've forgotten what it's like.'

'All the more reason not to cross Alex off your list. You have to admit, Ivy, it's pretty slim pickings around here.'

'True, though I'm not sure Alex is up for a relationship. Did you know he was divorced? He didn't say much about it, but I got the impression he'd had a rough time,' Ivy said, recalling the way Alex's demeanour had changed when the topic had come up.

'Nerissa hasn't mentioned it.' Laurie tapped a finger to her lip, her eyes going unfocused for a moment as she thought about it. 'And I'm sure Jake would have said something to me if he knew about it.' She turned her attention back to Ivy, a wicked smile forming. 'Maybe you could strike a deal with each other.'

'A deal?' Ivy didn't like the sound of it one bit. 'What are you talking about?'

Laurie spread her hands wide. 'You need to get back in the saddle, so to speak.'

Ivy wished she hadn't taken a sip of her water just then because it snorted straight up her nose. She mopped at her face with a napkin and spluttered until the horrible sensation faded. 'Alex isn't a bloody horse,' she gasped when she could speak again.

'But he might be worth a ride or two.'

'*Laurie!*'

'*Ivy!*' Laurie mimicked, her smile unrepentant. 'Come on now, if you can't talk about these kinds of things with me, who can you talk about them with?'

'Well, I can't say I'd planned on talking about it with anyone.' Using her napkin, Ivy fanned her hot neck and face. 'It's not exactly something that's been on my priority list.'

Laurie's expression immediately turned sympathetic. 'I know, and I'm not saying you should jump his bones the next time you see him, but it's not like there are lots of eligible bachelors in the Point – unless you count Nick—'

'No-o-o-o!' They both giggled. 'Poor Nick,' Ivy said a few minutes later. 'It's not that he isn't good-looking, it's just... ' She pulled a face, hoping Laurie would understand she meant no insult to her brother.

'A bit close to home?' Laurie suggested before heaving a sigh. 'It's a shame, really, because the two of you would be perfect for each other. And,' she added with a softer, more heartfelt sigh, 'if the two of you fell in love then I know he'd be more likely to stay here in the Point.'

'Is there any likelihood of him leaving?' Ivy couldn't keep the surprise out of her voice as it was the first time she'd heard any hint of Nick being unhappy.

'If he gets the funding he needs from the bank for the warehouse development then I think he'll stay, but he's been restless for a while and Aurora Storm did a real number on him when she was here. He didn't really say anything but I think it messed him up a lot.'

Ivy sat in silence as she absorbed what Laurie had said. The prospect of Nick moving away shocked her to the very core. He was an important part of her little world, and she would be devastated to lose him. Hot on the heels of that thought was the realisation of just how much she'd withdrawn from everyone during the last stages of her mother's illness. She'd wrapped her grief around her like a cocoon, the silken strands so tight they'd muffled everything else that was going on outside her own life. One of her friends had been suffering, and she'd had no idea about it. She didn't like admitting that everything had been a one-way street in terms of support. The world might have stopped turning for her, but it hadn't for other people. They still had their own worries and hurts, disappointments and heartaches. She needed to do better. 'Poor Nick, I had no idea he's been having such a hard time.'

Laurie reached out and squeezed her hand. 'He's never been one to wear his heart on his sleeve, and, besides, you've had enough to deal with without worrying about my big brother's broken heart.'

'Still, I can't help feeling bad. I've taken so much from everyone, it's about time I stopped looking inwards so much and started paying more attention.'

'Nobody feels that way,' Laurie reassured her. 'But I do agree it'll be good for you to focus on other stuff. That's why I'm pleased you'll have a chance to expand your business if this venture with Alex comes off.' Laurie paused, giving Ivy an appraising look. 'Did you ever mention to him that you had that leaflet about the bookshop because you were thinking of buying it for yourself?'

Ivy shook her head. 'There didn't seem to be any point once Harry set me straight on my financial situation. I can't go forward with it and I'd hate for Alex to feel guilty that he's able to achieve something I can't just because our circumstances are different. If I do get to work with him in the shop, then it's the best of both worlds because he's the one carrying all the risk.'

'That's true,' Laurie conceded. 'But it also puts all the power in his hands because he'll be the one that owns the business, so if he changes his mind or the two of you fall out then you'll be back to square one.'

The same thing had occurred to Ivy, too, but no one else was beating down her door offering any solutions to her predicament, so she didn't see a way around it. 'I could offer to take on a part of the business, but I'm not sure I want to rush into tying myself up in another property problem when I still have to extricate myself from the one I'm already in. My priority has to be finding somewhere to live. Between the money I'll need to secure something halfway decent, if something halfway decent ever comes on the market,' Ivy added with a groan, 'and having enough cash left over to invest in building up stock to sell, I don't see how I can afford to take on even a small share of the bookshop.' And there was no guarantee Alex would be interested even if she could. If she made him an offer and he turned it down, they'd risk starting off on the wrong foot. God, why was everything so hard?

'So, apart from Wendy's flat, which will never be mentioned again,' Laurie said, cutting across her spiralling thoughts with a wry grin, 'have you had any other luck on the housing front?'

Ivy shook her head. 'There's just nothing about. Alex wondered about Nerissa's flat above the surgery, but I'm not sure they'd want me wandering in and out, or the noise of my sewing machine whirring at all hours when the kids have to get up for school.'

'I'm sure she and Tom would be more than willing to help you out if they could, but the flat's already been promised to Linda when she gets home at the end of the month.' Jake's mum was currently away on a world cruise.

'She's definitely coming back to the Point, then?' There'd been some doubt over that as she and Jake had been estranged for a long time and, although they were back on much better terms, Laurie had confided in Ivy that Linda was worried her presence would somehow put pressure on Jake and Laurie's relationship.

'It took a lot of back and forth between them, but Jake has finally convinced her that we want her in our lives. I can't imagine not being able to see Mum and Dad every day.' Laurie clapped a hand over her mouth. 'I can't believe I said that. I'm so sorry!'

Ivy reached across the table because, in all honesty, she hadn't taken it as anything other than a fact of Laurie's life. 'You can't tread on eggshells around me, Laurie. Promise me that you won't. Mum's gone and I had a long time to prepare for it. It hurts and I'm sure it will always hurt, but she's in a better place because neither of us could have borne her suffering much longer.'

Laurie gave a reluctant nod. 'It was still thoughtless of me.'

'But I want you to be thoughtless around me!' Ivy said, tugging on Laurie's hands to be sure she had her full attention. 'Not careless, but carefree. You are my best friend and I never want you to diminish one single ounce of joy because you think it might hurt me. Okay?'

'Okay.' They held each other's hands tight for a long moment, strengthening the bond they'd both almost destroyed over a silly falling out. 'If you need somewhere to stay, you know you can come and live with me and Jake.'

'I appreciate the offer, but that's never going to happen.' She would move into one of the local bed and breakfast places before she did that. Staying with them on the night of the funeral had been exactly what she'd needed, but the cottage was too small for anything other than odd overnight stays like that. Jake and Laurie both worked long hours, they needed their downtime together. Besides, the last thing Ivy wanted was to be a third wheel in their relationship.

'Well, it's there if you need it. I've already spoken to Jake about it and he was in complete agreement.' Laurie's jaw had that stubborn set to it that told Ivy it wasn't the last she'd hear about it.

'I was thinking more along the lines of one of Nick's apartments, but from what you were saying earlier, it sounds like the development might not go ahead?'

'Oh, that would be perfect!' Laurie's face lit up. 'And I'm still really hopeful he'll get the go-ahead, especially now Jake and I are adding our savings to his. The bank are just dragging their feet a bit. Actually, you should talk to Nick sooner rather than later because if he could say he has one of the flats already sold, I'm sure that would help sway things in his favour.'

Ivy held up a hand. 'Whoa! I don't even know what he's asking for them, and I don't know what I can afford until the cottage sells and we untangle all the costs associated with that.'

'Sorry, I jumped the gun a bit there, didn't I?' Laurie sighed. 'It sounded like such a perfect solution to everything, I got a bit carried away.'

'I'm definitely going to talk to him,' Ivy assured her. 'I just have to be careful not to promise him anything until I know where I stand. Besides, that's a longer-term solution because even if it all goes ahead, it'll be months before the apartments are ready. I'll still need somewhere to live once the cottage is sold.'

'There's always my old room at Mum and Dad's,' Laurie mused.

The prospect of sheltering under the Morgans' roof, even for a little while, held a desperate kind of appeal – one Ivy knew she needed to fight against. It was time to stand on her own two feet. To face and address her problems head-on. She could lean on Laurie, Jake and the rest of the Morgan family for support, but she couldn't hide behind them. The only person who could be allowed to hold Ivy's future in their hands was Ivy herself.

7

Alex picked up the bowl of salsa, another of olives and feta cheese squares, and a large one full of his favourite hot and spicy flavoured tortilla chips. He managed to snag the neck of his bottle of beer between his ring and little fingers then headed through from the kitchen to the living room. About halfway down the hall the false economy of his actions became clear as he almost dropped the salsa and ended up balancing it against his chest. Then came the logistical battle of unhooking the bottle and getting it onto the coffee table without spilling it, while still balancing everything else. He finally managed his task in about twice the time it would've taken him to make two trips to the kitchen. In his defence, he'd not been able to think straight since the estate agent had called him that morning. His immediate reaction to being told there was an offer on his house had been to want to pick up the phone and call Ivy to share the good news. But they already had their evening chat scheduled so he'd forced himself to be patient. He'd tried to distract himself with a round of writing sprints, but even though he was enjoying getting to grips with his secret project he couldn't focus for more than five minutes at a time. When he was a grand total of three hundred words up for the hour, most of which was repeating stuff from half a page earlier, he'd given up.

A quick check of his watch told him he had a few more minutes before Ivy was due to FaceTime so he decided a pre-emptive pee would probably be a good idea. Having taken care of that, he washed his hands only to catch sight of the smear of salsa now decorating the front of his clean white shirt. With a curse, he stripped it off and shoved the marked bit under the bathroom tap, hoping to wash the tomato sauce out before it had time to stain. In his haste he turned the tap on too hard and sent a spray of water jetting onto his face and across his chest. *For fu—* The jaunty ring of his phone echoed up the stairs and he ran from the bathroom, grabbing a towel as he went, and took the stairs two at a time. 'I'm here, I'm here,' he said, drying his face and chest with one hand as he accepted Ivy's call.

'All set for another exciting movie night... *Oh, sorry!* Did I get you out of the shower? I was sure you said seven-thirty.'

Alex lowered the towel to look at the screen properly, only to see Ivy had averted her gaze. He was holding his phone at an angle that showed off far more of his bare chest than he'd realised, and he quickly tilted it up. 'No, you're right on time. I had an unfortunate encounter with a white shirt and some salsa.'

Ivy glanced back at the screen, and when it was clear he was no longer treating her to a show she straightened up to face him properly. 'Have you got any baking soda?'

'Have I got any what now?'

She laughed. 'Baking soda. It's good for getting tomato stains out if you mix it with salt and form a paste.'

How did women know this kind of stuff? Was this the reason they always went to the bathroom in pairs, to pass on secret household tips? 'I can say with all authority that I don't have any salt in the house, never mind baking soda.'

'Who doesn't have salt?' She huffed in obvious disbelief.

'Me. For one,' Alex replied, trying not to sound defensive. It wasn't that he couldn't cook, it was more that he'd got out of the habit of it. When Tom and the kids had been living nearby he'd gone over there when he'd felt the urge to cook as it was always more fun feeding a group rather than just himself. As things like condiments had run out at home, he'd never got round to replacing them, his shopping consisting mostly of ready meals, stuffed pasta and premade sauces, which already had more than enough salt in them.

'Oka-a-a-ay, then. Why don't you sort yourself out and give me a call back when you're ready?' The way Ivy dragged out the first word made it clear he'd not been successful in hiding his snappish tone.

'No, don't go. It's a bit of a sore subject, that's all.' He headed back upstairs, phone still in hand, to find something else to wear and to rescue the shirt. 'I was running it under the tap when you called, hence the unintended flashing.'

She laughed. 'I was going to fetch my purse and start throwing cash at the screen.'

He grinned, glad they were past the moment of tension. 'The sight of my...' he glanced down, casting a rueful eye at the slight bulge at the waistband of his jeans '... one-pack isn't really worth a fiver.'

Her pretty, merry laugh deepened into something rich and earthy that did strange things to the area a bit below his waistband. 'I was thinking coins rather than notes.'

'Harsh!' Alex chucked the phone on the bed, giving Ivy a view of his rather dusty ceiling light while he rummaged in his chest of drawers for a clean top. Dragging on the first T-shirt that didn't look too creased – ironing was another thing he'd mostly given up on, like cooking, and dusting – he tugged it quickly over his head. As he reached to retrieve his phone he saw that, rather than being plain black, his top had a picture of The Avengers on it. It had been a gift from his nephew, Max, a couple of Christmases previously. Not wanting to leave Ivy counting cobwebs on his ceiling any longer, he picked up his mobile. Though there'd been no hint from her she considered their movie nights as anything like a date, he'd wanted to look his best – hence the white shirt, and his freshly trimmed beard. Between the superhero T-shirt and the fact his kitchen cupboards were full of crap, he wasn't exactly selling himself to her. Thankfully, the T-shirt went uncommented on. 'So, what have you been up to?' he asked, hoping to distract her while he finished faffing around.

'I had lunch with Laurie on Thursday, which was nice.'

Something in her tone didn't sound quite right, making Alex pause in the process of wringing out the white shirt one-handed. 'You don't sound sure about that.'

Ivy shoved her hand through her glossy red curls with a sigh. 'Lunch was lovely, but I had a run-in with one of the local busybodies, which I could've done without. I'm not proud of the way I behaved if I'm honest.'

'Tell me?' he coaxed. By the time he'd got the shirt loaded in the machine on a hot wash and had settled on the sofa, he'd heard the whole story of her row with Bev. 'Sounds like she had it coming.' She wrinkled her nose in that way that made him want to lean through the screen and kiss the tip of it. Even if he was never going to admit it to Ivy, he was past pretending to himself that he didn't have a whopping great crush on her. He hoped that by acknowledging it, he could keep up his guard and not say anything that would make her feel uncomfortable and, in time, it would pass, as this precious new friendship cemented itself and they started working together.

'Maybe so,' Ivy said, pulling him back from his musings. 'But I still wish it hadn't come from me. I'm not the sort of person who enjoys confrontation, and I've been feeling sick about it ever since.' She shook her head, her curls bouncing around her face as though she was trying to physically shake off the feeling. 'Enough of that. I'm not letting Bev and her big mouth spoil our evening. Not when we've got such a scintillating movie to watch.'

Alex laughed. 'We can watch something else if you like?'

She pulled a horrified face. 'Clearly you're not a completionist! Why, I bet you're the sort of person who doesn't finish a book they're not enjoying?'

'Who does?' The idea had always seemed like madness to him. 'Life's too short for that kind of nonsense.'

'But how do you sleep not knowing how something ends?' She sounded completely baffled at the idea.

'I sleep just fine. If it's not for me, it's not for me. The end, or, should I say, not the end.' She just shook her head at him as if she couldn't believe what she was hearing. Surrendering to his fate, Alex reached for his remote control. '*Inferno* it is, then.'

They'd made it about forty minutes in when Ivy said, 'I didn't think it was possible, but this might be worse than *Angels & Demons*.'

Alex chuckled. 'Ready to quit?'

'Not on your life! It's almost become a challenge now. I'm just amazed Tom Hanks came back for a third time.'

'Maybe he's a completionist, too,' Alex teased, making her laugh so hard she made the most unattractive snorting noise, which he still managed to find adorable. Bloody hell, he was in big trouble when it came to her.

'Or, maybe they made him an offer he couldn't refuse,' Ivy said when she'd recovered herself.

'More than likely. I wonder if it made any money.' He reached for his laptop and did a quick search of the IMDB website. '$220 million against a budget of $75 million. Not blockbuster figures, but most film producers would probably bite your hand off for those kinds of numbers.' He did another search. 'Less than a third of what *The Da Vinci Code* made, though.'

'I honestly have no clue what is going on. The book can't be this much of a mess, surely?' Ivy mused.

He shrugged. 'No idea, I only read the first one.' They exchanged a look through the screen and started laughing.

'I've downloaded them all onto my Kindle as well as the fourth one, so I'll let you know.' When he raised his eyebrows at her, it was her turn to shrug. 'Completionist.' She settled back against the stack of pillows she'd propped against her headboard. 'I wonder how Dan Brown feels about all the criticism he gets.'

'I'm sure he weeps into a pillow stuffed with dollar bills every night,' Alex said, in a tone as dry as the Sahara desert.

'Oh, I know he's made a ton of money from his books, but still, it must be hard having people tear down something you've created.'

'That's why your editor warns you never to read reviews.' When she raised her eyebrows at him, Alex realised he'd slipped up. He didn't like lying to her and if they were going to be working together she was going to see him at his laptop at some point. He opted for a partial truth. 'I've been dabbling a bit, and it's what everyone says in my online writing group.' Technically, he was dabbling with his thriller idea, but it still felt a bit too close to a lie for comfort. Not for the first time, he cursed himself for ever writing that stupid tell-all about him and Jo.

Eyes bright, Ivy sat up. 'You're writing a book? Now the whole bookshop thing makes more sense to me! Ooh, what's it about? Tell me everything!'

Her enthusiasm was infectious and the guilt over misleading her lessened somewhat as he explained about the writing prompt. 'I'm still feeling my way around it and I'm not sure if it will come to anything, but it's a lot of fun trying.' Which was true. For the first time in forever he felt excited rather than terrified when he opened his laptop. His plot was all over the place and there were more holes than in a slice of Swiss cheese. 'It's hard to explain without sounding crazy, but it tastes right in my head.' He laughed. 'I'm not sure that makes sense, even to me.'

'No, I get it, I think. It's like when I find something in a charity shop and the material or something about the cut of it appeals to me. I see the potential of what I can do with it, how I can put my own twist on the original design and make it unique.'

She did get it, and he felt another strand adding to the connection growing between them. 'Speaking of the bookshop...' Alex let the smile on his face grow wider and wider.

'No?' Ivy's grin spread to match his own. 'Really?'

Alex nodded before quickly holding up crossed fingers. 'Well, I got an offer on the house this morning and the agent reckons they're in a really strong position to go ahead, so I hope you're ready, because it looks like we're going to do this.'

8

'So,' Alex Nelson said as he stopped in front of Cavendish's Books and Ephemera and held his arms out wide, 'what do you think?' He did his best to sound enthusiastic, but in the full glare of the late April sunshine, there was no denying the rundown state of the place.

The two men with him maintained a stony silence as they ran critical eyes over the shop's fading façade, further deflating Alex's attempt at positivity. Stepping closer, his father, Archie, dragged a finger down the filthy glass of the window before holding it up to display the dirt and grime he'd collected. 'I think,' he replied in a tone acidic enough to strip the peeling paint from the window's frame, 'that you have finally lost the plot.' Producing a pristine handkerchief from the pocket of his red moleskin trousers, Archie made a show of wiping the muck from his finger.

'Tom?' Alex turned to his older brother for moral support. A bit of back-up was the least he could provide, given the fact he'd been the one who'd relocated to the Point first. If Tom hadn't turned his life upside down the way he had, Alex wouldn't even know

Mermaids Point existed, never mind be the new owner of the local bookshop. So, really, this was all his fault.

'It needs a lot of work,' Tom said, scratching his chin as he continued to take a visual inventory of the work needed to the outside of the building.

'It has character; tradition,' Alex protested, trying not to think about the estimates lurking in his email for decoration and essential repairs. The bones of the building were remarkably sound for its age, but it was clear from the avocado-coloured bathroom suite in the upstairs flat alone that it was in dire need of a cosmetic overhaul.

'Well, we can only hope old Cavendish was better at record-keeping than he was at maintenance,' Archie said as he cupped a hand to shield his eyes as he peered through the murky window into the shop's interior. 'And his cleaning,' he finished with a sardonic mutter.

'You don't think I would've bought the place without checking the finances out, do you?' Alex hoped his father couldn't hear the bit of bluster behind his outraged retort. Of course, he'd checked the accounts for the bookshop before he'd gone ahead with the purchase, he just might have done it through a pair of rose-tinted spectacles. If the profits – a term that one might perhaps apply loosely to the very thin margin between incomings and outgoings recorded by Mr Cavendish in a red leather-bound ledger – were a bit on the low side, Alex chose to see that as an opportunity for the business to grow. Especially with the new direction he was taking with Ivy. Speaking of whom... He checked his watch and wondered where she was because she'd promised to be here for a bit of moral support.

'Perhaps we should have a look inside? You'll get a better feel for the place, Pop,' Tom said to their father, ever the diplomat.

'It'll have to be pretty damn special to make me feel better about

Alex throwing good money away on this white elephant,' Archie grumbled. 'This isn't what I had in mind when I helped you get onto the property ladder.'

'I never asked you for a penny,' Alex snapped, wishing like hell he'd never accepted his father's offer to help him buy his house. The terrace house Alex had owned in London had earned a tidy profit even after clearing the mortgage, and he still had a substantial balance in the bank from his book royalties. There was enough to pay his father back for the deposit, but his mother had assured him they didn't need the money any time soon and he should keep hold of it to invest in the bookshop. It had meant he was able to secure a smaller mortgage on the shop, which would take some of the pressure off if it took a while to get the business really up and running. That smaller monthly outgoing to meet the mortgage had also enabled him to punch up the refurbishment budget so he'd be able to open that much quicker, which was a win-win as far as he was concerned. So he'd bitten the bullet and allowed the debt he owed his parents to remain.

But Alex had known he'd made a terrible mistake when his father had shown up on his doorstep with a notebook full of 'helpful' suggestions. Not even the endless rounds of golf he liked to play were enough to keep a mind as sharp as Archie's occupied full time. There'd never been any opportunity for him to meddle in Tom's work, but, because Alex had chosen to follow in his footsteps into the financial services sector, Archie had always treated Alex's career as an offshoot of his own. He'd been furious with Alex for quitting his job in the City – although how anyone could've expected him to set foot in the same building as his ex-wife and the friend who'd betrayed him was beyond comprehension. Somehow he'd decided he now had a financial stake in the bookshop, and he was determined to have his say – on everything.

'Your mother would've never let me hear the end of it if I didn't help now, would she?' Archie said with a shake of his head.

As irritated as Alex was with his father, he was glad of the distraction before the ugly memories of Jo's betrayal could dig their claws in. 'I've still got enough cash to repay your loan if you are that worried about my choice to buy the shop. Say the word and I'll transfer it back and you can leave me to be foolish in peace.' Alex drew out his phone and tapped on his banking app because, seriously, getting Archie off his back would be worth it even if it meant he had to paint the shop himself with the cheapest whitewash he could find in B&Q.

'Don't be so bloody daft.' Archie dismissed the idea with a wave of his hand.

'I'm serious, Pop. The house is sold. The shop is bought and there's no going back now.' Not that Alex would change his mind about things even if there had still been time to wriggle out of the deal. There was nothing left for him in London other than a gutful of unhappy memories. 'If you can't be excited for me, then at least shut up about it for five minutes.'

Tom did a very poor job of concealing a bark of laughter behind a hasty cough, doing nothing to improve their father's bad mood. 'What did a man do wrong to raise two such ungrateful sons?' Archie glowered at them both beneath his impressive set of eyebrows.

'I guess the apple doesn't fall far from the tree, eh, Pop?' Tom said, giving their father a gentle nudge in the ribs. 'Come on, now, stop giving Ally such a hard time. I, for one, am delighted with his decision to relocate to the Point.'

Alex beamed at that. He'd been a bit worried about what Tom thought about him tagging along after him like some little lost lamb. It really hadn't been his intention, but in those few short visits he'd made to the Point, it had already started to feel like home. 'Cheers, Tom. That means a lot to me.'

Tom slung an arm around his shoulders. 'How could I not be thrilled at having a babysitter on tap?' Laughing, he dodged out of reach when Alex swung a mock punch towards him. 'Sorry, that was too easy!'

Archie reached out an arm, blocking Alex when he started to pursue his rapidly back-wheeling brother. 'Behave yourselves! What will the locals think to see the pair of you brawling like teenagers in the street? Your brother has his reputation to think of.' There was just a hint of a smile as he said it.

Tom made a show of brushing down the front of his still-pristine polo shirt. 'Yes, Alex, don't you know who I am?'

'You're an idiot, that's what you are,' their father said, tone drier than his favourite afternoon Martini. 'Come on, then,' he said, turning his attention to Alex. 'Open up and let's see what we're really dealing with.'

* * *

Drawing out the bunch of keys he'd collected from the estate agent that morning, Alex cast one last look up the road, expecting to see Ivy's red curls shining in the sunlight, but there was no one else around. Hoping the hold-up was nothing serious, he slotted a large iron key into the lock of the shop but instead of twisting it, he cast a warning look over his shoulder at his father. 'Not a word, okay?'

Archie sighed but drew his fingers across his lips in a zipping motion. 'I'll be as good as gold.'

Alex exchanged a disbelieving look with Tom, but let it go. If Archie managed to keep his opinion to himself for longer than five minutes, that would be more than either of them expected. 'Right, then, here we go.' He turned the key, swung open the door and stepped back. 'Welcome to Mermaid Tales and Treasures!'

The first thing he noticed as he stepped inside was the drop in temperature. Though it was warm out in the direct sun, the heating was either off, or set only high enough to prevent the pipes from freezing, and a distinct chill lay over the interior of the shop. The second thing he noticed was a terrible smell. 'Christ,' he exclaimed, wafting a hand in front of his nose. 'What the hell is that stink?'

'Cat piss,' his father said, with an air of bitter familiarity. 'My grandmother had this tabby cat when I was a kid. Poor thing was half-blind and incontinent. She probably should've had it put down, but they seemed to be the only thing keeping each other going. When it finally died, she was never the same and she faded away a few months later. Cat piss and aniseed balls are the two smells I will always associate with those grim Sunday visits.' He looked a million miles away, caught in the web of unexpected memory, and Alex found himself exchanging an uncomfortable look with Tom. His instinct was to reach out to comfort their father, but Archie didn't take kindly to anything he thought of as fussing so they reluctantly let him be while he wrestled with his ghosts.

'Find something to prop the front door open, will you, Tom, while I unlock the back door?' With any luck they could create a through breeze and air the place out a bit.

'Good idea.'

Alex weaved his way around a stack of boxes piled up in the middle of the floor, wondering how on earth a cat could've possibly got in. Reaching the back door, he spotted a previously unnoticed cat flap cut into the bottom of it and had his answer. Vowing to get the thing screwed shut as soon as possible, he unlocked the door and yanked it open, sucking in a lungful of fresh air. He kicked one of the cartons closer, using it to hold the door open before returning to the main shop floor, where he was pleased to see

Archie had recovered himself and was now nosing about behind the counter.

'There's a note here for you,' his father said, pushing it towards Alex.

Picking it up, he scanned over the copperplate script, which looked as though it had been written with a fountain pen.

Dear Alex,

I do hope you will be as happy as I have been these many years in this place. There's a special magic in selling books that's unlike anything else. It's not about the pounds, shillings and pence – ask your parents, or more likely your grandparents about that.

Alex paused to smile at that before continuing.

It's about awakening the imagination. The joy of introducing a child to a series that will expand their minds and open their hearts is hard to put into words, you'll know it when it happens.

I know you'll want to put your own stamp on things and I give you my blessing to change whatever you wish. Everything that has been left behind belongs to you. Again, you are free to keep or dispose of it as you see fit.

Wishing you every success in the world,

Sincerely,

Leonard Cavendish

P.S. If Lucy shows up, please let Barbara Mitchell know as she's taken him in, and it might take a few weeks for him to adjust to his new accommodations.

'Who the hell is Lucy?' Alex wondered aloud.

'That'll be Lucifer, Mr Cavendish's cat,' Ivy's bright voice came from behind him. 'Sorry, I'm late.' She wrinkled her nose. 'Oof. Lucy is not happy about the change in circumstances, by the smell of it. Poor old thing, have you checked to see if he's still here?'

Alex could only shake his head as he tried to take it all in. He'd never been a cat person, or a dog person for that matter, although it had been impossible not to lose his heart to Toby, the golden retriever his brother had somehow inherited from his predecessor. Maybe there was an unwritten rule in Mermaids Point that every business came with its own pet. He couldn't say he liked the sound – or the smell – of a cat called Lucifer, though. 'We've only just let ourselves in.'

'I'll have a hunt around for him,' Ivy said as she approached the counter and offered her hand to his father. 'You must be Archie. I'm Ivy. It's lovely to finally meet you.'

'Likewise, my dear.' His father took her hand and held it between both of his own for a moment. 'Alex didn't tell us we were expecting such lovely company this morning.' He cast a sly look in Alex's direction.

'Well, I know where your son gets his abundance of charm from,' Ivy said with a laugh as she extricated her hand. 'And I'm so excited about the shop that I couldn't wait to get started.'

'So, you two will be working together, eh?' Archie cast another interested look between Alex and Ivy.

'Ivy needs somewhere to sell the things she makes and I thought it would be a great way to increase footfall,' Alex said, stepping forward to block his father's line of sight with Ivy before she caught wind of what was written all over Archie's face. 'Behave,' he muttered the warning beneath his breath before stepping out from behind the counter. 'I'll help you look for the cat, and show you around the place. I don't suppose you've had reason to go upstairs before?'

Ivy shook her head. 'I only know the layout in here. I'd like to get a look at the back room you mentioned, too.'

'Sure thing. Do you want to start there?' They would need to check all the rooms and he wanted to make sure the space he'd offered her would work for what she needed, otherwise they'd have to go back to the drawing board and come up with another plan.

'We'll search in here, make sure the cat's not hiding behind any of the shelves,' Tom offered.

'Yes, yes. Take your time.' Archie waved them away with that enthusiastic smile that told Alex he'd have to have a serious chat with Pop sooner rather than later. It was one thing for Alex to admit to himself he had a thing for Ivy, it was another entirely for anyone in his family to decide to go into the matchmaking business, particularly his father, who was about as subtle as a steamroller.

'Come on through,' Alex said, ushering Ivy quickly out the back, shooting another warning look at his father over his shoulder.

* * *

The door to the storage room Alex had earmarked for Ivy's use was locked, so at least they didn't have to worry about the cat being trapped inside it. It took Alex several attempts to find the right key on the ring he'd been given by the agents as only the front and back door ones had been labelled, and the rest were generic Yale so it was a process of trial and error. 'You might be better off taking the internal keys off and leaving them in the doors,' Ivy suggested when he eventually found one that fitted the lock.

'Good idea. I'll also have to get a full set cut for you so you can come and go as you please.' He pulled his phone from his pocket. Loads of things were bound to occur to them as they explored the building so he might as well start a list now. While he was doing that, Ivy squeezed past him, curiosity making her impatient. When he joined her in the storeroom a few moments later she was staring about her in wide-eyed wonder. 'What do you think?'

She turned those shiny eyes on him. 'I think it's perfect. I had no idea there'd be so much natural light.' She gestured to the row of windows set high along the back wall.

Alex grimaced at the state of them. Though they had some sort of opening mechanism, they were too high to reach without a ladder and they looked as if no one had attempted to in years. 'It'll be even better once we give them a clean.' He retrieved his phone and made a note to buy a ladder, and a load of cleaning supplies. That done, he turned his attention to the contents of the room. The walls on both sides were covered floor to ceiling with shelves that were stuffed with anonymous cardboard boxes, what looked like old biscuit tins, which he sincerely hoped didn't still contain actual biscuits, tubes one might use for drawings or paintings and other random containers too numerous to count. This, he assumed, would be the ephemera of the shop's current name. It would take forever to sort through them and he was tempted to hire a skip and junk the lot. Before he could do that, though, he would have to do something about the dust-sheet-covered piles of furniture stacked here, there and everywhere. Lifting back the corner of the first, he winced at what looked to be a set of ugly kitchen cupboards, the Formica peeling off the edges of the cheap chipboard. 'Why on earth would anybody bother keeping these?' he wondered aloud.

'Perhaps Mr Cavendish was a bit of a hoarder?' Ivy suggested. 'Some people struggle to let go of things, especially when they've been on their own for a long time.'

'Hopefully, it won't all be this crap,' Alex said, worried he'd over-promised Ivy a ready stock of things she could refurbish and sell.

'Oh, I can make use of those, don't worry,' she assured him. When he raised his brows in disbelief she grinned. 'And I thought writers were supposed to have good imaginations.' After sweeping the dust sheet to the floor, she crouched in front of the cupboards to give them a closer look. 'I can turn these into storage boxes or toy boxes with a bit of elbow grease and love.'

'If you say so.' Not convinced even Ivy could work enough magic to make them look like anything other than exactly what they were. 'Let's see what else there is.'

They had the rest of the dust covers removed in short order and Alex was relieved to see there were some decent pieces of solid furniture, including an old rocking chair that had once been very well loved from the state of the worn seat cushion and the difference in the patina of the wood on its curved arms. 'Oh, I was hoping to find this!' Ivy exclaimed. 'Mr Cavendish used to sit in it when he did story time.'

'Story time?'

Ivy nudged the back of the chair, sending it rocking backwards and forwards in a slow, hypnotic rhythm. 'Yes. He used to run it every Saturday when we were kids and I loved it. We should think about setting something like that up again. Maybe not every weekend, but it would be a good draw for the community as well as visitors if the weather isn't great. I could run some craft activities for some of the sessions so you wouldn't have to do a story every week.'

'Me?' Alex held his hands up in protest. 'What the hell do I know about reading stories to kids?'

Setting her hands on her hips, Ivy tilted her head and gave him a disbelieving look. 'Oh, come on, you must've read Emily and Max stories when they were little.'

'Well, yes, but that was different. I know them.'

'And you'll get to know the kids who come to story time.' She said it with a blasé wave as though the matter were already settled.

'I'll think about it,' Alex said, more to get her off the subject than because he had any real intention of following through. He could see the appeal of doing something to draw younger members of the community into the shop and he was happy for Ivy to do her craft things, or whatever, but he had no intention of sitting in the rocking chair himself.

'It was just a thought. I wasn't trying to tell you what to do or anything.' Ivy turned her back to him, but not before he caught the colour creeping up her cheeks.

Damn, he was really going to have to think before he spoke if she was going to take everything as a criticism. 'It's a good idea,' he assured her. 'You just caught me off guard with it, as, apart from Em and Max, my experience with kids is sadly lacking.' When she cast him a quick, shy glance he reached for her hand and tugged her towards him. 'Let's get something clear right from the start. I might own the bricks and mortar, but as far as I am concerned this is a joint venture. I want you to feel free to speak your mind and I promise to be open to all suggestions, okay?'

She released her breath in a sound of relief and nodded. 'That's great. And I'm sorry if you felt pressured around the story-time thing. If you don't want to do it, I'm sure we could find someone else who will. If we ask around we might be able to put a rota of volunteers together. Some of the parents or even the grandparents who bring the children along might like to take it in turns. I'm sure we could get someone like Sylvia to do a few sessions. She works at the school as a classroom assistant so the kids already know her. A familiar face would kick things off nicely.'

'That sounds more like it.' Alex whipped out his phone and opened a separate note. 'We could try sessions for other parts of the community, too, unless there's already somewhere that caters for things? I don't want to be treading on anyone's toes.'

'There's a village hall which runs a few events but that's mostly for larger groups. They have a pensioners' lunch club on Wednesday and a Mums and Tots session, but we could get a copy of their schedule to make sure we don't clash with anything. No one is going to protest at being given more choice, especially in the winter when they're otherwise stuck at home.'

'Any luck?'

Alex turned to see his brother and father filling the doorway and for a moment the question confused him. Luck with what? 'Oh! The cat? No, the room was locked, so he can't be in here. Sorry, we got caught up making plans for the future.' He regretted his choice of phrasing as soon as he saw the knowing grin forming on his father's face. Thankfully Pop kept his trap shut, for once.

'I take it you didn't find him?' Ivy asked. 'Poor thing. Hopefully he made his way out the cat flap, but we'd better get back to the search.'

They quickly checked the rest of the ground floor, closing doors behind them as they went to minimise the chances of the cat slipping past them if he was still lurking around. Tom and Archie volunteered to check the large, cobbled yard while Alex and Ivy headed upstairs. The door to the flat was open, and they were greeted with a whiff of something even less pleasant. Exchanging a quick grimace with Ivy, Alex started paying attention to where he was walking. They tried the kitchen first, which was in decent condition having been upgraded the previous year, according to Mr Cavendish when he'd had a tour of the place. Hence the presence of the old kitchen cupboards downstairs, he supposed. There was no sign of the cat, but they found the source of the smell in the shape of a turd so large Alex wondered if it had been left by a dog rather than a cat.

'Great.' More out of hope than expectation, he checked the cupboard under the sink and found an old dishcloth, the dried-up end of a bar of soap and a bottle of cleaning spray with a few squirts left in it. With a quick swallow, Alex scooped up the mess in the cloth and hurried back downstairs to leave it outside the back door until he had chance to dispose of it properly. Returning to the kitchen, he washed his hands as best he could with the stub of soap while Ivy sprayed the floor.

'Probably best to let it soak in for a while before we mop it up?' she suggested.

'I'll sort it out later once we find the culprit,' he agreed, wiping his damp hands on the back of his jeans. 'Let me open this, though,' he said, leaning forward to unlatch the window over the sink. Leaving the room to air out, he closed the door behind them, and they turned their attention to the rest of the flat.

The living room looked a bit more tired than he remembered now the furniture had been removed, leaving vibrant patches on the carpet that only served to show how badly faded the rest of it was. He was glad he'd decided to put the furniture he was keeping into storage rather than moving straight in. It would be much easier to strip out and redecorate while it was empty instead of working around things. Tom had agreed to put him up for a couple of weeks while he got the flat straightened out. It didn't take more than a quick glance to show the cat wasn't lurking in a corner and, again, he closed the door. He'd just turned towards one of the two bedrooms when he heard piteous mewling coming from what he remembered as being the bathroom.

The door was ajar so he pushed it back and came face to face with the biggest, ugliest black cat he'd ever seen. Perched on the closed lid of the toilet, it twitched one battered ear at him, the other flopping at an odd angle as though it hadn't survived a fight intact. 'Hello, boy,' Alex said, extending a hand gingerly towards the mangy-looking beast. 'It's all right.' The cat gave his outstretched fingers a look of utter disdain before swiping out at him with a paw tipped with a set of lethal-looking claws. Alex snatched his hand back, clutching at the deep set of scratches. 'Hey!' he yelled, in shock. The cat's hackles rose and it hissed at Alex before jumping off the toilet seat and shooting past him out into the hall.

'Poor thing, you probably frightened him,' Ivy said, showing absolutely no concern for the blood beginning to well on the back of his hand.

'Frightened *him*?' Alex exclaimed in disbelief. 'That big bastard doesn't look like he's scared of anything.'

With a tut and a shake of her head, Ivy turned her back on him and started crooning for the cat. 'Here, Lucifer. Here, Lucy. Where's my gorgeous boy? Did the nasty man frighten you?' On and on she went, making kissing noises and calling to the cat in a tone of affection Alex could only dream of her ever using with him. Deciding to leave her to it, he rinsed off his hand in the avocado-green bathroom sink, wishing Mr Cavendish had upgraded the bathroom at the same time as the kitchen. He was just blotting his hands dry on the back of his jeans when Ivy reappeared, the appropriately named Lucifer cradled in her arms. 'I found him in the back bedroom. He doesn't look to be in bad condition, so I'll give Barbara a call and let her know we've found him.'

'Great,' Alex said, giving the smug-looking cat a glare. He was curled up against Ivy's chest as meek as a kitten and Alex wondered how she could hold the beast because he looked as if he weighed a ton. 'Are you sure he's not part panther escaped from one of those exotic private collections?'

Ivy laughed as she nuzzled the top of Lucifer's head. 'He's a big old softie, aren't you, precious?'

Alex rolled his eyes, hoping she didn't make the damn thing feel too welcome or they'd never be rid of it. 'Let's get him back where he belongs, eh?'

'Good idea. Here, can you take him while I call Barbara?' Ivy shifted her grip and held the cat out towards him. Lucifer immediately started yowling and struggling and Alex had to admit he wasn't any more keen on holding him than the cat appeared to wish to be held.

Taking a step back, he banged his hip on the bathroom sink and had to bite back a curse. 'Why don't you take him downstairs and put him out in the yard before he decides he needs to pee – or worse – again?'

'Yes, that's probably a good idea.' Ivy nestled the cat back against her shoulder and Alex could've sworn the cat smiled at him as though he had scored a great victory.

They headed downstairs, cutting off Archie and Tom, who were making their way up to meet them. 'Ah, you found our intruder, then?' Pop said, reaching out to scratch the top of the cat's head. To Alex's disbelief, Lucifer turned his face to nuzzle Archie's palm, even giving it a little lick.

'He was hiding in the bathroom. Alex gave him a fright, didn't he, darling?'

It was clear to Alex from the smattering of kisses she placed on Lucifer's head who the darling was, and it wasn't him. 'All I did was open the door,' he protested, holding his injured hand up for his brother to see when they reached the ground floor. 'And this is the thanks I get.'

'Let me have a look?' Tom took his hand and examined the scratches. 'You'll probably be okay, but I'll clean it properly when we get back to the surgery.' He pressed his fingers against the deepest scratch, making it bleed again. 'This looks a bit deep so it's good to try and make sure any dirt is out sooner rather than later.' Taking a clean handkerchief from his pocket, he held it tight against the wound. 'When was the last time you had a tetanus jab?'

'What? You must be joking! How the hell should I know?' Alex tried to pull his hand free, but Tom held on. 'It's not that bad, stop making a fuss,' he continued grumpily.

Tom gave him his best stop-being-a-big-baby look before

raising his voice to call out. 'Hey, Pop? Do you remember the last time Alex had a tetanus shot?'

Archie stuck his head around the back door where he'd followed Ivy out into the yard. 'What's that?'

'Tetanus? Alex?' Tom said, waving Alex's injured hand around.

'There was that time we went blackberry picking and he got himself tangled in that barbed-wire fence. Now then, how old was he? Nine? Ten?'

'I was six,' Alex huffed. 'And how was I supposed to know there was a fence hidden by the bushes?'

'Well, if you hadn't been so busy stuffing your mouth with fruit you might not have fallen head first into the bloody bush in the first place,' Archie said with an unsympathetic shrug. 'We'll have to check with your mother later, but that's the only time I can recall you needing one.'

'That's settled, then,' Tom said, in a tone that brooked no argument. 'You're having a shot when we get back, just to be on the safe side.'

Alex sighed, but conceded. 'Okay, if you really think it's necessary.' He cast a baleful glance at the cause of all his troubles, who was currently rubbing his head against Archie's shin as if he'd found his new best friend.

Ivy appeared at that moment. 'I've spoken to Barbara and apparently Lucifer and Carlotta had a set-to last night, which is probably why he ended up back here.'

'Carlotta?' Alex had no clue who or what Ivy was referring to.

'Barbara's tabby cat,' Tom supplied helpfully. 'She's the reason we ended up with Toby when Doc shacked up with Barbara. Seems like she doesn't like other cats any more than she does dogs.'

'Well, Lucifer can't stay here!' Even if the bloody thing hadn't tried to take his hand off, there was no way he could have a cat hanging around the place while they were trying to do the refurbishment.

'Of course, he can't,' Ivy said, and he was grateful if a tad surprised to have her on his side, especially given the way she scooped the cat up and was cuddling him once more. 'Barbara is going to take him back and hopefully he and Carlotta will get used to each other. If not, we'll have to look for another solution.'

Alex did not like the sound of that, nor the way she was nuzzling at the damn cat once more. Was it possible to be jealous of a cat? He rather suspected it was and wondered just how pathetic that made him.

9

The next week flew by in a flurry of activity and Ivy was grateful for the distraction. Going to the bookshop every day to help Alex clear the shelves and pack up the stock he'd bought as part of the purchase kept her away from the cottage so she didn't have to think about Alun showing people around her home – not that it looked as if it was going to be her home for much longer. The improvement in the weather had seen an uptick in interest and there'd been several people who'd previously holidayed in the Point and left their details with the agent, as well as one or two locals looking to expand their current portfolio. No one had made an offer as yet, but one of the visiting couples had made an appointment for a second viewing and Alun was sure it was only a matter of time before someone moved forward on the cottage.

Unfortunately, she wasn't any further forward with her own search for somewhere to live. Jake's mum, Linda, was back from her cruise and had moved into the apartment at the surgery. With Alex still living there and his parents popping down every weekend to help out, things were a bit crowded in the Nelson household, and Ivy got the impression Alex was as glad of the distraction of getting the shop sorted out as she was. At least he was making progress with his flat. The wallpaper had been stripped and the carpets taken up and thrown in a skip in the back yard, together with the ugly bathroom suite. A local plasterer had been in to skim the walls and now they were dry, the combined forces of the Morgans and the Nelsons had a painting party planned for tomorrow where between them they hoped to get the place decorated throughout. Ivy had been included by default, and she was happy to help out. Anything would be better than sitting at home worrying about things that were out of her control.

It was the not knowing where she stood that was the worst thing. Until someone made an offer she didn't dare speculate on what she would be able to afford. The asking price still seemed wildly over the top to her, but Alun seemed quietly confident, and she supposed he knew his business better than she did. With a sigh she turned her attention back to the box she'd filled, sealing the top with the tape gun they'd found under the counter and writing a large 'W' on each side. They'd decided to pack the shelves alphabetically so they'd know what was in each box regardless of how it was stacked in the back room. They'd already filled the actual stockroom from floor to ceiling and decanted the furniture from what would eventually be her workroom into the large double-doored garage, which was at the far end of the yard. The block containing the garage had originally been part of the blacksmith's workshop and stables, which had given the street its name. The properties on either side of it had long been converted into housing or retail units and Ivy had a feeling the garage was where the entrance to the yard had originally been. It had doors facing out onto the street as well as into the yard itself and seemed watertight enough that the furniture they'd piled up inside it would be fine for a few weeks. Alex's car would have to remain at the surgery until they could make room for it, but that didn't seem to be a problem.

Tom seemed so happy his brother had decided to make a home for himself at the Point that Ivy thought he'd do pretty much anything to help make it happen – including spending what little downtime he had after serving the medical needs of the village working side by side with them.

It was rare it was just her and Alex about the place because someone or other was always dropping in to see how they were getting on, and lending a hand even if they could only spare an hour or two. For those who were tied to their businesses, like Tom with the surgery, or Laurie with the café, it was more difficult, but Nick had been in more days than not. Although he'd secured funding in principle, he was now stuck waiting for the council to make up its mind about his conversion project and it was still too early in the season for the boat tour company he ran with his uncle to be doing much business. 'Is this one ready to go?' Nick asked her as he and Alex returned from their latest trip to the back room, pointing at the box she'd just sealed.

'Yes.' Ivy set the tape gun on the shelf she'd just emptied and shoved her hands into the small of her back while she tried to stretch out a twinge. She wasn't used to bending over so much, but her job was a lot easier than Nick and Alex's as they were the ones carrying the boxes she filled, so she didn't like to complain. At least she was sleeping well at night because she was too exhausted at the end of the day to do much else. It was a good kind of tired, too, the kind that made her grateful for a hot bath, the kind that told her she'd done something productive. And it was so much better than the foggy, desperate kind of tired she'd carried with her towards the end of her mum's life and for the first few weeks afterwards. She might not know what was going on in terms of her long-term living arrangements, but life in general felt as if it had a purpose.

* * *

'Are you all right?' Alex asked. From the concerned look he was giving her, he must've noticed her stretching.

'I'm fine, just a bit stiff.' She knuckled her back again, straining to reach the big knot just beneath her shoulder blades.

'Here, let me.' Before she could respond, Alex had brushed aside her hand and replaced it with his own. 'Here?' he asked, pressing into the spot.

'Up a bit.' When his fingers prodded just the right place she had to bite her lip not to cry out because it really hurt. She nodded her head, closing her eyes against the discomfort.

'Am I hurting you?' His voice was close to her ear and she wasn't sure if she shuddered from the slowly unravelling crick in her back or the sensation of his breath against her skin.

'Yes, but don't stop because I think you've nearly got it,' she said, trying not to think about how close he was standing to her. Not for the first time, she sent a silent curse towards Laurie because ever since she'd suggested Alex could be the solution to her sex drought, it was hard to think about anything else whenever she was around him. No, that wasn't strictly true. She'd been drawn to him from the first moment they'd met in Tom and Nerissa's kitchen, but Laurie saying it out loud had broken down a wall inside Ivy's head, almost as if she'd been given permission to think about herself and her own needs for the first time in forever.

Alex laughed, the husky sound scrambling her brains even further, and when he dug the tips of his thumbs into the exact right spot to release the knot in her back she couldn't stifle a moan of relief.

'Hey, if you two want me to leave, just say the word,' Nick said, choosing the worst possible moment to walk back into the room.

Stepping away from Alex's magic hands, Ivy turned her flaming face towards the bookshelf and reached blindly for the next stack of books to pack. Unfortunately, she'd used the last of the boxes and was left holding the pile in her hand. She couldn't look at Alex, and meeting Nick's eye wasn't much easier, but she forced a bright laugh. 'I seem to have run out of boxes. Can you make me up some more?'

'Say no more.' At his knowing grin, she realised her mistake because the flat-packed boxes were stacked against the wall in the storeroom meaning Nick would have to leave her and Alex alone once more.

'It's not like that!' she called after Nick's retreating back. 'Alex was helping me with an ache in my back, nothing more.' *Shut up, Ivy, for the love of god just shut your silly mouth and stop digging.*

When the hole she was praying for failed to materialise, she risked a quick glance towards Alex, who was leaning against the shelves across from her, an expression on his face she couldn't quite read. 'It's not like what?' he asked softly.

Oh, boy. 'Well, you know.' She raised a hand to gesture, forgetting she was still clutching a stack of books, which clattered to the ground. Ivy crouched to retrieve them, her hand colliding with Alex's as he bent to do the same. His fingers caught hers before she could pull away, the touch an electric energy that zinged to every nerve ending in her body. She froze, the sensible bit of her brain yelling warnings to retreat now while the baser part of her nature positively hummed with the rightness of the contact.

'Ivy?' There was so much loaded into that one word: hope, anticipation, a rough touch of need that spoke to her.

'Not now,' she whispered, keeping her eyes locked on the books scattered at her feet.

'Okay.' He lifted her hand and she felt the softest brush of his lips across her knuckles and then he was gone, calling out to Nick in a jokey tone about giving him a hand because the last batch of boxes he'd made up had all leaned to one side. Ivy stared at the spot where he'd kissed her, wondering what the hell she'd set in motion. She could've said 'no'. Could've cut things off right there and then and they'd both have been able to move on without causing any difficulty between them. That would've been the sensible move, the one that kept her defences secure and her mind focused on the future. Risking it all because she couldn't keep her hormones in check was crazy. No. That wasn't fair to Alex. This draw she felt towards him was more than simply physical. She liked him, wanted to get to know him better, to ease the sadness she sensed in him and soothe the edges of her own pain at the same time.

Maybe there was still a way to salvage things before they got out of hand. As Laurie had said, things didn't have to get serious between her and Alex. They were both adults and free agents, so no one else was going to get hurt if they gave in to something she sensed they both needed. If they acknowledged their attraction and dealt with it in a mature, sensible way then there was no reason for things to get complicated. She would have to give the matter some more thought.

They managed to keep out of each other's way for the rest of the day. Even when Nick had to take himself off in the afternoon for a meeting with his architect, things didn't get too awkward. Alex produced a portable radio from somewhere and tuned it into the local BBC station. The chatter of the presenters and the easy, familiar pop music they played served as a buffer to fill the silence. Ivy couldn't remember the last time she'd listened to the radio, preferring her ever-growing list of podcasts, but she found herself fascinated by the range of topics covered, all with a local flavour.

'Probably not what you are used to listening to?' she asked Alex with a laugh after an enthusiastic discussion between the afternoon presenter and a local steam-railway volunteer.

'It's great,' Alex replied with a grin as he hefted yet another full box towards the back room. 'It might be good to have on when we are up and running, not too loud, but we're not a library. Besides, it's good research for an outsider like me to get a feel for what's important to the community. I've never lived anywhere other than London. Moaning about how crowded the Tube is feels like a privilege when villages like the Point struggle to maintain even a regular bus service.'

'It's all I've ever known. Even when we were teenagers and desperate to go out, going into town was a big deal. We only did it a couple of times a year because it meant clubbing together enough money for taxis there and back.'

Alex set the box down at his feet and shook his head. 'I think I've fallen out of most of the nightclubs in London in my time.' He met her gaze with a rueful smile. 'I'm not sure I ever actually enjoyed it much, it was just what we did.'

'We used to have parties on the beach in the summer. We'd light a fire and sit around listening to music and passing a bottle of whatever had been liberated from someone's family liquor cabinet.' She cringed as a long-forgotten memory surfaced of her and Laurie sharing half a bottle of sweet sherry, much to their later regret.

Alex laughed. 'We used to send our oldest-looking mate into one of the corner shops to try and score a big bottle of gut-rot cider. It's amazing we survived our teenage years, really.'

'That trick would be hard to pull off in the Point when literally everyone knows who you are,' Ivy said with a wry grin. 'We soon grew out of that phase and were happy enough with a bottle of Diet Coke to share. It was more finding somewhere we could hang out without feeling like we were being watched all the time.'

'I can understand that. The novelty of being part of a community that watches out for each other is something that really appeals to me after the relative anonymity of London, but I guess there are some who pay a little too much attention – like your friend Bev, for example.'

Ivy rolled her eyes. 'She's no friend of mine, but I was glad to see the knitting ladies seem to have forgiven her.' She really didn't want anyone to feel ostracised because of her; besides, with any luck Bev might have learnt her lesson. A companionable silence settled between them as they returned to the never-ending task of packing up the books. Mr Cavendish had added more shelves over the years, blocking out a lot of the natural light, which resulted in the interior feeling quite gloomy. The sections she remembered from her youth had gradually been eroded for a simpler fiction/non-fiction split with titles alphabetised by author. She supposed that would have been easier to manage but the shop had lost some of its atmosphere, or perhaps she'd romanticised the magic of her childhood experiences a bit too much.

The song on the radio faded to an interview with someone from a village a few miles along the coast who, according to the introduction, had set up their own jewellery-making business. Her attention caught by the topic, Ivy set down the books she was holding and wandered closer to the radio. It was hard to get a visual impression of what was being discussed, though the interviewer was doing his best to describe a couple of items. Alex must have noticed she'd stopped working because he came and joined her. 'What are they talking about?'

'Shh.' Ivy waved a hand at him because the interviewer was asking the woman about how easy she'd found it to set up a website. Brushing past him, she grabbed one of the markers they'd been using to label the boxes and, finding a scrap of paper on the counter, began to make a note of the website provider as well as the address of the jeweller's site.

'Good on her for getting a proper plug in there,' Alex said as the brief interview wound up. 'Are you thinking of buying something, then? I've noticed you're a jewellery fan.' He nodded at the onyx pendant dangling from a silver chain, which had been Ivy's choice from her mother's collection that morning.

'This is a tribute to my mum,' she explained, closing her fingers briefly over the pendant. 'It was one of the things I promised I would do, wear something of hers every day and smile as I put it on.'

Alex's eyes softened. 'That's a lovely idea. My mum's got some gorgeous stuff, which I know Jo used to covet.' He shrugged. 'I guess it'll go to Emily in time.'

'Your ex?' Ivy guessed, wondering if it was a good idea to pry. He'd not mentioned his divorce other than that one time, but if she was seriously going to think about getting involved with him, even on the most casual level, it seemed like a good chance to test the lie of the land, so to speak.

'Yeah. She always liked to dress to impress, and Mum has some fancy pieces Dad has bought her over the years. Jo said they were wasted on the kind of bores who went to golf dinners.' He shook his head, a sardonic smile on his face. 'She always was a bit of a snob, which was a bit rich given her dad used to drive an HGV. Some people like to pretend they're something they're not, I guess, and she was one of them. I don't think it even occurred to her that she was insulting my folks when she said it.'

He hadn't cut off the conversation, so Ivy ventured a little further. 'Perhaps she was a bit insecure about it?' Ivy's dad worked in a warehouse in a big retail park on the outskirts of the nearest large town. Regardless of how much he'd let her down over the years, it had never occurred to Ivy to be ashamed of what he did. It was honest, hard work and many of the locals did things that required physical labour. Their ancestors had mostly earned their living from the sea, which was not a job for the faint-hearted, even nowadays with the technological advancements. As the fishing jobs had been lost those that hadn't transitioned into supporting the tourist trade had been forced to seek work outside the Point.

Alex shrugged. 'Perhaps she was. I thought her parents were very nice, on the handful of occasions I got to meet them. She wasn't big on family visits.'

'Do you miss her?' Ivy blurted before she could stop herself.

He laughed. 'Jo? Not a bit. I was very bitter at the time of our split and I...' A shadow crossed his face. 'I did some stuff I regret now. When I look back I can see we were never a great fit.'

So he wasn't pining for her at least; that was one less thing to worry about. 'I'm sorry for prying.'

'It's fine. I mean, it's not a topic I like to dwell on, but I don't feel the need to pretend she doesn't exist or anything like that.' He gave Ivy a considering look. 'What about you? Any relationship secrets you want to share?'

'I'd need to have had one in order to have something to share.' Ivy snapped her mouth shut a moment too late to hold in the unguarded words.

He gave her a look so loaded with sympathy that she wanted to die a little inside. 'I guess things were tough when you had your mum to look after.'

'Yeah, and I wasn't exactly spoiled for choice, either. It's hard to fall in love with someone when you remember them picking their nose and flicking it in your hair at primary school.'

Alex grimaced. 'God, little boys are such beasts. I should make a list of all the girls I was terrible to, look them up and send them flowers to apologise.'

'If the boys I went to school with did that, I'd have bouquets for the next month.' She giggled. 'Oh, it wasn't that bad, really, but the few I dated never really sparked into anything serious. And like you said, it was difficult sometimes with Mum and having to cancel plans at the last minute if she wasn't feeling good.'

'What about you and Nick?'

Startled at the question, she looked up to find Alex watching her intently. She tried not to blush at the idea he'd perhaps been speculating about her the way she was about him. '*Nick?* What made you ask about him?'

He lifted one shoulder in an overly casual gesture. 'You guys are very affectionate with each other, so I wondered if there was any history, that's all.'

She supposed it might look like that to an outsider. 'In spite of our mothers' grand plans, Nick and I have never been more than friends. He's like a big brother to me.'

'But your mum wanted there to be more?'

'Only in that way best friends who grow up and have children of the opposite sex close in age might speculate about them getting together. She never pushed me towards him, just dropped a few heavy hints, which I chose to ignore.' She shook her head. 'I adore Nick to pieces, but not in that way.'

'Good to know.'

Was it? Biting the inside of her cheek to hold back a grin, Ivy did her best to appear nonchalant as she pushed aside the notes she'd made about the jewellery maker. 'Well, we'd best get the rest of these books packed up.' Though she didn't look back, she could feel Alex's eyes on her all the way.

* * *

By the time they'd packed and stacked the last box, it was after five and all Ivy wanted to do was crawl into a hot shower and stay there for an hour. Every inch of her exposed skin felt as if it was covered in a layer of grime from handling the dusty books, and she'd sneezed so much she was sure her nose must be glowing. Now the shop area was cleared, it needed a thorough clean before the carpenters Alex had hired came in the following week to take down the shelves and repair and polish the floor. They were taking the shelves back to their workshop to strip and paint the ones Alex was keeping, and had offered to keep the rest in return for a discount on their bill.

'What time do you want me in tomorrow?' she asked Alex as he double-checked the back door was secured for the night.

'It's been a long day, so not too early. I think Nerissa has plans for a cooked breakfast to set us up for the day, so about ten, if that suits you?'

'Sounds good,' she agreed, already thinking about the lie-in she could have. As she waited for him to lock the front door behind them, a thought occurred to her. It was Saturday night and the first one in weeks when they wouldn't be watching a movie and chatting over FaceTime. They'd moved on from the Dan Brown adaptations and had been taking it in turns to choose something to watch. 'It'll be weird not talking to you later.' When he frowned, she realised she'd had the first part of the conversation in her head so no wonder he looked confused. 'Saturday night is movie night...'

'Oh! Yeah, it completely slipped my mind. Whose turn was it to pick?' The knowing grin he gave her said he knew it was her turn but was trying to cheat anyway.

'Mine! You made me watch *The Waterboy* last time, remember? I'm not sure I trust you to choose again.'

'Adam Sandler is a comedy genius,' Alex huffed, before giving her a sly grin. 'His worst film would still be better than whatever romcom nonsense you are planning on foisting on me.'

Ivy was having none of that. 'Who was the one sniffling at the end of *Dumplin*?' she scoffed, giving his arm a little nudge.

'I had something in my eye!' Alex protested. 'Hay fever season must've started early.'

The trees and hedgerows around the village were in full bloom and yet she'd not heard a single sneeze from him. 'Do you even get hay fever?'

He shrugged. 'Maybe?'

God, he was such an idiot. Her smile drooped as she realised this was the end of their banter for the evening rather than just the start of it. 'It seems a bit daft to FaceTime when you're five minutes down the road.'

Alex shoved the bundle of keys in his pocket with a sigh. 'And the odds on me being able to hide upstairs without Max barging in every five minutes is highly unlikely. He's been my little shadow since I moved in.'

'Aw, he loves spending time with his Uncle Alex.' She might not have siblings, but Laurie and Nick were close enough to blood as far as she was concerned. How lovely would it be to be the favourite aunt to their children one day? She really hoped she got the chance to find out.

'He's fantastic, but also a pain in the arse when I want five minutes to myself. Hopefully the novelty will wear off once he gets used to the idea that I'm here for the duration. Not that I'm complaining, well, not much, anyway. I missed the hell out of them all when Tom relocated. It'll be great being able to spend time with him and Emily on a regular basis.' Alex rested his shoulder against the shop window and grinned. 'I wouldn't be too surprised if my folks didn't end up moving down here at some point as well.'

'There's a very good golf course about ten miles north of here,' Ivy said, remembering what he'd said earlier about golf dinners.

'Is there?' Alex's brows perked in interest. 'I'll drop a quiet word to Mum. She's dead keen on the idea, but I know Pop will find it harder to give up easy access to the city. Maybe she can book a round for next time they are visiting and surprise him.'

'She plays as well?' Ivy couldn't say it was a sport she'd ever been that interested in, she only knew about the course because it was something the village used in their promotional material to lure the tourists.

'Ladies' vice-captain. I think she's got a better handicap than Pop, not that anyone dares mention it around him.' Alex grinned. 'At least it's something they enjoy doing together.'

'And they look well on it,' Ivy said, thinking about how fit and trim Archie and Philippa always looked. She cast a quick glance behind her. She wanted to keep on talking to him, but the surgery and her cottage were in opposite directions. 'Well, shame about movie night, but we can pick it up again once things settle down a bit.' *Unless...* As tired and in need of a hot shower as she was, she wasn't ready to say goodnight. 'You could come over to mine and we could watch something together. If you want to, I mean. I'll understand if you'd rather go home and relax. And things at home are a bit all over the place because I've got clothes and toys I've made everywh—'

Alex pressed a finger to her lips to stem the stream of nervous words. 'I'll see you at seven.'

Well, that was easy. 'Okay, then!' Ivy checked her watch. 'If I hurry I can catch Luca before the deli closes and pick up a sharing platter, maybe a pizza as well if you'd like.' *And a couple of beers,* she added to herself, racking her brain to try and remember what brand he liked.

'Perfect.' Alex took a couple of steps backwards. 'I'll see you in a bit.'

'Yes. See you.' And with that, Ivy spun on her heel and hurried towards the high street to catch Luca. She had less than two hours to grab some provisions, have a shower and make the cottage look vaguely presentable. She also needed to work on her pros and cons list about whether or not to make Alex an offer he hopefully wouldn't refuse.

* * *

Ivy got home feeling even more frazzled, having been held up by Luca and his lovely wife, Maria. It hadn't taken long for word to get around about the planned changes at the bookshop and her involvement in it and they wanted to know all about it. Their encouragement and enthusiasm were a great lift, but they could've done with better timing. Opening the door, she kicked the pile of post waiting on the mat out of the way and hurried through to the kitchen, where she dumped two loaded bags of shopping on the table and began to sort through the contents. The bottle of wine she'd bought for herself went straight in the freezer, together with a couple of bottles of beer from the six-pack Luca had worked out was probably the brand Alex preferred from her vague description of the label she'd only seen through her phone screen. It looked as if it might be the right one, and Luca had assured her it was a decent brand so she would just have to hope for the best.

They'd sold the last of their platters, so she'd ended up with little sample boxes of everything they had behind the fresh counter. She would let Alex choose, and whatever was left over she would work her way through over the coming week. The four seasons pizza she slid onto the top shelf of the fridge had been a calculated gamble with its four-in-one selection – again, there was bound to be something Alex liked. And if he didn't, she thought with an eyeroll at her own silly panicking, he could go hungry. Or go to the fish and chip shop.

Shutting the fridge on that thought, she returned to the hallway to take off her coat and risked a quick peek into the lounge. It was in a much worse state than she remembered, with clothes draped every which way over the back of the sofa and chairs. Plastic crates covered the floor, filled with the patchwork bears and rag dolls she'd made using the offcuts of material. With her workroom upstairs being so small, she'd carried each finished item downstairs and now it looked as if a rainbow bomb had gone off. Her mum's old room didn't have much furniture in it, the specialist hospital-style bed she'd needed having been returned to the local health service back in January. The wardrobe and dressing table remained where they were, the contents waiting for Ivy to sort them out. She didn't like going in there much so had left everything untouched, apart from her mother's jewellery chest, which now sat on her own dressing table.

She and Alex could huddle around her laptop at the kitchen table, she supposed, but the chairs in there were hard and the old-fashioned strip light was quite harsh after a long day. If she was brutally honest with herself, the only place suitable for watching a film was her bedroom, which might give Alex the wrong – or the right – impression. She checked her watch. It was after six, too late to call and cancel, especially when he would want to know what had changed in the space of an hour. No, she would have to brazen it out. One look at the state of the lounge would be enough to explain the reason they were going upstairs without Alex necessarily reading too much into it. Mind made up, she hurried upstairs to see what she could do to perhaps make it look a little less as if she was inviting him to her bed...

10

The temperature had dropped in the past couple of hours, making Alex glad he'd tugged a jumper on over his usual T-shirt and jeans as he strolled down the path along the front. The spring tide was high thanks to the full moon, and he paused for a moment to watch the frothing white foam crash up onto the beach. It was like something out of a painting, and London seemed so very far away. He'd only been in the Point a few days, and he was already addicted to everything about the sea. He kept his bedroom window open at night, listening to its different moods, the soft shush of a calm, cloudless night, the boom and roil when it was whipping up as it was now. He closed his eyes, drew in a deep breath and felt the rightness of the moment settle into his bones. This was his place in the world. All he had to do now was not stuff everything up. Given his track record, the odds were hardly in his favour. The self-deprecating thought was enough to make him laugh at himself and he turned from the lure of one beautiful thing to another and began the short walk to Ivy's cottage.

Although she had said she'd grab them something to eat from

the deli, Alex didn't want to turn up empty-handed. With Nerissa's blessing, he'd raided the kitchen cupboards at the surgery for snacks. His sweetheart of a soon-to-be sister-in-law – if Tom pulled his finger out and got around to proposing to her, that was – had handed him a bottle of white wine with a wink and, with a couple of beers thrown in, he hoped he had most things covered.

When she'd first invited him over, he'd wanted to jump for joy, or grab her up and kiss away the pressure that had been building inside him all day. *Not now.* God, those two words had been on a permanent repeat loop since she'd whispered them, and he'd tortured himself trying to read the right meaning into them. If she hadn't been feeling something along the same lines as him, she would've said no, right? Or perhaps that was just wishful thinking on his part and she'd been looking for a way to let him down gently. He flashed back to that cheesy kiss he'd laid on the back of her hand and something withered inside him. What the hell had that been about?

Still bemused at himself, Alex turned the corner into Ivy's street. His eyes went immediately towards her front door and saw she'd put the outside light on. It was a simple thing, but it warmed something inside, as if she was welcoming his approach. He seized the feeling and gripped it tight in his mind before it had the chance to get carried away. Things were at such a delicate stage between the two of them, he couldn't afford to get it wrong. She was the key to his success here – and not necessarily just on a personal level. The week they'd spent in close proximity sorting out the shop was enough for him to know he'd been right in asking her to get involved with the project. She had an innate sweetness about her, a quiet warmth that reminded him a little bit of Nerissa. And he didn't think it was his personal bias towards Ivy making him feel that way. Everyone she interacted with came away with a smile. She would be a magnet to customers, young and old alike. *Not now,* she'd said, and he would take her at her word and leave the next move up to her. Even if that meant *not now* ended up being *not ever.* With that promise fixed firmly in his mind, he reached the cottage and knocked on the door.

It took a few moments for Ivy to answer. The first thing he noticed was her hair, the curls much tighter than he was used to seeing and he realised they were still damp from the shower and not fluffed out around her head as was her usual style. 'Sorry!' she said, stepping back to let him in. 'The place needed a bit more tidying up than I'd anticipated so I'm running a few minutes late.'

'You didn't need to bother on my account,' he assured her, moving to the side to let her close the door. Something rustled under his foot and he bent to rescue a pile of post he'd inadvertently stepped on. 'My turn to apologise,' he said, handing her several envelopes, the top one bearing the damp outline of his training shoe on it. 'I came via the seafront and the path was wet from the spray, I guess.'

'It's fine. I should've picked them up when I got home. Come on through.' She took the small stack and led the way to the kitchen. 'Always bills or junk,' she said with a laugh, tossing them on the table.

A white envelope with the thickness that spoke of quality missed and Alex bent to retrieve it for her. 'Doesn't look like a bill,' he said as he dropped his backpack onto the table next to the rest of the post. 'I brought a few things with me. Is it okay to put them in the fridge?'

'Hmm? Oh, sure,' she said in a distracted voice as she turned the envelope over in her hands. 'I wonder what it is.'

Alex looked up from emptying his bag and couldn't hide his grin. 'I believe the usual practice is to open it and find out.'

'Good point,' she said with a laugh. 'I'm glad I have you here to do the clever thinking stuff.'

Leaving her to open the post, Alex carried his drinks to the fridge and opened it. The shelves were packed with so many treats his mouth began to water. Ivy must've all but cleared the deli out, and he approved of her actions wholeheartedly. On the pretence of making room, he started lifting out the little boxes and peeking inside at the contents. There were fat vine leaves stuffed with feta and tomatoes, shiny black and green olives glistening in garlic-infused oil, charcuterie slices and bite-sized squares of focaccia. It rather put the peanuts and pretzels he'd filched from Nerissa's cupboards to shame. 'That's a feast fit for a king. You've really pushed the boat out tonight, thanks.'

When she didn't respond, Alex turned to find Ivy staring at a square of white card with neat black printing on it. 'Everything all right?'

Dazed eyes rose to meet his. 'It's an invitation to my father's wedding.'

'Well, he didn't waste any bloody time!' Alex exclaimed, appalled at the crassness of Kevin and Wendy rushing to the altar so quickly after Jen's passing. 'He's not seriously expecting you to go, is he?'

'It's not like that,' Ivy said, setting the invitation aside and picking up a letter. 'He didn't send it, Wendy did. She wanted me to know before anyone else and says she's not posting the rest of the invites out until Monday.' She waved the letter with a sigh. 'I can't believe he's managed to talk her around but listen to this: "I understand why you felt the need to give me that old letter Kevin sent to your mum, but he's explained everything to me. He didn't want me to be disappointed about having to wait, and he didn't want to put Jen under any more strain with her being so unwell. So, you see, he was stuck between a rock and a hard place".' Ivy shook her head. 'He's really done a number on her.'

'I guess people believe what they want to when it comes to relationships.' Alex could sympathise with Wendy because he'd made enough missteps with Jo to know how easy it was to deceive yourself when you loved someone badly enough.

'I suppose you're right.' Ivy set the letter down on top of the invitation. 'Well, it was bound to happen at some point, and at least she had the foresight to warn me before the rest of the village finds out. She doesn't expect me to go but wanted to give me the option. Maybe she thinks she still might be able to build bridges between me and Kevin.'

The way she said it made it clear to Alex that wasn't likely to happen any time soon. Ivy had taken the news amazingly well, all things considered, but he didn't want her to spend the evening dwelling on what must still be hurtful, no matter how brave a face she was putting on things. 'Right, then,' he said with forced joviality. 'There's a fridge full of goodies to soften the pain so tell me what godawful chick flick you're going to make me suffer through tonight.'

He was pleased he'd hit the right note when her eyes lit up with mischief. 'You're going to love it, I promise. I should warn you that we'll have to watch it upstairs as the lounge is a disaster zone.'

A faint hint of colour rose on her cheeks, and Alex made himself take a step back to give her a touch more space. 'Whatever's easiest for you.' He held out his hands. 'Load me up and point the way.'

A few minutes later he was carrying a tray filled with snacks, plates and napkins up the stairs and trying his best not to notice how round and plump Ivy's bottom looked in the navy yoga pants she wore. It didn't help that the material they were made from looked so soft and strokable. Trying to remind himself of his early promise not to push things, he forced his gaze higher. She'd paired them with a long-sleeve fire-engine-red top, which should've clashed with her hair, but didn't. Vibrant colours suited both her looks and her personality. They reached the top of the narrow stairs and Ivy nudged open a door immediately to the left. 'You can put the tray straight on the bed, if you like,' she said, turning her back on him to set the bottles and glasses she was carrying on her dressing table. The pretty pale quilt he was used to seeing on the bed was covered with a tartan picnic-style blanket and the pillows had been supplemented with a pile of cushions. Doing as he was bid, Alex then toed off his trainers and set them outside the bedroom door. 'You didn't have to do that,' she said with a smile as she offered him his beer.

'I should've thought to take them off when I arrived.' He touched a hand to the blanket. 'This looks nice.'

'It won't matter if we get crumbs on it. Go ahead and make yourself comfy.' She took a sip of her wine, then placed her glass on the bedside cabinet on the left of the bed before setting out the food from the tray so it would be in easy reach for both of them.

Alex leaned back experimentally before adjusting the cushions on his side to make a curve he could settle into. They were soft without being too squashy. 'I might have to steal a couple of these cushions,' he said, tucking a spare one under his elbow so he could recline on his side and still reach the food. 'Did you make them?'

Ivy nodded with a pleased smile. 'Yes. It took me ages to find the right filling for them. I was thinking about making a few giant ones we could put out in the children's book corner.'

'That would work,' he mused, picturing the revised layout he had in mind. He hadn't set anything in stone, wanting to see how much room they had once the extra shelves had been cleared out, but he liked the idea of a cosy spot where little ones would feel welcome. Maybe they could source a couple of low plastic tables and chairs as well, especially if Ivy wanted to do her craft activity sessions. Things like that and the floor cushions would be easy to bring in and out of storage. 'We should create a couple of other reading spots as well, for adults.'

'Definitely. This is fun, isn't it? I'm so glad you're happy to accept my input on the plans for the shop.'

'We're a team,' he said, patting the empty space next to him. 'We'll succeed or fail together so we need to make these kinds of decisions together.' She flopped down on the cushions beside him, sending a gentle waft of her perfume towards him. It was sweet but not sickly-sweet, reminding him of something from his childhood. 'Do you mind me asking what scent you're wearing? It's driving me mad.'

Ivy sat up abruptly, a look of consternation on her face. 'Is it too strong? It's a matching shower gel and body lotion so I might have overdone it.'

He shook his head, patting the space next to him once more. 'No, nothing like that. I've been catching hints of it around the shop all week and it reminds me of something, but I can't work out what for the life of me it is. Something good, I promise.'

'Oh, thank goodness,' she exclaimed, settling back again. 'I'd hate to be one of those women who chokes anyone who comes within a few feet of them. I swear some of them are practising chemical warfare.'

'You're not in any danger of being banned under the Geneva Convention, I promise.'

'Phew! I could do without a NATO invasion this weekend, I've got plans.' They laughed. 'To answer your question, it's cherry blossom. Laurie gave me a set for Christmas from L'OCCITANE. I was going to save it for special occasions but then decided it would sit in the bathroom cabinet forever if I did that, so I use it most days.'

Wondering how long it had been since someone had done

something special for her, Alex made a note to find out from Laurie when Ivy's birthday was. There must be a nice restaurant some-where within driving distance he could take her to. It didn't have to be a date or anything if she didn't want it to be, just a treat, because she deserved to be made to feel special. 'Doing something nice for yourself is a good thing.'

She turned that sweet, shy smile on him. 'I had the same thought when I was in the deli earlier and couldn't make up my mind what to choose so I went for everything.'

'A bold move, and one I appreciate.' Alex pulled the nearest pot towards him and fished out an olive. 'If we don't start the movie soon it'll be midnight before it's finished.'

'Good point.' Ivy helped herself to one of the stuffed vine leaves. 'Oh, I think these are my favourite,' she said with an appreciative murmur Alex did his best to ignore because it made him want to nibble on her the way she was devouring the vine leaf. 'Should I put the pizza in now, do you think?'

He surveyed the spread between them. 'I'm not sure we need it, unless you're starving.'

She shook her head. 'Let's see how we get on with what we've got. I can always pop it in for a half-time snack if we're peckish later.'

Picking up the remote control, Alex handed it to her. 'Go on, then, do your worst.' To his surprise, she'd chosen *Blended*, an Adam Sandler movie, and not one he'd seen either. 'You didn't have to pick this for me,' he protested as she started the film.

'I didn't. I know I wasn't keen on *The Waterboy*, but *50 First Dates* was fun and this one has him teaming up with Drew Barrymore again so hopefully it'll be good. I think it's a romcom so it's a good compromise of what we both enjoy.'

It proved to be a great choice and they were soon both caught up in the silliness of the film about two single parents thrown together in the same hotel suite. 'Do you want any more to eat?' Ivy asked him after about half an hour.

Alex shook his head. 'I can't eat another bite.' He probably could, but he'd regret it. When she started popping lids back on the pots, he grabbed the remote and paused the film. 'I'll give you a hand.'

'Thanks. Do you want another drink?'

There was about an inch left in his bottle, but that wouldn't last long. 'Are you having another?'

She nodded. 'Only half a glass though or I'll be nodding off. It's been a busy day.'

While he was reluctant to end the evening early, he didn't want to outstay his welcome. 'We can finish the film another time.'

'Oh, no, I'm fine. I'm a bit tired, but not sleepy as such. I wasn't trying to drop a hint for you to leave, I promise.'

'Well, just say the word when you do want me to.'

* * *

Five minutes later, the food was cleared, their drinks refreshed and the pair of them were semi-sprawled across the small mountain of cushions and pillows. Ivy had turned off the lamp on her dressing table, leaving only the small lamps on either side of the bed to cast their low, warm light. It should've made it easier to concentrate on the TV screen suspended from the opposite wall, but it heightened his awareness of where they were. Ivy was only inches away and he couldn't work out if he could feel the heat of her body, or just wanted to feel it so badly he was imagining things.

'You okay?' Her voice was little more than a whisper.

'All good,' he murmured, forcing himself to pay attention to the antics on the screen.

He'd just got back into the film when Ivy changed position and her head ended up half resting on his arm. 'Sorry,' she said, quickly shifting back to her side of the bed.

'I don't mind,' he found himself saying. His pulse thudded loudly in his ears. One beat, two beats, three, and then she was rolling over to nestle against his side. With a silent warning to himself to move with great care, Alex raised his arm so she could settle her head more against his chest then let it fall so the tips of his fingers were just grazing the small of her back. Her palm settled on his ribcage just below where her cheek rested, and she relaxed against him with a soft sigh. The feeling of rightness he'd experienced on the seafront earlier came back to him, deeper this time. If they never had more than this moment, it might be enough because it was so close to perfect as made no difference. Allowing himself the indulgence of a gentle brush of his thumb against her back, he settled back to enjoy the rest of the film.

The film ended with its perfect happy ever after and Alex had to smile to himself at how easy they made it look. *If only.* His arm had gone to sleep about twenty minutes earlier, but he hadn't dared move it in case he disturbed Ivy and she changed her mind about snuggling. He hadn't really thought of himself as the snuggling type before, but he could get used to it with her.

As Netflix did its usual trick of cutting off the credits to make recommendations of other things to watch, Alex knew it was time to make a move. 'I should probably get going. We've got another busy day tomorrow.'

'Okay,' Ivy said, sounding a little sleepy.

When she didn't move he closed his eyes on a brief prayer for the shreds of gentlemanly behaviour not to desert him. 'I need my arm back,' he said gently.

'It's mine now, sorry.' Ivy cuddled in a little closer and Alex didn't know whether to laugh or groan in despair.

He pressed a kiss to the top of her head. 'If you don't let me go, we might end up doing something we regret.'

She raised her head just enough to look up at him. 'What if we didn't regret it?'

That was the million-dollar question, wasn't it? 'I'm not sure I'm what you need right now,' he admitted. 'However much I might wish I could be.'

She sat up properly then, crossing her ankles and curling her arms around her raised knees. 'What if I said I'm not looking for something permanent?'

Whatever he'd been expecting her to say, he was damn sure it wasn't that. 'What, like a friends with benefits arrangement?' Did those even exist in the real world?

She shook her head. 'Not quite that casual, but something in between that and a big commitment.' Reaching out, she placed a hand on his chest, as if she was staking a claim to him. 'I like you, Alex, and I think you're one of the most attractive men I've ever met – in lots of ways.'

So far so good... 'But?' he said, because there was clearly a but coming.

'But,' she echoed with a grin, 'the last thing I want to do is spoil our friendship, and I definitely don't want to stuff up our working relationship – sorry if that sounds a bit mercenary.'

He sat up, trying to ignore the rush of pins and needles in his numb arm. 'That's been playing on my mind as well. I think we can make a real success of the shop and getting involved with each other is bound to complicate things.'

'Exactly. Plus, I've not been with anyone in a long time, and I don't want to rush blindly into something heavy with the first guy that turns my head.'

'Gee, thanks,' Alex muttered, trying not to be offended.

She poked his leg with her foot. 'You know what I mean, there's no need to get all huffy. Maybe I'm reading the situation wrong, but it seems as if things are still a bit raw for you.' Their gazes met and Alex nodded. 'I guess what I'm trying to say is perhaps we can help each other out.'

'By having sex, you mean?' Because he was still not sure what to think about any of this and he wanted to be crystal clear they were talking about the same thing.

'Not just sex,' she said, hiding her face against her knees. 'God, I didn't know this would be so hard to talk about. I wish I'd never said anything.'

'I liked it earlier when we were cuddling,' he offered, regretting being quite so blunt.

'Yes, that was nice.' She raised her head, her cheeks two spots of pink on her pale skin. 'There's lots of ways to be intimate, and I think that's what I'm craving more than anything.' She bit her lip as she met his eyes for a moment. 'But sex would be nice sometimes, too.'

Though it was tempting to drag her down on top of him and throw caution to the wind, Alex worried it would be a bit of a disaster if they rushed straight in. 'I'm happy to take things slow.'

'How slow?'

He couldn't resist teasing her. 'Do you want to make a list of what's allowed?'

'I do like a list,' she said with a laugh as she uncurled the death grip around her legs and held up a finger. 'Item one, movie-night cuddles.'

'Agreed. Where do you stand on kissing?'

'I'm amenable to kissing,' she said in a voice much more serious than the twinkle in her eye.

'Duly noted. Anything else?'

She shrugged. 'I think that's fine for now. I'm not sure we need to go on proper dates or anything as we'll be spending so much time together anyway.'

He recalled what she'd said earlier about not having any special occasions to save her bath stuff for and shook his head. 'I reserve the right to take you out to celebrate when the shop opens at the very least.'

'Agreed.'

They looked at each other for a long moment, and again Alex felt an awkwardness he wasn't comfortable with. 'Let's see how we feel about all this in the cold light of day, okay?'

'Okay.' A flash of something crossed her face and he suspected it was the same mixture of relief and disappointment he was experiencing.

Although he was pleased they'd talked so openly, he also hoped they hadn't messed things up. She followed him to the doorway, where he paused to pick up his trainers. With his free hand he touched her cheek. 'You look all done in. Go to bed and I'll see myself out.'

'I need to lock the door behind you.'

She leaned into his palm and any awkwardness between them melted away. He dropped his trainers so he could cup her face properly. 'I'll do it and post the key through the letterbox. Stay up here in the warm.' Bending his head, he brushed a kiss across her lips. He'd meant to stop at that, but she followed him up as he began to move away, claiming a second kiss, then a third, before easing back. An errant curl had caught on her eyelash, and he brushed it away before pressing a final kiss to her temple. 'I'll see you in the morning. Sleep tight.'

'You too.'

She remained framed in her doorway as he gathered up his trainers and jogged down the stairs. He shoved his feet in them without bothering to undo the laces and removed the key from the lock. He was about to open the door, when he remembered he'd left his backpack in the kitchen, and did a quick about-face to retrieve it. Ivy was still waiting at the top of the stairs so he raised a hand for a final wave and she lifted hers to her lips and blew him a kiss before stepping back into her room out of view and closing her bedroom door. When he'd locked up and posted the key he rested his forehead briefly against the door, hoping they were doing the right thing.

11

When her alarm went off the next morning it took Ivy a few moments to pull herself from the depths of sleep. Rolling over to shut off the annoying chirping of her phone, she groaned at the pain in her shoulder and realised she'd slept in the same position all night. She couldn't remember the last time that had happened and wondered if it had anything to do with the pillow she'd been cuddling that still bore a faint trace of Alex's aftershave. A flurry of images invaded her brain from the evening before and she pushed them aside before they could overwhelm her and she started second-guessing her decisions. Her eyes strayed to the long-abandoned yoga mat rolled up next to her wardrobe. They had a busy day ahead with the flat-decorating party at Alex's and a few minutes' gentle exercise would help to warm her muscles for the exertions ahead as well as help her work through how she felt.

Her pyjamas were loose enough to be comfortable, so Ivy put them back on after she'd pulled on her sports bra and a pair of soft cotton pants. She opened her curtains enough to let in the early morning sunshine and a refreshing breeze from the window, then unfurled her mat on the patch of carpet between the end of her bed and the wall. Her warm-up stretches eased the stiffness in her shoulder and by the time she sank down onto the mat in a cross-legged position she felt ready to process the busy whirl of thoughts she'd been ignoring. Closing her eyes, she focused on her breathing and tried to remember what her instructor had told her many moons ago about letting whatever was in her mind just come. The rise and fall of Alex's chest beneath her ear; the way his laughter had rumbled through her; the faint brush of his fingers at the base of her spine; that kiss. Oh, she wanted to linger on that kiss, but she inhaled again and gave it a mental push as she slowly blew out her breath. A jumble of feelings followed: happiness, a hint of embarrassment at how forward she'd been, excitement at the thought of seeing Alex again in a couple of hours, worry that he might have changed his mind. What would she say when she saw him? How should they behave around everyone else? Would he want to keep it a secret? Did *she* want to keep it a secret?

No.

Whatever else she might be concerned about, the idea of her and Alex sneaking around as if they were doing something shameful didn't sit well with her at all. It was too reminiscent of her father's behaviour, and he was the last person she would ever model herself on when it came to relationships.

'Maybe you should just speak to Alex?' she said out loud as she opened her eyes and let herself come back to the present moment. With a laugh at her internalised drama, Ivy uncurled herself from the mat and went for a shower.

When she returned to her room it was to find a message on her phone from Alex.

Morning. Hope you slept well x

Her tummy doing a little flip at the sight of the kiss, she sat on the end of her bed and tapped out a reply.

Best sleep in ages. I had a lovely time last night and I'm looking forward to seeing you later x

Alex's reply came back almost immediately.

That's a relief and makes the half-hour I spent stressing over whether to message you worth it. See you soon.

He added three little kissing-face emojis, which she returned, delighted he'd been honest about his own sense of hesitation. Between that and her little yoga and meditation session she felt free to enjoy what promised to be a fun day surrounded by the people she cared about the most. What better way to spend a Sunday than that?

As she left the cottage it seemed as though the spring weather was determined to reflect her upbeat mood. The sky was blue as far as the eye could see, with only a few lazy drifts of fluffy cloud to mar its duck-egg perfection. Almost every house she passed had a window or two propped open to welcome in the fresh, if still slightly cool, air. One of her neighbours had put a pair of terracotta flowerpots on either side of the doorstep that were brimming with tulips in every sunshine hue from bright-yellow to the deep-red of an early evening sky. Just seeing them made Ivy smile and she paused to snap a quick photo on her phone so she could show Alex. They might need to seek permission from the council, but if they could do something similar outside the shop it would add to the welcoming feel they hoped to generate. They could change the floral display as the seasons turned, maybe complement them with thematic window displays. Mind buzzing with ideas, she opened her voice notes app and started recording them.

She'd just turned the corner into Farriers Way when her phone pinged with a message from Laurie to say they'd called in at her mum and dad's and were now all on their way. Unable to resist sharing her news, Ivy paused a few steps from the entrance to the bookshop and sent her a quick reply.

We kissed last night!

Laurie is typing...

AND??????????

Giggling, Ivy sent a GIF of a woman swooning. A few seconds later Laurie sent one back showing Phoebe and Rachel from *Friends* jumping up and down with excitement. Ivy was still laughing at that as she let herself in through the front door. She left it on the latch, knowing the Morgans were just a few minutes behind her, and paused to take in the space. Even with too many shelves the shop floor still looked a lot larger without all the books filling them. She wandered between the bookcases, trying to imagine what the room would look like if it were completely empty. It had a strange footprint that made it clear the space had been repurposed several times before ending up as it looked now.

What she'd already come to think of as her part of the shop had a lower ceiling and standing here it was clear to see that several older buildings had been knocked through at some point to create the shop as it was now.

The main area had an almost double-height ceiling to accommodate the tall shelves before the room extended down a longer arm on the right-hand side towards the corner where the children's books had always been located. Alex had shown her an AI copy of the floor plan, which had made the wonky L shape more pronounced than she'd realised. It also helped to make sense of the slightly odd layout of the upstairs flat, with its long, narrow kitchen and bathroom running along the rear of the building and the bedrooms at either end, with the sitting room roughly above the children's area on the ground floor.

The junk room – soon-to-be her workshop – was directly behind Ivy's section, and she made her way towards that back wall, wondering how solid it was. If it was a newer partition, it might not cost too much to open it up so she could add space for a small dressing room. It would also be easier to keep an eye on the shop on quiet days and still work on new projects. She gave the wall an experimental rap with her knuckles and winced at the contact with the hard plaster. It was a lot more substantial than the plasterboard partitions that the builders had erected when they'd converted part of the ground floor of the cottage to accommodate her mother's bedroom and wet-room area. She could at least ask the question and see what Alex thought. It was his money they were spending, after all. It was also a 'nice to have' rather than something she desperately needed so it could wait. Assuming they made a success of everything there would be plenty of time at a later date to think about phase two improvements like the one she had in mind. The most important thing was to get the flat and the shop up and running as quickly as possible. A knock sounded on the front door and she turned to see Laurie, Jake and Laurie's parents letting themselves in.

'Good morning, sunshine!' Andrew greeted her with his usual bear hug. 'How's tricks?'

'Good, thanks. I was just daydreaming about what the shop might look like in a few weeks,' Ivy replied as she moved from Andrew's arms to accept a kiss on the cheek from Sylvia, who, like everyone else, was wearing a variation of worn jeans and shirts or T-shirts that they didn't mind getting a few paint splatters on. Ivy had opted for an old pair of men's dungarees she'd shortened and patched several times as the denim wore through because they were the most comfortable thing she owned. They were already covered in paint, varnish and spots of glue from her own efforts, so nothing they had planned for today was going to be a problem.

Footsteps thundered down the wooden stairs and Laurie just had time to give Ivy a knowing wink before Alex bounded in, his own jeans ripped at the knee by age rather than a fashion choice. Trying not to pay too much attention to how well his black T-shirt fitted to his body, Ivy hung back until the others had said hello. When his smile widened just a touch as his eyes settled on her, it gave her enough courage to step into the space beside him and slip her arm around his waist. She gave him a quick squeeze, which broadened his smile even more as he bent down to brush the briefest of kisses on her lips. 'Everything all right?'

'Everything's great,' she said, doing her best to ignore the flurry of reactions around them. 'Do you have a plan for today?'

'Pick up a brush and get stuck in, basically,' he said as he walked her to the foot of the stairs and ushered the others up. 'Pop and Tom have already started in the main bedroom and the kids are doing the woodwork in the bathroom because they can squeeze around the pipework easily. Mum and Nerissa are in the kitchen, I think.'

'We'll sort ourselves out, son, don't you worry,' Andrew said with a smile as he placed his foot on the bottom step. 'You'll be in and settled before you know it.'

'I hope so. I don't want to outstay my welcome at Tom and Nerissa's.'

* * *

Ivy would've followed Andrew and the others but Alex grabbed her wrist and tugged her around the corner out of sight. Before she knew what was happening, he had her trapped between his warm body and the wall and she wasn't in any hurry to get away. 'Hello,' he said, brushing an errant curl from her forehead.

'Hello,' she replied, trying not to grin as her arms curled around his waist and her tummy did little flip-flops of anticipation. He didn't disappoint, bending his head to capture her lips in a soft, tender kiss that blurred seamlessly into something deeper and altogether more intense than anything they'd shared previously. Ivy's fingers bunched in the back of his T-shirt and for a moment she wanted to pull it free from the waistband of his jeans so she could touch his skin. Alex sank his hands into her hair, gripping her head just a touch roughly as he tried to pull her closer into him even though their mouths were already fused, their bodies touching from chest to hip, and more. His tongue teased hers, curling around and coaxing hers into his mouth before pressing forward as though he would fill her up. Her hands slid lower to cup his bottom as she rolled her hips in a frantic effort to ease the sudden tension building inside her. With something like a groan, Alex all but wrenched himself away and turned his back. Thankful the wall was behind her to hold her up, Ivy tried to unscramble her brain and remind herself their friends and family were just a few feet away. She could hear his heavy breathing, or perhaps it was her own gasps echoing in her ears, it was hard to tell.

'That,' Alex said, through what sounded like gritted teeth, 'was a big mistake.' Worry threatened to douse her passion until he turned to face her with a rueful grin and gestured towards the unmistakable bulge in his jeans.

'Oh. I see.' Hoo boy, did she see.

'That's not helping,' Alex said in a pained voice.

Ivy dragged her eyes from his groin to his face. 'Sorry.' She said it without a flicker of remorse, and he shook his head.

'You're going to be trouble, aren't you?'

'Only the best kind,' she promised him with a cheeky grin. Goodness, she'd forgotten quite how much fun flirting could be. 'I'd better get upstairs before we're missed. I'll tell the others you're locking up and you'll be up—' she couldn't resist a quick flick of her eyes back down to the source of his discomfort '—in a minute.'

'You might want to do something about your hair,' Alex called softly behind her as she started up the stairs. Her fingers flew to the curls he'd mussed and she combed them through as best she could before reaching the landing on the first floor, where an impromptu party seemed to have broken out with the Nelsons and the Morgans all shuffling around each other in the narrow space as they exchanged greetings.

'Ivy!'

She was just in time to open her arms and catch Max, Tom's son, as he threw himself at her for a hug. He'd already shot up a couple of inches since she'd last seen him and he was at the awkward stage of being all limbs and not quite in control of his rapidly changing teenage body.

'Hello!' she said, giving him a squeeze before stepping back to consider him. 'Goodness, if you keep on sprouting you'll be taller than me in no time!'

Max grinned. 'I'm almost as tall as Mimi already,' he said, referring to his step-grandmother, Philippa, by her preferred nickname.

'All the best things come in little packages,' Philippa said, giving his hair a ruffle as she smiled at Ivy. 'Hello, my dear, would you like a cup of tea before you get started?'

'That would be lovely. Can I give you a hand?'

Philippa shook her head. 'I'm not sure there's room for another in the kitchen at the moment.' She reached behind Ivy to poke her husband, Archie, in the arm. 'Back to work, you.'

Archie laughed, a big sound that came deep from his belly and made Ivy think he'd do a cracking job as Father Christmas. 'That's me told. Come on, son.' He clapped Tom on the shoulder. 'Looks like tea is for the newcomers and us workers will have to do without.'

Philippa rolled her eyes and gave Ivy an exasperated look. 'They started all of ten minutes before you got here.' She turned her attention back to her husband. 'Finish one wall and you can have something from the box of treats Laurie brought with her.'

'You know how to incentivise a man,' Archie said with a waggle of his eyebrows that made his words seem a lot less innocent.

'Away with you!' Laughing, Philippa shooed him off before placing a hand on Ivy's shoulder and steering her through the others towards the kitchen where the other women had gathered. Someone had brought a radio with them and placed it on the kitchen windowsill. It was tuned to the local radio station, which played a decent mix of hits from the sixties right through to the latest chart-toppers. Michael Bublé was singing away merrily about the perfect woman he hadn't met yet, his warm tone adding to the friendly atmosphere.

* * *

With all the commotion, Alex didn't appear to have been missed. Certainly nobody said anything other than to offer him a cup of tea when he entered the kitchen a few minutes later. He accepted a mug from his mother, sending Ivy a ghost of a wink before he fell into conversation with Andrew about the best way to divide everyone up. They decided it would be too awkward to try and tackle the narrow landing with so many people around, so Ivy was dispatched to the second bedroom with Sylvia and Andrew while Alex, Jake and Laurie headed for the sitting room to make a start in there.

Andrew rubbed a hand over one wall with a thoughtful expression on his face. Ivy guessed the colour had once been magnolia, but it had yellowed somewhat with age. 'It seems sound enough to paint on without any undercoat, but let's see what colour Alex has chosen before we make a decision.' He pried the lid off the larger can waiting on the dust sheet already spread out to cover the floor and they moved closer to survey the shade. It was cream with just a hint of apricot to give it a touch of warmth.

'Oh, I like that,' Sylvia said. 'It'd look lovely in the dining room at home.'

Andrew rolled his eyes. 'How did I know this was going to end up with more work for me?'

She patted his arm, not an ounce of remorse in her expression. 'We want to make the best impression on the fostering team, don't we, now?'

'I'm sure they won't care if we paint our dining room walls in a colour almost identical to what they already are,' Andrew muttered, but Ivy noted with a smile that he took a quick photo of the lid of the can nonetheless.

'I didn't know you two were thinking about fostering,' she said to Sylvia as they watched Andrew pour a generous amount of paint into the roller tray.

'We talked about it at Christmas. With Laurie gone and Nick all but out the door with his new project, we had a terrible case of empty nest-itus.'

'Well, I think it's a lovely idea and any child would be blessed to come and live with you.' Ivy meant every word even as her heart sank a little. She hadn't mentioned it to them, but staying with Andrew and Sylvia had been on her list of possible options in the event the cottage sold before she had time to find somewhere else to live. Since the initial flurry of viewings it had all gone quiet, but she knew better than to hope things would stay that way. Determined not to feel sorry for herself, she turned the conversation. 'How's Nick getting on with his planning application?'

'Bloody council finally bothered to respond, but only to send a load of questions back, most of which he'd already answered in the original submission.' Shaking his head, Andrew slapped the lid back onto the paint pot with slightly more force than was probably necessary, an unusual show of irritation. 'That's why he's not here today. We left him at the kitchen table going over what he needs to address with the architect next week. The damn place is crying out for affordable homes for you young people, you'd think they'd be biting his hand off. And it's not like the harbour is ever going to return to what it once was, so why not repurpose the warehouses?'

'Shh. Don't get yourself all worked up about it again,' Sylvia said as she rubbed a comforting hand along his upper arm. 'I have a really good feeling about Nick's project, and once people see the potential, hopefully a few others will come forward with ideas.' She glanced over at Ivy with a smile. 'I mean, look at what Ivy and Alex have planned for this place for a start. I have faith that their generation will be able to drag the Point into the modern ages while still being respectful of our traditions.'

'You're right, as always, my heart.' Andrew bent to kiss his wife. 'The future of the Point is in good hands and I'll be having a stern word with anyone who tries to stand in their way.'

A glow of warmth spread through Ivy. With Sylvia and Andrew behind them, how could they possibly fail?

'Right, let's get to it, then,' Andrew said, clapping his hands together. 'Ivy, do you mind rubbing down the skirting boards while I tackle the walls?'

'Sounds like a plan.' Ivy reached for one of the sandpaper

blocks stacked together with the other decorating tools they'd need throughout the day.

'What about me?' Sylvia asked. 'Shall I do the same with the door?'

'Good idea, my love,' Andrew agreed. 'Once you've done that and Ivy's made some progress on the skirting you could go behind her with a brush and do the edges, if you like.'

With everyone assigned their tasks, they set to it, silence settling over the scrape of the sandpaper and the softer squish of the extendable roller Andrew was using to cover the main section of the back wall. They worked away for a while until Andrew set his roller down in the tray and fiddled with his phone. The local radio station blared out from the handset, playing an eighties' classic by Queen and David Bowie. 'That's more like it.' Andrew set his phone on top of a stepladder that had been erected in the corner and began humming along to the music.

They'd been working steadily for about an hour when a shout came from one of the other rooms. 'What's that all about?' Andrew asked, setting down his roller.

Ivy managed to get to the door and squeeze in between him and Sylvia just in time to see a streak of black fly along the landing followed by a red-faced, furious Alex. 'If I catch you in here again, you little shit, it'll be violin-strings time!' he yelled.

'What on earth is going on?' Sylvia exclaimed, although Ivy had a sneaking suspicion, which was confirmed by Alex's frustrated gesture at the carpet. A trail of pale-blue-painted paw prints led from the sitting room where he'd been working.

'That bloody cat decided to stroll right through the roller tray I'd left on the floor.' Alex shook his head in disgust. 'Just as well I'm getting the carpets replaced next week.' He cast a glare down the landing. 'Look at him, just sitting there like he owns the damn place!'

Ivy edged her way into the corridor to where Lucifer was sitting by the top of the stairs, trying to wash his paws. 'Oh no, don't do that!' she cried out, running to scoop the cat up. 'You'll make yourself poorly.'

'With any luck he'll poison himself and do us all a favour,' Alex muttered, even as he pulled a cloth out of his pocket and tried to wipe the remaining paint spatters from one of Lucifer's paws. 'Stop trying to bite me. I'm only trying to help you!' he snapped at the cat when Lucifer made a lunge for his hand that almost spilled him out of Ivy's arms.

'Here, let me.' Sylvia bustled over and took the cloth from Alex. 'Come on, bring him into the kitchen so I can wet this cloth properly. It's only a bit of emulsion so should wash off easily enough.' They carried Lucifer into the kitchen between them where he sat on the draining board with Ivy barely having to hold him while he held up each paw in turn for Sylvia to clean off. '*Such* a good boy, aren't you?' the older woman crooned, earning a snort of disgust from Alex.

'He's the devil incarnate,' Alex groused. 'I'm nailing up that cat flap, later, just watch me.' Turning on his heel, he marched out of the kitchen.

Ivy and Sylvia exchanged a look, trying not to laugh. 'Poor Alex, he's really not a cat person, is he?' Ivy said, stifling a giggle as she lifted Lucifer off the board. 'Come on, mister. Let's get you back outside before you cause any more dramas.'

* * *

By the time they stopped for lunch, Ivy's neck and shoulders were sore from hunching over the skirting boards and she was glad to get up and stretch. The cat had thankfully got the message after she'd put him out of the front door earlier and locked it behind him, and hadn't made a reappearance. Ivy did feel some sympathy for Lucifer. The bookshop had been his territory for a long time, and it wasn't his fault he'd been turfed out.

Philippa and Nerissa had been busy in the kitchen and a small mountain of sandwiches had been stacked on a plate on the sideboard together with a selection of fresh fruit, bowls of crisps and a selection of home-baked treats from Laurie's café. As Ivy waited for her turn in the little procession past the food, Alex slipped in beside her and slung a casual arm around her waist. 'How're you guys getting on?' he asked her with a grin.

'If I never see another skirting board, it'll be too soon,' she groaned.

'Laurie said much the same thing, earlier,' he said, giving the small of her back a sympathetic rub. 'Why don't you change out for something else this afternoon?'

Ivy shook her head. 'I'm okay, really, and I think we're all in the same boat when it comes to bending and stretching, whatever job we do. I've rubbed them down and I'm halfway through the undercoat so I'm making good progress. Besides, even with the extendable roller I'd hardly be able to reach the top of the walls,' she said with a rueful grin.

Alex dropped a kiss on the top of her head. 'You are a bit of a short-arse, it has to be said.'

'Hey!' She balled her fist and pretended to punch him in the ribs. 'Be nice or there'll be no more kisses for you.' She said the last in a low voice meant only for him.

He ducked his head. 'But you like my kisses.' The murmured words against her ear were like a hot caress and they shivered through her as she recalled the feel of him pressed against her from shoulder to knee earlier.

God, he was so sure of himself and the effect he had on her, it would be maddening if what he'd said hadn't been completely true.

Still, there was no way she was letting him get away with it. 'They were okay,' she said in her best attempt at sounding bored. The space in front of them cleared at exactly the same moment so she stepped out from his hold and made a beeline for the food, keeping her back to him so he wouldn't see her grin. He was beside her in a flash and she handed him a paper plate before he could get any ideas. He shot her a look that made it plain the conversation wasn't over, but when she'd filled her plate and crossed the room to wriggle into a small space next to Laurie he didn't try and follow her.

With everyone in the kitchen there was hardly room to move, but they managed well enough with a bit of shuffling around and the odd smiling apology for a bumped elbow here and there. The radio was still playing in the background, the music half drowned out by the hum of conversation as they discussed the progress made so far.

'Now this isn't a request hour,' the DJ on the radio said, catching Ivy's attention just as Andrew shushed them all. 'But I'm going to make an exception for this one. It's come in from Andrew and Sylvia Morgan, who will be very familiar to the residents and visitors of Mermaids Point as they run a delightful gift shop on the seafront there. Andrew's texted in because he wants to let everyone know about a brand-new business that's opening in the Point very soon. Mermaid Tales and Treasures is going to be replacing the old Cavendish's Bookshop, and will be selling bespoke gifts, clothing and furniture as well as continuing as a bookshop.'

'What did you do?' Alex asked Andrew, his cheeks showing hints of a faint blush, the smile on his lips one of surprise and delight.

'Shh, listen,' Andrew replied, waving him into silence as the DJ continued his spiel.

'Well, I don't know about you all, but I'll be popping over to check it out as soon as it opens. Andrew wants to send his congratulations to Alex Nelson and Ivy Fisher, who are the proud new owners of the shop.'

Ivy cast a horrified glance towards Alex, but he didn't seem bothered about the DJ's misunderstanding of their situation in the slightest and was still grinning his head off about Andrew's surprise.

'And he's dedicating the next song to you. Alex, Ivy, I hope you guys are listening and you get in touch as I'd love to hear more about your new venture, and I'm sure my listeners will too. And what better way to celebrate than with this classic number from Kool & the Gang.' The familiar introduction filled the kitchen as everyone broke into a round of applause and cheers.

Crossing to Andrew, Ivy gave him a hug. 'That's so lovely of you, thank you.'

Andrew held her away from him so he could look down at her, beaming for all he was worth. 'We couldn't be more proud of you...' He broke off to shake hands with Alex, who'd come over to join them. 'Of the both of you. The Point needs investment and innovation to survive and if it comes from within the community, then that's even more reason to celebrate.'

'Thanks, Andrew.' Alex shook his hand again before turning to give Ivy a hug. 'Looks like I'm part of the community, now, too.' Ivy hung onto him for a few seconds, hoping that was indeed the case and that they both had a long-term future to look forward to in the Point.

12

The next couple of weeks passed by in a blur of aching muscles, dozens of petty frustrations, and an ever-decreasing bank balance. Decorating the flat had been a lot of fun, but the shop was a different matter. Alex might find the wonky gloss on the skirting boards in the bathroom charming because it made him think of Max giggling afterwards as Tom did his best to remove white splodges of paint from his son, including a big patch in his hair. His customers might not take as kindly to amateur efforts, so Alex had stuck with his plan to use a professional decorating firm to make the finishing touches. He watched them now as they rolled up their dust sheets and stowed their ladders away, chatting over whether they had time to nip for a quick pint on the way home, and felt a quiet sense of satisfaction spreading inside him.

'You look like the cat that's got the cream,' Ivy said as she came to stand beside him as he waved the decorators off. Her curls were bound back from her face with a bright-pink scarf decorated with cartoon sheep and she was wearing the same baggy dungarees she'd been all but living in lately. There was a smudge of dirt on her cheek and the shadows under her eyes were dark as bruises.

She looked pale and tired, and he wanted nothing more than to bundle her upstairs and tuck her in his newly delivered bed so she could sleep for the next twelve hours. If he said anything about her taking it easy she'd roll her eyes and tell him off. Shouldering so much responsibility at an early age had left her with an independent streak a mile wide. Jo had always enjoyed being coddled, which had fed into his natural protective instincts, causing an imbalance in their relationship he would hate to replicate with Ivy. There was a difference between *caring* for someone and taking care of them, and Alex was still learning to walk that line. Slinging an arm around her shoulders, he tugged her against him. 'Don't mention that bloody cat,' he growled, making her laugh.

Lucifer had still not got the message and kept popping in through the cat flap whenever he felt like it. It didn't help that Ivy cuddled him like a baby and Alex was sure he'd seen her sneak the beast a treat from her pocket when she thought he wasn't watching. Given how taken she seemed with the cat and its persistence in thinking the bookshop was still its home, Alex had attempted to make friends, but the damn thing hated his guts. But that was a problem for another day, for now he was going to concentrate on the positive. 'Whisper it, but I think everything is starting to come together,' he said to Ivy, leading her back onto the shop floor.

His eyes surveyed the room as he tried to see beyond the echoing space to how it would look once it was finished. At Ivy's suggestion, they'd had the walls painted brilliant white. He'd personally been in favour of adding a bit of colour, but she'd insisted the room should be as neutral as possible, a blank canvas to be filled with the colour of the book covers, brightly patterned clothes and the colourful knick-knacks they intended to sell. The only exception was the revamped children's area, which was painted the same pale-blue as the spring sky and covered in white fluffy clouds, which Ivy planned to fill with quotes from classic stories. The carpenters had finished the shelving and would be in tomorrow to start fitting it. Once that was done, they could start filling the shelves. They had two more weeks until the tentative deadline they'd set themselves for reopening. Barring any last-minute disasters, he was feeling more and more confident they were going to be ready in time to make the most of the late May bank holiday weekend. 'You were right about the colour.'

'It does look good, doesn't it?' She rested her head against his chest, and he allowed himself a moment to soak in the feel of her cuddled up against him. Spending so much time in each other's company had put him on a fast-track to falling for her. She was like the spring flowers popping up all over the village – bright and pretty and full of the promise of wonderful days to come. He hated leaving her and going home alone. They were still taking the physical side of things slow, and he didn't mind that, he just liked *being* with her. By the time they finished for the day, he was bone-tired and more than happy to walk Ivy home and share a quiet dinner and snuggle for a couple of hours in front of the TV before one or other of them started yawning their heads off. As much as he'd longed to follow her upstairs to bed and curl around her until the morning, he ended up trudging back to Tom and Nerissa's because he was waiting for Ivy to make the next move.

At least he wouldn't have to keep avoiding his brother's searching looks when he walked in the door for much longer. Tonight would be his last night at the surgery because the furniture he'd placed in storage was being delivered tomorrow and then he could officially move into the flat upstairs. Though he hadn't said anything, it didn't take a mind reader to know Tom had deep reservations about Alex and Ivy's relationship. It was a bit rich given his own situation with Nerissa, but that was annoying older brothers for you. Speaking of which, he checked his watch and sighed. 'I promised Tom I'd have dinner at the surgery with them tonight as it's my last night, so I'll have to get going in a few minutes.'

Ivy smiled up at him. 'He's going to miss having you around, the kids too, I bet.'

'I'm not so sure about that. With Linda back from her cruise it's a bit much when we all sit down together. Not that she isn't pulling her weight,' he added hastily when he saw Ivy's smile fade. 'I think she's so grateful for somewhere to stay while she sorts herself out, she's cooked most of the meals even though Nerissa's told her there's no need.'

'It must be hard for her not having a place of her own.' Ivy's voice was bleak and Alex wanted to take himself out in the back yard and give his arse a good kicking at his clumsy words.

'Anything new from the estate agent?' Ivy had mentioned a viewing over the weekend, but she hadn't said anything and he hadn't liked to ask. There was no point in avoiding the subject now though, since they were both clearly thinking about it.

'Alun sent me a text on Sunday after they'd been to say he thought they were very keen, but not a word since.'

Hating to see her so down, Alex opened his arms and let her settle against his chest with a sigh. 'Whatever happens, we'll sort it out. You don't have to deal with this on your own.'

'I just wish I didn't have to deal with it at all,' she muttered. 'Oh, goodness, I need to stop feeling sorry for myself.' Though he wanted to hold her to him, he forced himself to let go when she pulled away and lifted her head to meet his gaze with a determined look in her eye. 'It is what it is, right?'

'Worst-case scenario, there's a spare room upstairs,' he said with a wink. He'd hoped to make her laugh, but her slightly appalled expression told him he'd well and truly missed the mark. 'I promise I'd clean up after myself and I always put the toilet seat down afterwards.'

'I couldn't possibly move in with you!'

Ouch. Well, didn't that make him feel special? 'I wasn't suggesting we *live* together,' he snapped, feeling the rejection strike like a punch in the gut. 'I was just pointing out that if you can't find somewhere else, then you'd always have a roof over your head.'

He half turned, but she stopped him with a gentle hand on his arm. 'I'm sorry. I didn't mean to hurt your feelings.'

Alex forced himself to shrug. 'It's fine, really. After all, we're just fooling around and having a bit of fun together.' He knew he sounded like a petulant teenager, but he couldn't help it. She'd got well and truly under his skin and for all they'd promised to take it one day at a time, he wasn't sure he'd ever be able to get her out of his system. Perhaps this was a warning sign and he should take heed? Especially as it seemed as if he was the one with all the complicated feelings.

'Wow. Okay, then.'

When she spun away it was his turn to reach out and stop her. 'Wait, I'm sorry, I don't know what's got into me.' He let go of her arm and scrubbed his hand over the back of his neck. 'That's not strictly true. I know things are supposed to be casual between us, but I'm, ah, I'm having a hard time with that.'

Stepping into the space he'd left between them, Ivy raised her hand and placed it over his thumping heart. 'There's a difference between taking things carefully and being casual. I don't want you to think that I'm taking you for granted *or* taking advantage. That's not my intention at all.'

He covered her hand with his and pressed it against his chest. 'I don't feel taken for granted, I promise. And I want to be clear that my offer of you staying here wasn't meant to put you under any kind of pressure – the opposite, in fact.'

She glanced down and then back at him. 'Does this class as our first fight?'

He laughed, thinking about the time Jo had thought he'd been flirting with the receptionist at work and dumped a plate of spaghetti bolognese in his lap. 'And our last one, I hope.'

'I'm not sure that will be possible, unless we call it a day.'

He wondered if she could feel the way his heart stuttered at those words. 'Is that what you want?' She shook her head. He should take the win and drop the whole thing, but he wanted to clear the air between them so there was no more room for misunderstandings. 'But—'

'I don't want to hurt you.' She flexed her fingers against his chest as though she were placing a protective cage around his heart. 'And,' she continued in a much quieter tone, 'I don't want to get hurt either.'

He placed a finger beneath her chin and tipped her head so he could meet her gaze. 'Do you think that's what's going to happen?'

She sighed. 'I don't know. I thought I could do this and not get too caught up in my emotions. I wanted you to stay last night. I've wanted you to stay every night since you first kissed me.' Her cheeks turned a delightful shade of pink as she admitted her desires to him.

'I've wanted to stay every night, too, but I didn't want to rush you into anything you weren't ready for.'

She closed her eyes for a second. 'It's been so long, Alex. Almost too long and the more I think about it, the more I worry it's going to all go horribly wrong and then I'll have messed it all up and I'll never be able to look you in the eye again, never mind work side by side with you every day.'

She sounded so earnest, as though she truly believed that him getting the chance to make love with her was going to be anything other than one of the best moments of his life. He thought about the way she melted into him every time they kissed and couldn't help but laugh. 'I don't think we've got anything to worry about when it comes to chemistry, do you?'

Ivy stared at him for a long moment, then grabbed his hand. 'You're right.'

* * *

Before Alex knew what was happening they were heading up the stairs towards his flat. 'What are you doing?'

'I'm putting a stop to this nonsense right now,' she replied, keeping a steady pace as she pulled him along behind her.

'Oh.' It was all he could not to step on her heels in his haste as they cleared the last few steps. When they reached the open doorway to his room and the stark emptiness of his new bed struck him, his brain took over from his libido. He didn't have so much as a sheet to cover the bare mattress, his linens boxed up with the other belongings that were being delivered the next day. 'Maybe this isn't such a good idea.'

Ivy looked from him to the bed and back again. 'It's not exactly The Ritz, but it'll do.'

'You deserve something better than this.' He'd had a whole plan in his head for several weeks down the line. In his mind's eye, the shop would be up and running and he'd be properly settled into his flat by the time she gave him the signal she was ready to take things further. He'd cook her a nice dinner, open a decent bottle of wine and treat her to lots and lots of foreplay on the sofa before he so much as suggested they retire to his room for the night.

Releasing his hand, Ivy sat on the edge of the bed and gave a few experimental bounces. 'It's nice and firm.'

'Stop it.' He was the one with the flushing cheeks now.

Ignoring him, Ivy lay on her back and scooted to the middle of the mattress. Spreading her hands on either side, she stroked the white satiny finish. 'Soft.'

'Ivy...'

He could only stare in frustrated amusement as she raised one hand from the mattress and placed it on the skin of her throat just above the hollow of her collarbone. 'Very soft.'

With a groan of defeat, he kicked off his trainers and clambered onto the bed. Crouching over her, he kept his arms locked and braced his knees on either side of her hips so their bodies weren't touching. 'There's no rush.'

Reaching up, she cupped the back of his neck and tried to draw him down. When he resisted, her wicked smile faltered. 'If you say no to me now, I might not find the courage to be this brave again.'

Alex lowered himself to his elbows, letting his chest rest against hers but keeping enough of his weight held back that she'd be able to push him off or wriggle away if she changed her mind. 'Promise me you don't feel forced into doing this,' he pleaded with her.

She cupped his face. 'I want this.'

Easing a little lower, he pressed his mouth to hers in a soft, slow kiss. When her tongue nudged against his lips he opened them on a sigh and let the kiss deepen. Her arms curled around his shoulders, pulling him closer, and he gave her a little more of his weight as he let the moment carry him along. Whatever his plans might have been, they were nothing compared to the sweet reality of having her beneath him, and when her legs rose to cage his hips he surrendered to her will and let the need building between them act as their guide. Her fingers tugged at the back of his shirt and he broke their kiss long enough to reach down and yank it over his head and toss it aside. Her hands shifted to the front of his body to shape the muscle there and play with the scattering of dark hair on his chest. 'I like this,' she said, looking up at him through her lashes.

'That's good because I wasn't planning on waxing it,' he replied, making her giggle. Pulling her hands away before they could explore too far and make him lose his mind, he pinned them loosely above her head. He studied her face for a long moment, seeing only a reflection of the desire he felt inside him. 'You're so beautiful.'

'Kiss me.'

Letting go of her hands, he slid his arms beneath her and pulled her up from the bed to meet him as he lowered his mouth to hers once more. The kiss went on and on, driving the need in him to touch her but wherever his hands roamed they encountered only denim. 'I hate these bloody dungarees,' he muttered against her lips as he fumbled at the clips near her chest. 'How the hell do they open?'

Laughing, she pushed him away so she could unfasten the clips and Alex rolled to the side onto his back. His wallet in his back pocket was an uncomfortable lump beneath him and he reached around to pull it free. He tossed it over the edge of the bed, realising a moment too late that they would need the condom tucked away beneath the inside flap. When he said as much, Ivy clambered off the bed and retrieved it, tossing it back to him before shedding her dungarees with a shimmy of her hips. His fingers froze on the leather in his hand, his breath catching in his lungs as she reached for the bottom of her T-shirt and slowly pulled it over her head. The inch-by-inch reveal of her creamy skin sent Alex's brain into freefall and all he could do was lie there and watch her and wonder what the hell he'd ever done to be this lucky. From the moment he'd seen her in his brother's kitchen in those fire-engine-red wellington boots he'd been smitten, even if he hadn't been prepared to admit it at the time.

'What are you smiling about?' she asked in a shy voice.

'You in your red wellies.'

Placing a hand on one hip, she cocked her head and gave him a quizzical look. 'Is this some kind of kink for you – red wellies? Because I've got to say I'm not sure I'm into that.'

Alex laughed and just like that any awkwardness about the timing, or the less than perfect location of his all-but-empty flat, didn't matter one bit. Taking the step from friends to lovers was a big risk, but it was one he was more than ready for now. He held out a hand to her. 'Come here and let me show you how beautiful you are.'

13

Though he hated leaving her so soon afterwards, Alex couldn't let the family down and skip his last dinner at the surgery. Ivy had made it clear to him she didn't want him to either, so they parted ways on the doorstep of the shop with a promise Alex would come and see her as soon as he could get away. He watched as she walked away, wondering if she would have any regrets about their unconventional first time together. Though it had been everything he'd imagined, and more, he was still a little uneasy about the less than romantic setting. When she reached the top of Farriers Way, she turned to wave, giving him such a gorgeous smile it was all he could do not to run after her and drag her off to her much more comfortable room and indulge his passion for her. His phone beeped with a message from Tom asking him how much longer he was going to be, and by the time Alex glanced back up, Ivy had vanished from sight. With a regretful sigh and a reminder it would only be a few hours at most before he could be with her again, Alex tapped a quick on-my-way reply and stuffed his phone back in his pocket.

He'd barely taken two steps before he stopped in his tracks at the sight of the bane of his existence curled up on the shop windowsill. One of the many things still on his to-do list was to get the cat flap on the back door closed up. 'Don't even think about it,' he said, pointing a warning finger at the big black cat. Lucifer drew back his lips and hissed at Alex before turning his attention to what could only be described as an intimate ablution. Alex considered whether he should go back inside and shove a box up against the cat flap to block it, but he was already late for dinner and, given what he and Ivy had just got up to, he definitely needed a shower before he sat down with everybody.

Five minutes later he let himself in the kitchen door at the surgery and gave Nerissa an apologetic look when she paused in the process of lifting a roast chicken from the oven to greet him. 'Sorry, I'm late. Give me a few minutes to sort myself out and I'll give you a hand.'

She smiled. 'Don't worry about it. Linda is the perfect sous chef,' she said, casting a fond look towards her friend, who was mashing potatoes in a large pot with terrifying efficiency. 'Besides, your brother is dealing with an urgent call so we might have to hold off for a few minutes anyway.' There was no such thing as off-duty in a little village like the Point. Even with access to the NHS 111 service, most people still called the surgery number if they had a medical problem, regardless of the hour, and Tom always answered.

'Well, at least let me set the table,' Alex offered as he crossed the room and headed towards the stairs.

'I've already done that,' Max said, coming the other way. 'We're eating in the dining room tonight because it's a special occasion.'

Despite Nerissa's protestations, Alex still felt guilty about keeping them all waiting when it was obvious they'd gone to so much trouble, Alex ruffled Max's hair and promised him a quick go on his PlayStation after dinner.

* * *

The meal was wonderful, and as much as Alex was looking forward to moving into his own place, he was going to miss the fun and laughter around the table as much as the brilliant home-cooked food. Not that he couldn't cook, or that he didn't take his turn in the kitchen and with other chores, it was just never the same when cooking for one. His thoughts drifted to Ivy and he allowed himself a little smile. With any luck, he'd be cooking for two more often than not, because he planned on tempting her to stay with him at every possible opportunity.

'Look out, Uncle Alex! There's a dragon behind you.' Max's warning dragged his attention back to the game blasting on the TV in time for Alex to watch his virtual avatar get chomped in half.

'And that's my cue, bud,' Alex said, tossing his control onto the coffee table before reaching for the remote and muting the deafening blare of the game.

'Aww, a few more minutes,' Max pleaded.

'It's almost bedtime,' Nerissa said as she walked into the lounge. 'Did you finish all your homework?'

Max started to nod before turning it into a shake. 'But it's only some reading before Chemistry tomorrow, I can do it on the bus.'

Nerissa paused and looked at him. She didn't say anything, didn't need to because Alex was ready to shrink back against the cushions and he wasn't the one on the receiving end of her look. It wasn't a glare, because Nerissa wasn't one for losing her temper, especially when it came to the kids. Her weapon of choice was quiet disappointment and she wielded it with the rapier-like accuracy of a master dueller.

'I'll do it now as soon as I've tidied up.' A shame-faced Max scrabbled around as he unplugged his game and packed it away in the cupboard as quickly as possible.

Nerissa waited until he'd finished before putting an arm around the boy's shoulders and pressing a kiss to his temple. 'Go on up and I'll bring you a hot chocolate in a few minutes, okay?'

Max's mood lifted in an instant, like the sun popping out from behind a dark cloud. 'Thanks, Nerissa. Night, Uncle Alex!'

'Night-night.'

* * *

Linda had retired to her little apartment upstairs for the evening and Nerissa was making sure Max had done his reading by the time Alex was ready to head out. He'd just tugged on his jacket when the back door opened and a weary-looking Tom trudged in, medical bag in hand. 'Everything all right?' Alex asked, taking the bag from his brother and setting it on the table so Tom could take off his own coat.

'Yeah, fine. Keith's got a nasty chest infection, and of course, he left it too long before seeking help. Bloody fool was out on his boat this morning even though he can barely draw breath. I didn't want to leave it until tomorrow so I ended up driving into town to the late-night pharmacy in the supermarket and filling his prescription for him.' Tom paused to take a look at him. 'You off out somewhere?' he asked with a frown.

Though he had no reason to feel awkward, Alex found himself shuffling his feet as he muttered, 'I'm going over to Ivy's.'

Tom raised his eyebrows. 'Spending an awful lot of time together, lately, aren't you?'

'I like her,' Alex retorted, unable to keep from sounding defensive. 'Besides, we're both free agents so I don't see that it's anyone else's business what we do.'

'Didn't say it was.' Tom's gaze was level. 'I just hope you're not throwing yourself headlong into things like you usually do.'

'What's that supposed to mean?' Alex snapped, folding his arms across his chest.

'Marrying Jo.' Tom raised his hand and tapped his index finger as if he was about to reel off a list.

'We were together for ages,' Alex protested.

'But you had more than a few doubts and still went ahead with it,' Tom reminded him.

'So I made a mistake. I'm not a dumb kid any more.'

'What about your new career as a writer? I thought that was supposed to be the next big thing and then suddenly you've dropped that and now you're going to be a shopkeeper.'

Alex felt his face flush. 'I haven't dropped it. I'm still writing.' Not what he was supposed to be working on, but his spy story was starting to come together in the few minutes he could grab here and there. 'Once the shop opens I'll have more time to focus on it.'

Tom snorted. 'If you say so.' Turning his back on Alex, he walked over to the sink, rolling up his sleeves as he did. He soaped his hands thoroughly before casting a look back over his shoulder. 'Have you told Ivy about your writing?'

'Not exactly,' Alex admitted, feeling like a sulky teenager. 'She knows I'm writing but not about that stupid 'Heartbreak Kid' stuff.'

Drying his hands, Tom set his back to the kitchen counter and gave Alex a searching look. 'Why not? If things are going as well as they appear to be with her, why haven't you told her?'

Alex shoved his hands in his pockets with a sigh. 'Because I'm not particularly proud of that book, or who I was when I wrote it, okay? I don't want her to know *that Alex* because he was a bit of a dickhead. I'm not that person any more.'

'He's still a part of you, though,' Tom said, his voice gentle. 'How can you build a relationship with her if you only let her see the good parts of you? Don't you owe it to her to be honest?'

'She knows about Jo, if that's what you mean.'

'But she doesn't know you used your relationship with her as a basis for your book. Or that you've got more books to come in the same vein. You can't write about Ivy without her permission, for god's sake.'

'I'm not! I wouldn't!' Alex scrubbed a frustrated hand across his bearded chin. 'I'm not doing any more "Heartbreak Kid" books, I'm working on something completely different.'

There was no mistaking the look of shock on Tom's face. 'Since when? Why didn't you tell me?'

Alex shrugged. 'I'm still working it out, okay.'

Tom moved to the kitchen table and pulled out a chair. He pointed to it before pulling out the one at right angles to it and sitting down. 'Talk to me. I feel like we haven't talked for ages and I have no idea what is going on with you.'

Reluctantly, Alex slid into the empty chair. 'You had enough on your plate.'

Tom's expression was one of hurt this time. 'I'm never, ever too busy to talk to you, Ally. Don't ever think that, please.'

Feeling like an absolute heel for making Tom upset, Alex reached out and placed his hand over his brother's. 'It's not your fault, it's mine. I haven't felt like talking because I'm still trying to sort things out in my own head. I got really stuck trying to write the next book and I didn't want to admit it, so I lied to everyone, including myself, that it'd be all right.' He sighed. 'That all blew up before Christmas when I had lunch with my editor. I finally came clean about what a hole I was in. She was so understanding, and with the pressure off a bit, I managed to get on track with my writing again.'

'That's great news,' Tom said. 'Not the getting stuck bit, but I'm glad you're working again.' When Alex remained silent, Tom raised his brows once more. 'Why am I sensing a "but" here?'

'Because the book I've been writing isn't the one I'm contracted to deliver,' Alex confessed with a groan. 'It's a spy novel, hopefully the first in a series if I can manage it. It started out as a writing exercise, something to help me get some words on the page, and it worked. A bit too well as it turned out because the character just leapt into my head fully formed and I can't stop thinking about him.' It wasn't only that, though, and Alex decided it was time to come clean about the *real* problem. 'I just couldn't do it, go back to being "The Heartbreak Kid", you know? I made a load of notes after my meeting with Immy and thought I was back on track. She was so brilliant about missing my deadline that I couldn't face letting her down again, so I let myself believe I'd found a way around all the doubts. I grabbed onto the idea of writing a fictional account of someone trying to get back onto the dating scene like a drowning man grabbing for a lifebuoy. I spent the rest of that afternoon making all these notes and researching ideas.' He sighed, seeing now he'd been masking the real problem. 'But then I came here for Christmas, and I spent some time with Ivy...'

'And you wanted the real thing, not a fictional version?'

Alex nodded. 'It didn't help that I lost my bloody notebook, either. Without those notes, my head felt like this empty void again and I was back to square one.'

'But you're excited about writing this spy novel?' Tom asked, then immediately shook his head. 'No, tell me another time. Let's focus on the important stuff for a minute. What's the situation with your editor?' When Alex pulled a face, Tom threw his hands up in frustration. 'Bloody hell, Ally!'

'I know! I know!' Alex hung his head for a moment. 'I kept meaning to talk to her, but I couldn't find the words, especially when she'd already been so understanding. It felt like I'd be taking the piss, you know? Besides, I've been so caught up with getting the shop I haven't been able to find the time to call her.'

Tom gave him a long look before bursting out laughing. Alex

could only stare as Tom all but doubled over, he was laughing so hard. Every time he paused to catch his breath, he would look at Alex and start all over again until there were tears leaking from the corners of his eyes.

'It's not funny,' Alex muttered.

'Oh,' Tom gasped as he wiped at his face. 'Oh my god, Ally!' He collapsed into another fit of giggles then shook his head as though he could shake off his amusement. 'I don't believe it,' he said when he could finally breathe properly. 'You must be the only writer who procrastinated so hard they actually bought a bloody bookshop!' His lip wobbled as though he was going to start laughing again.

'Shut up, you bastard,' Alex swore, feeling his own middle start to shake. 'It wasn't like that!'

Oh – but hell – Tom might just have a point, though.

The idea he'd bought the shop just to avoid dealing with the mess of his book contract had never occurred to him for a second. Until now. A wild panic hit him and he grabbed for Tom's hand. 'Oh shit, what have I done?'

It was too much for Tom, who started howling with laughter again and Alex couldn't do anything other than join in. They were still at it when Nerissa walked into the kitchen, hands planted on her hips. 'What on earth are you two carrying on about? I'm trying to get Max settled and all I can hear is you two braying like a couple of donkeys!'

Alex and Tom exchanged a look and burst out laughing again. 'This idiot,' Tom said between gasps, 'bought a bloody shop rather than make an awkward phone call.'

14

It was the Wednesday before the bank holiday weekend, and somehow they'd actually made it. Ivy checked her watch, trying to ignore the butterflies dancing in her stomach. Half an hour to go until opening. At least they'd given themselves a couple of days to troubleshoot any problems before an onslaught of tourists poured into the Point, and *hopefully,* through their front door. She hurried to the curtained area at the back where she'd created a private dressing area for customers who wanted to try things on and gave herself a quick once-over in the full-length mirror. She'd chosen a pair of smart black trousers, which had a bit of hidden stretch in them so would be comfortable on what she hoped would be a busy day. The tunic top with an asymmetric hem she'd slipped on over a black wide-shoulder vest was a sample she'd run up after a last-minute idea the previous weekend. She hadn't had time to make any to sell, but she could at least be her own mannequin and show-case the design. Grimacing at her reflection, she checked her teeth and rubbed a tiny spot of red lipstick off the front of one of them. She glanced at her watch again to see exactly two minutes had passed.

Alex was upstairs, waiting to be interviewed by the local radio station about their grand opening, and she'd already tuned the radio on his workstation to the correct channel in anticipation. He'd asked Ivy if she wanted to join him, but she didn't want to steal any of his thunder. The shop was his and all of the financial risk was his so he should enjoy his moment in the spotlight. Spotting one of the little wooden duck figurines she'd bought from a whole-saler and decorated, Ivy hurried over to the shelf where it was standing and turned it half an inch to the left. Leaving the head and body of the duck as they were apart from a coat of clear protective varnish, she'd decorated the over-sized boots in a riot of colours and patterns. Some had bright-pink or yellow flowers painted on them, others rainbows and smiling sunny faces. The one she'd adjusted on the shelf had shiny pea-green boots with thick black soles.

Giving the duck an affectionate pat on the head, Ivy turned her attention to a little hedgehog she'd bought from the same supplier, hiding away on a lower shelf. Instead of boots, the smiling hedgehog had a red and white polka-dot cotton bandana tied around his neck, which she'd run up on her sewing machine using a scrap of discarded fabric. She loved quirky things and hoped they would appeal to their customers too. Alex had shaken his head when she'd shown him the plain wooden pieces and asked her who on earth was going to want a duck wearing massive boots. He'd given her a laughing hug when she'd shown him a couple of the finished ones, but she hadn't missed the fact he'd pinched one off the shelf and set it on his workstation in the middle of the shop.

Thoughts of Alex inevitably conjured the sight of him breath-less and laughing as she'd clambered off him that morning after a most energetic bout of wake-up sex. 'Insatiable,' he'd panted while reaching for her and pulling her tight against him. He did rather have a point, she thought with a wicked grin, because she hadn't been able to stop herself from pouncing on him every time they were alone. Hard to believe, looking back over the past fortnight, that she'd been worried about not being able to rediscover the sexual side of her nature. It was as if a huge part of herself had been asleep and for the first time she felt fully alive, fully herself. Just thinking about him now was getting her all hot and bothered, which was a very bad idea given the fact they were due to open the doors in – she checked her watch for a third time – exactly twenty minutes.

For want of something to do that would keep her mind off the man upstairs, Ivy headed out the back to the small kitchenette and retrieved a watering can and a pair of protective gloves from beneath the sink. Carrying the filled can carefully through the shop, she opened the door and gave the large planters the council had thankfully given them permission for, a quick once-over. The colourful pansies she'd planted the previous week were bedding in nicely and provided bright splashes of orange, purple and yellow between the miniature conifers. She would be able to swap them out with other seasonal flowers over the coming weeks and months and ensure there was always a pretty display. Next to the planters were a pair of terracotta pots each containing a rosebush that was already coming into flower. The pink-tipped creamy buds were just beginning to open and would be in full bloom in the next week or two. The garden centre had assured her they would provide scent, as well as colour, and as she bent to breathe the delicate perfume in, she was glad she'd asked their advice. She gave the pots and planters a quick top-up from the can and brushed away a stray bit of soil from the edge of one of the planters.

A soft meow sounded behind her and the next moment Lucifer was weaving around and around her ankles. 'Just as well I put black trousers on, isn't it?' she said, bending to give him a scratch between his ears. 'Now, mind my lovely plants, won't you? Don't let me catch you having a snooze in one of the planters.'

Lucifer butted his head against her palm, demanding a few more strokes, before he crouched on his back legs and sprang over the planter to land gracefully on the windowsill, where he settled down to clean his fur. Hoping Alex didn't spot him, Ivy left the cat to his daily ministrations and carried the watering can back inside. For all his threats and bluster, Alex still hadn't got around to blocking up the cat flap. As a consequence, Lucifer was paying almost daily visits to the shop and had even been found having a snooze in the middle of Alex's bed the one time he'd forgotten to close the door to the flat before coming down in the morning. As she entered the shop she was just in time to hear the breakfast show host saying, 'And here's Alex's song of choice to start what we all hope will be a beautiful day for him. Get yourself down to Mermaid Tales and Treasures, folks, and support your latest local business!' The opening chords of U2's 'Beautiful Day' echoed from the radio as Alex's footsteps thundered down the stairs.

'What did you think?' he asked. He'd chosen dark-navy jeans and a blue and white checked shirt with the sleeves rolled to the elbows and pristine white trainers for his outfit. He'd trimmed his beard to the length she preferred, maintaining a full coverage of his face without straggling down into mountain-man territory. Anything shorter than that and it played havoc with her skin, leaving her looking like a blotchy slice of salami.

'I was so busy trying to distract myself from clock-watching that I was outside watering the pots and I missed it,' she confessed. 'I'm so sorry! I'm sure you were great, and I promise I'll catch up later on the station's website.'

'Well, hopefully I didn't make a complete idiot of myself. It absolutely flew by and it seemed like I was saying goodbye only moments after it started, but that was probably the adrenaline. The DJ was brilliant, and covered all the points we sent in the briefing email. I think he mentioned the name of the shop about five times in as many minutes.'

'That's fantastic.' Tugging off her gardening gloves, Ivy pressed a hand to his chest as she popped up on tiptoe and planted a kiss to his lips, leaving a smear of red behind. 'Oops.' She giggled, reaching up to rub it away with her thumb. 'I'll have to remember not to kiss you on the shop floor.'

'Or you could just stop wearing lipstick,' Alex said with a grin as he ducked his head and nuzzled the spot behind her ear that always turned her into a puddle of melting desire. 'Because I have no plans to stop kissing you.' His gaze strayed behind her, and he straightened up. 'Action stations, here's our first customer!'

'Give me one second!' Ivy gathered up the watering can and scuttled out the back so she could check she hadn't smeared her lipstick all over her face. Regardless of what he said, they were going to have to set some ground rules because how embarrassing to have almost been caught smooching by their very first customer!

By the time she'd regained her composure and joined Alex out the front there were already half a dozen customers in the shop, including Nick. 'I'm the family representative,' he declared, giving her a quick hug before shaking Alex's hand. 'Everyone sends their love and I've got a shopping list.' He pulled a piece of paper out of his back pocket. 'Right, Dad wants the new Jack Reacher.'

Ivy led him towards the books, where they'd set out a bestseller section for hardbacks and paperbacks, and took a paperback from the display. 'We've got that. What's next?'

Nick pulled a face. 'Mum's been watching *Bridgerton*, which can't be a good thing at her age.' Ivy laughed as he continued, 'She wants a copy of the first three novels if you've got them.'

'We've got them.' Ivy gave him a knowing grin. She'd adored the racy Netflix adaptation of the popular series of historical romance and had assured Alex they would be able to sell multiple copies of them, especially when the holidaymakers arrived and were looking for something fun to read on the beach.

Nick put on a pretend shocked face. 'Ivy Fisher! Don't tell me you've been watching that filth,' he said in an unmistakable impression of gossipy Bev from the knitting circle.

'Twice!' she said with a giggle as she led Nick along the rows and rows of crisp, colourful book covers and spines until she found the complete set of the novels standing in a proud line, face out where they would catch a browsing reader's eye. She added the first three books to the Jack Reacher and clutched them against her chest. 'Any more for any more?'

'Laurie said something about a duck with rainbow wellies for the shelf in the café. She said you'd understand,' he finished with a shrug that clearly said he didn't get it at all.

Ivy hugged the books to herself, delighted at her friend's kindness. Knowing Laurie, she'd put the duck in an eye-catching position and send anyone who enquired about it their way. 'I know what she means.'

'I'm glad someone does,' Nick said with an exaggerated eye roll. 'Have you got any stationery, or is it just books? I could really do with a proper notebook as the spiral-bound one I've been using is falling apart. Now the council have finally given me planning permission I need to be as organised as possible.'

'That's brilliant news! Hey, I'll need to see what happens with the sale of the cottage, but can we have a chat sometime about the flats?'

Nick grinned at her. 'You really want to live next door to me?'

'Well, I've got to live somewhere,' Ivy muttered, unable to keep the bitterness out of her voice.

'Shit. Me and my big mouth.' Nick drew her into a quick hug. 'Your name is at the top of the list, okay?' She nodded and he gave her another squeeze. 'Now, how about you help me find a notebook so I can make that list?'

It was impossible to feel down for long when someone like Nick had her back. 'I'm sure we can find something suitable for you, *Sir*,' she said, putting on a posh accent that made him laugh. 'We've got a few different styles on the display behind Alex's counter,' she continued in her normal voice. 'If you can't find what you need have a word with him, and he'll be able to check our supplier's online catalogue.'

Nick grinned at her. 'A natural saleswoman, if ever I heard one.' His expression grew more serious as he cast a quick glance towards where Alex was chatting to a woman in the children's book section. 'How's it all going?'

'Well, it's a bit too early to tell, given we've only been open half an hour, but we're hopeful. Alex was on the radio this morning so with any luck that'll bring a few more people through the door later.'

'Not the shop,' he said, shaking his head. 'I mean between the two of you.'

'Oh.' Nick hadn't been around much because he'd been so busy with his own plans for the warehouse conversion, so the only way he could know about her and Alex dating was if someone had told him.

'Don't worry, you're not a hot topic of gossip. I mentioned to Jake the other day about having a few beers with him and Alex and he said Alex might have other plans involving you. How long's it been going on?' He sounded more interested than anything else and Ivy felt her shoulders relax. They hadn't made a secret of their relationship around their close friends and family, so she shouldn't be surprised if it came up, she supposed.

'A few weeks. We're taking things as they come, but he's a good guy, Nick. I really like being with him.'

His face softened into a smile. 'I can see it in your eyes that you do. Well, I for one, am glad that you've found yourself a bit of happiness. And you can tell Alex from me, if he doesn't treat you right, he'll have me to answer to.'

Ivy crossed her arms and gave him a mock-glare. 'I'll tell him no such thing, so don't start going into big-brother mode. I'm more than capable of looking after myself.'

Nick tossed his head back on a laugh. 'Well, that's me told, isn't it?' His expression grew sad and serious. 'Just be careful of your heart, Ivy, that's all I'm saying.'

Wondering if he was thinking about his own brief fling with Aurora Storm from last year, Ivy couldn't help but feel sorry for him. Nick was such a great guy, he deserved someone who would fall in love with him the way Laurie and Jake had fallen for each other. The way... No, it was too soon to entertain such things. She liked Alex, but she wasn't ready for more than that. 'I'll be careful,' she promised. 'And I'll let Alex know about going out for a drink, I'm sure he'd love to catch up with you guys.'

* * *

The community of Mermaids Point did what it did best and came out in support. Whenever things fell quiet and Ivy started to worry they'd had all the visitors they were getting for the day, the door would open and more of their friends and neighbours appeared. Most had dropped in to pick up a book, but Ivy was gratified to have sold a couple of dresses and had taken three orders for tunic tops the same as the one she was wearing. The quirky little ducks had also proven a surprise hit and she was just wondering whether she had time to check the supplier's website for other things she might be able to customise when her phone pinged. Alex had been sending her flirty little messages all morning, from suggestive emojis to GIFS of famous movie kisses. Wondering what he'd sent her this time, she was already smiling as she unlocked the screen. The frisson inside her died the moment she read the header of the message. It was from Alun, the estate agent.

I know you're busy with the shop opening but please call asap. AW.

Alex was at the till and as well as the person he was serving there were a couple of others browsing, but nothing he couldn't handle. She caught his eye as she hurried out the back, holding her phone up so he'd know what she was doing. Letting herself out the back door, Ivy walked to the far end of the yard close to the garage doors. They'd found an old bench when they were sorting out the stuff piled high in the junk room and had put it here where it would catch the afternoon sun. She still hadn't found time to strip it and paint it, so she checked the surface for splinters before perching on the edge. Not giving herself time to dwell, Ivy clicked on Alun's name and waited for the ring tone.

'Alun Wise, good afternoon!' His hearty tone made the sick feeling in Ivy's stomach spread.

'Alun, hi, it's Ivy Fisher. I got your message.'

'Ivy! Thanks for calling me back so quickly. How's everything going with the shop? I'm out and about later so I was going to try and pop in, and Maureen said she was planning a visit.'

Ivy couldn't help but smile at the innate thoughtfulness. His wife was one of the three who'd ordered a tunic from her. 'She's

already been in. Everyone has been so wonderful and supportive.'
She took a deep breath. 'You didn't want me to call just so you could
wish us well, though.'

'No. Indeed.' Alun sighed. 'There's good news and there's bad
news. We've had an offer this morning for the full asking price on
the cottage. It's a cash buyer with no onward chain.'

It was what she'd been dreading. 'And the good news?' she
asked with a hiccupy little laugh.

'Oh, my dear girl, I know how hard this is for you,' Alun
murmured. 'I wish it were otherwise.'

'I know, Alun, me too.' Ivy forced herself to suck in a deep
breath. 'Tell me the rest.'

'The buyer is a few years off retirement, so they want to
maximise their investment and rent the property out before they
relocate here on a permanent basis. In order to get it up to scratch
before the season they want to proceed as quickly as possible.'

'How quickly?'

'Literally as soon as we can get through the formalities. If their
offer is accepted they've already lined up a surveyor who can
inspect the property tomorrow, and, as I said, it's a cash buyer so
they won't need to go through all the malarkey of securing a mortgage and whatnot. If you accept the offer then you need to be
thinking in terms of weeks rather than a couple of months.'

Though she'd been half expecting something like that since
he'd mentioned them being a cash buyer, it was still a shock to hear
it laid out in such plain terms. 'I... I need to think about it. I'll need
time to find somewhere to live...'

'I'm obliged to tell all parties concerned about the offer.'

Alun's voice was gentle as he delivered the brutal blow. In her
panic, she'd forgotten all about Kevin and his vested interested in
the cottage. 'You haven't spoken to him yet?'

'I wanted to talk to you first, but what with it being the full asking price and the lack of complication it's my duty to recommend the offer to both you and your father. Sales don't come much easier than this and I'm almost 100 per cent sure what Kevin will say.'

Ivy was too. Whatever her feelings, the cottage had to be sold. There was no point dragging things out because Kevin wasn't going to change his mind and she didn't have grounds to reject the offer, other than her own living arrangements issues. 'Looks like I don't have any choice, then, doesn't it?'

She was still staring at her phone ten minutes later when Alex opened the back door. 'There you are! Is everything okay?'

'Everything's great. The cottage has been sold at full asking price.' Even Ivy couldn't miss the wobble in her voice.

'Oh god, Ivy, I'm sorry.' Alex glanced behind him. 'One second,' he called back into the shop before turning back to her. 'We'll talk about this later, I promise. Take all the time you need, and I'll handle things in the shop.' He disappeared again before she could thank him.

Lifting her face to the warmth of the afternoon sun, Ivy closed her eyes and let the heat sink into her skin. She tried to centre herself, to draw the lessons from her yoga classes and exist in the moment. It was a struggle to calm her mind, to slow the beating of her heart, which was trying to leap out of her chest like a startled rabbit. Through a concerted effort she eventually fell into a slow rhythm of breathing and regained a modicum of control. Today was too important to screw up, not only for her, but for Alex too. She pictured the box in her mind and pushed all her feelings inside. In went the panic about finding somewhere to live, her anger at Kevin for putting her in this situation because of his unwillingness to act like a bloody grown-up, the rising wave of grief as the loss of her mum came roaring back to life. Into the box it went until she could slam down the lid and turn the mental key. It wouldn't stay locked for long, but all she needed to do was get through the next couple of hours and make sure opening day at the shop was the success Alex deserved it to be after all his hard work.

15

As the afternoon progressed, Alex's concern for Ivy grew. Though she was all smiles for the customers, he could see the effort it took. Even more worrying was the wall she'd pulled around herself when it came to him. He'd sent her a couple of texts, just silly memes, but they remained unread. Whenever their customers thinned out she made herself busy, disappearing out the back to find stock to replace sold items, or out the front to fiddle with the pretty pots she'd planted. If she watered those pansies one more time they'd float away, poor things. Lucifer had stalked in about an hour ago, taking a turn about the shop like an officer on the parade ground before hopping up onto the workstation Ivy had set up for herself and nudging her arm until she gave in and petted him. Though Alex still wanted to discourage the cat he said nothing, letting Lucifer offer Ivy some measure of comfort while Alex himself couldn't.

A late influx of well-wishers meant they stayed open longer than anticipated and by the time he saw the last person out and locked the front door it was well after six. He flipped the sign on the door to 'closed' and leant against it with a sigh. 'What a day.'

'We did well,' Ivy said without looking over at him from where she was straightening a rack of clothes.

Unable to stand the distance between them for a moment longer, Alex crossed the room and slid his arms around her waist from behind. When she stiffened but didn't pull away he let them drop but stayed close. 'I know we can't expect numbers like that every day, but it was so kind of everyone to go out of their way to make today a success.'

'Yes. Everyone was great.' Though she tried to make it appear as though she were focused on tidying the already neat rack, Alex couldn't help thinking she was trying to move away from him. He wanted to grab her, hold her tight against him until the bloody wall of ice she'd erected around herself melted away and she let him in. The only thing that stopped him was the stiffness of her movements. There was a brittleness to her actions, as though she were made of glass and one wrong touch might shatter her into a million pieces. The only other time he'd seen her like this was in the pub after her mother's funeral and he'd be damned if he'd be the one who tipped her over the edge again.

Shoving his hands in his pockets, he made a point of backing up towards his workstation, giving her lots of space. 'Right. I'd better make a start on cashing up.' He hesitated, wondering what to say next. He'd put a bottle of champagne in the fridge that morning, so they'd have something special to share to celebrate their first day. Given the way she was avoiding him, perhaps she might prefer a bit of time on her own to process the news from the agent. 'If you've had enough for the day, you're welcome to head home for the night. It's going to take me a while to get my head around a new reconciliation system so I'm not sure I'll be much company.'

She shot him a quick glance from under her lashes. 'I'll stay for a bit if you don't mind. Make sure everything is tidy ready for the morning.'

He nodded. 'Whatever you prefer.' Reaching for the dial on the radio, he turned the volume up a couple of notches so the drivetime show would fill the quiet and take the pressure off Ivy feeling as if she had to talk to him. Though he'd had a few practice runs with the till, Alex still made sure to follow the step-by-step instructions in the manufacturer's manual while he cashed up the receipts and reconciled them back to the daily stock report. He was aware of Ivy shifting in and out of his peripheral vision, but he was too worried about making a mistake to do more than glance up from his reports now and again.

Drivetime finished at seven, and somewhere in the back of his brain he noted the music had stopped and there was some kind of round-table discussion panel about the impact of climate change on coastal communities. He tapped his pen against his lip as he stared at the mismatched pair of figures before him. *What had he done wrong?*

'Are you listening to that?' Ivy asked him, setting down the duster and polish she'd been using.

'No. Feel free to find something else.'

'How's that?' she asked after switching over to an easy-listening station that promised smooth classics according to the ident playing. A slow eighties ballad started.

'Much better.' Alex caught her eye and was relieved when she gave him the ghost of a smile. Giving her time and space to work through her emotional turmoil over the sale of the cottage seemed to be the right call, so he turned his attention back to his books. There had to be a transposition error somewhere because the difference between his reconciliation and the till receipts was divisible by nine. It was one of the first things he'd been taught as a trainee accountant, and it had saved his bacon on many occasions. It was just a case of finding the blasted thing...

'If the wind changes, you'll stay like that,' Ivy observed, pulling his attention away from the reports once more.

'Huh?'

'Your face, you were frowning and...' She trailed off, waving a hand towards his desk. 'Never mind, I'm distracting you.'

'I could do with a little distracting,' he said, taking a chance and holding his hand out to her. When she stepped into his arms and rested her head against his chest, he held her against him and felt the tension seep from his body. Catching the rhythm of the song on the radio, he swayed them in time to the music. A soft sigh escaped her and he felt her fingers relax against his back. 'Do you want to talk about it?' he asked, pressing a kiss to the top of her head.

'No.' The word was so forlorn it all but broke his heart, but at least there was emotion in it, unlike her robotic responses earlier.

Letting the song work its magic, he continued to rock her gently until the final chorus faded out. Pressing his lips to her ear, Alex lowered his voice to a husky whisper. 'Do you want to come up to bed, drink champagne and do obscene things with me?'

She giggled. 'I haven't brought my red boots.'

With a laugh, Alex pulled back to see she was smiling up at him. 'We can improvise.'

'What about the books?'

Letting her go, he swept up everything on the counter, including the receipts bag. Most of their transactions had been by card so they were within the insurance limit if he put everything in the safe upstairs. 'I'll get up early and finish them.'

* * *

Half a bottle of champagne later, Alex slid an absent hand over the delicate curve at the base of Ivy's spine. Sprawled face-down as she was, it was hard to tell if she was awake and he didn't want to disturb her. 'Shower first,' she muttered into the pillow and he laughed.

'I wasn't actually trying to seduce you again.'

She lifted her head from the pillow. 'Well, that's disappointing.'

He grinned. 'Pour me another glass of champagne, then, and I'll see if I can rise to the challenge.'

'I should leave you for your terrible sense of humour, you know?' she said, but she was grinning as she pushed herself up enough to reach for the bottle on the bedside cabinet. Her tummy gave a huge rumble and they both stared down at it in surprise.

'Perhaps we should eat something before we have any more to drink?' he suggested as he reached for his phone and checked the time. 'Bloody hell, it's nearly half-eight. We should definitely eat something.'

'I still need a shower,' she reminded him.

'Good point. You go on and I'll get some food started and then we can swap, okay?'

By the time Ivy wandered into the kitchen dressed in one of his T-shirts and a pair of boxer briefs she'd pinched from his underwear drawer, Alex had chopped and browned a couple of chicken breasts and added them to a jar of carbonara sauce together with a handful of frozen veg. He'd measured out some pasta but it was a few minutes too soon to put it on to cook. 'Smells good,' Ivy said, taking a seat at the kitchen table, one leg curled underneath her. 'Anything I need to do?'

'Give it a stir now and again if you don't mind. I'll be back in five.'

They ate on the sofa, sharing the remains of the bottle of champagne between them. Alex had flicked the TV on out of habit and there was a documentary on about a train journey through the wilds of Sweden. The images were soothing, so he'd turned down the volume and let the pictures tell the story.

Ivy placed her empty bowl on the coffee table with a satisfied sigh and flopped back down on the sofa. 'I'm stuffed.'

'Feeling better?' He didn't want to push her, but she still hadn't said anything about the sale of the cottage and he didn't want her dwelling on it when he was there for her to talk to.

'Much.' She reached out a hand and placed it on his thigh. 'Thank you for this evening. I couldn't face going back to the cottage, tonight.'

'I get it.' Alex set his own bowl aside and raised his arm for her to snuggle under. 'Even though you knew it was coming, it must've been a hell of a shock today.'

Rolling onto her back, she rested her head across his legs so she could look up at him. 'I thought I was ready, but I wasn't. And I haven't even got the luxury of time to get used to the idea. The buyer wants to move quickly so I *have* to find somewhere else to live.'

Taking hold of one of her hands, Alex played his fingers over her knuckles. 'I meant what I said before about staying here if you want to. Wait!' he added when she tried to pull her hand away and sit up. 'Listen to what I'm actually saying before you react, okay?'

She narrowed her eyes at him, but settled back down. 'Okay.'

'I'm not suggesting we live together as a couple, or even that you need to think of it as a long-term arrangement. You'd have your own room. I *want* you to have your own room because I like how things are between us right now and I don't want to spoil it by rushing ahead of ourselves.'

'You think we should live together, but not live together?' She frowned. 'I'm not sure I understand.'

'We share the flat, but respect each other's boundaries. Like I said, you'd have your room, and I'll have mine. Any time either of us wants to shut that door and be alone, that's fine. If you want to stay in my room some nights, or invite me into yours, then I'm up for that, of course.'

'Of course,' she echoed with a wicked grin. 'And I could still look for something more permanent for myself.'

'Exactly.' He thought about what Tom had said to him before, about Alex's tendency to dive headlong into things and he knew his brother had a point. He liked Ivy. Liked her a lot, but there was no way he wanted to screw things up between them by rushing into something. They had all the time in the world. 'I just want to take the pressure off you trying to find somewhere to live in such a short space of time. The last thing you want is to end up paying over the odds or tying yourself to a lease on a place you don't like.'

'I've been keeping an eye out online and I know Alun would've given me a heads up if anything came onto his books that he thought was suitable. I'd really hate to move out of the Point, but there's nothing local unless I move into one of the bed and breakfast places on a short-term basis.'

'Which would be a waste of money. I don't need any rent from you, just a contribution to the running costs.' He wasn't even bothered about that, but he knew her independent streak would not take kindly to that idea.

'I could talk to Nick about how long he thinks it will be before one of his apartments are ready,' she mused. 'I mentioned it briefly to him earlier, but now I know the cottage has a buyer I should talk to him properly.' A frown creased her brow. 'And you're sure it wouldn't bother you if I moved in and moved out again, even if things are still good between us?'

He interlaced their fingers and gave hers a little squeeze. 'Whatever you want to do, I promise I'll be fine with it.'

'I don't ever want to feel like this again,' she said, in a soft, pained voice. 'Like I have no control over my life because someone else is calling the shots. I hate the idea of even renting somewhere, because there's no guarantee a landlord won't change their mind or decide to sell up. I need the security of bricks and mortar, a place I can truly call my own.'

He understood. As much as he hoped things would work out between them, there was no guarantee of anything; experience had taught them both that already. If they broke up, he would be okay because he had the flat and the shop, but what would Ivy have? He couldn't expect her to shoulder all the risk. 'I think you should definitely talk to Nick.'

A meow sounded from the door, and they both sat up to stare over the back of the sofa. Lucifer sat on the threshold, expectant gaze trained on Ivy. 'Oh dear,' she said, giving Alex a sheepish grin. 'We must've forgotten to close the door when we came up.' Scrambling off the sofa, she bent to gather the cat and gave him a cuddle. 'Come on, let's see if I can find you something to eat in the kitchen.'

Alex sighed. 'There's a can of tuna in the cupboard.' When Ivy turned a delighted smile upon him, he knew it was time to admit defeat. 'He sleeps in your room, okay?'

* * *

Alex woke the next morning to find Ivy still fast asleep beside him. Wanting her to get as much rest as possible after the shock of the day before, he slipped from the covers and padded into the kitchen to make a cup of coffee. Five minutes later, he was settled at the table with his reconciliation laid out before him. As though it had been waiting for him, the transposition error popped out almost immediately and within a few minutes he had everything signed off and ready. Putting the accounts back in the safe, he checked his watch and saw it was still too early to wake Ivy, so he settled down on the sofa and flicked open his laptop. He hadn't had much time to write over the past few days so it was a good opportunity to try and bash out a few words.

As he waited for the document to open he thought again about how brave Ivy had been the previous day. Traumatic as it must be to be losing the security of her home, she was facing it head-on, chin raised and determined to front it out. It was enough to put a man to shame. With a sigh, he closed his Word file and opened his email and composed a brief message to his editor telling her they needed to talk about his contract and asking her to call him at the earliest opportunity. It barely seemed as if he'd pressed the send button before his mobile was ringing and he rushed to answer it before it woke Ivy up.

It was Immy. 'Alex, please tell me you're not about to give me some sort of horrible news before I've even had my first cup of coffee?'

She sounded more resigned than angry. With a half-laugh, half-sigh Alex settled back against the sofa cushions. 'Forget the instant and stick the machine on because you're going to need a lot of caffeine, I'm afraid.'

When they ended their call about twenty minutes later, Alex could only marvel about his own stupidity in putting it off for so long. Immy had been disappointed, but far more understanding than he'd had any right to hope she would be. There was enough left over in his refurbishment account that he'd offered to refund the part of his advance he'd received for delivering the first book. Immy hadn't thought that would be necessary, given how well it had sold, but said she appreciated the offer. She finished by saying she would have to speak to her divisional director and would get back to him when she could.

Knowing there was nothing he could do other than wait, Alex headed to the kitchen to pop the kettle on. It was time to wake Ivy and focus on the positives. As he looked out over the rooftops he caught the faintest glimpse of the sea. It was barely a sliver, a thin blue strip several shades darker than the sky above, but it was enough to remind him how lucky he was. He had a wonderful woman asleep in his bed, a business that had got off to a roaring start, and he lived in one of the most beautiful places in the country. Things could be a whole lot worse.

16

The sale of the cottage moved faster than even Alun had expected, so Ivy was absent a lot over the first few weeks of June while she faced the unenviable task of condensing a lifetime's worth of memories into what would fit into her new bedroom above the shop. She'd decided sleeping at the cottage was too hard, so they'd hired a van one Sunday and with the help of their friends they'd decanted the contents of her bedroom from there to the flat. Tom had agreed Alex could park his car at the surgery for the time being so they could use the garage behind the shop for storage, but it was still a wrench for Ivy to decide what to keep and what to part with.

She wasn't sure how she would've managed without everyone pulling together. Linda had the most time on her hands so she'd filled in at the shop whenever Ivy had needed to be at the cottage. Packing up her mum's things had been harder than expected, but Laurie had given up as many evenings as Ivy needed to laugh and cry with her and somehow they'd got through it. Jake had some charity contacts through the work he did with the local paper and had put Ivy in touch with one that provided furniture and other household essentials to previously homeless people who had been rehoused. They'd been so grateful that in the end it hadn't been that hard for Ivy to let most things go.

Though it would be months yet before her apartment at the harbour would be ready, making plans for how she would decorate and fill the space was a good distraction as the legal wheels turned at breakneck speed and Ivy was closing the door to the cottage for the last time. And by the Friday before Father's Day she had dropped the keys off with Alun. The irony of the date hadn't been lost on her, but once Kevin and Wendy were married – and hopefully the rumours proved true and they were planning to leave the Point – she wouldn't need to have anything more to do with him. Alun and Harry had both been wonderful, acting as a buffer between her and Kevin. Any appointments to sign paperwork and the like were kept entirely separate so there was no chance of her bumping into him. Both he and Wendy seemed to be keeping a low profile and Ivy hadn't heard a word since the letter Wendy had sent with the wedding invitation.

When Harry had called to let her know the final funds transfer had gone through and her share of the money was sitting in her bank account, the only thing Ivy had felt was relief that it was all over. As she'd logged in to double-check the money really was there, it was as if she'd taken the final step away from her childhood. This was what her mother had wanted for her. It was time to move forward in the next chapter of her life and make the very most of the freedom and opportunity the money in her account was offering her.

Though she was still uncertain about their unconventional set-up, Alex had stayed true to his word and put no expectations on them spending every night together. If anything, it was Ivy who was the one who made the first move that inevitably decided their sleeping arrangements. They'd fallen into something of a domestic routine when it came to things like cooking dinner, because it seemed like a false economy to cook individually when they could take turns. The rest of the chores they'd sat down and divided between them. The kitchen was a shared area they both kept clean as they went, and Ivy had accepted the bathroom cleaning in exchange for Alex hoovering and dusting the lounge and hall and putting out the bins. Their bedrooms they looked after themselves, partly to preserve that sense of privacy, but mostly because Lucifer still wouldn't let Alex over the threshold into Ivy's room without trying to scratch or bite him. The nights they did choose to spend together had, therefore, defaulted to Alex's room, which he didn't seem to mind. Still, Ivy was going to have to do something about the cat because it wasn't fair on Alex.

Before Ivy tackled Lucifer though, she was going to have to find something to wear on Monday. She'd sworn to herself she would ignore Kevin and Wendy's wedding, but as the date had approached she'd found herself wondering whether she'd be better off going after all. It would draw a line under everything, send a message to the rest of the village that she was fine with them getting married. If she could forgive and forget, maybe everyone else would too.

'Why do I care what they think?' She sighed, abandoning her fruitless staring at the contents of her wardrobe before scooping Lucifer off the end of her bed and depositing him back in his basket in the corner. It was a pointless exercise because he'd be stretched out on her clean quilt cover the moment her back was turned, but she still went through the motions in the vain hope he'd get the message one of these days. 'And what am I going to do with you? You're really going to have to be nicer to Alex, you know,' she continued as though the cat could understand her. 'It's his home, after all. Once my flat is ready you can't expect him to keep letting you stay here.' Nick was going full steam with the conversion works and, thanks to the money now sitting safely in her bank account, she'd been able to agree a price in principle with him that didn't feel as if she was taking advantage of his good nature.

Lucifer raised his head from where he'd been licking his unmentionables and levelled a stare at her.

'I'm serious. Barbara won't have you back after that last scrap with Carlotta, so you'll either have to move over to the harbour with me or you'll be off to Cats Protection.' He lowered his head to resume his bathing routine as though he knew it was an empty threat. For all his cantankerous behaviour and the black hair he kept shedding on her crisp white sheets, she'd already grown hopelessly attached. 'Well, at least try not to bite him any more, okay?'

'Who's biting who?' Alex had barely spoken before Lucifer shot out of his basket and Ivy had to all but throw herself on the cat before he could launch himself at Alex.

'Come on, give me break!' Alex protested when Lucifer hissed at him from the safety of her arms. 'I stayed this side of the threshold.' Alex pointed to his feet where there was a clear gap between the end of his toes and the metal carpet strip that separated her room from the hall. He scowled at the cat before looking up at Ivy. 'I only came to let you know that dinner will be ready in about ten minutes.' He stalked off, looking every bit as disgruntled as he was entitled to be.

'Now look what you've done.' Ivy dropped Lucifer back in his basket, pushing him away gently when he tried to climb out and weave around her ankles. 'No. No more cuddles for you until you can behave yourself.' With that she left him sulking in the corner and shut the bedroom door behind him.

'It's not going to work, is it?' she admitted to Alex as she entered the kitchen after washing her hands.

'He's not so bad around the shop. Maybe we could try shifting his basket back downstairs again,' he replied, keeping his attention on the pot he was stirring on the stove. He'd told her earlier he was making spaghetti bolognese, and the flat smelled of rich tomato sauce and Italian herbs.

'We can try,' she agreed, not feeling hopeful after the way Lucifer had howled and mewled until they'd let him upstairs. Alex had already placed a couple of mats on the small square table so she added plates, cutlery and glasses while he flicked on the kettle to boil ready to rinse the spaghetti. 'Can I do anything else?'

'No, you're fine, just a couple more minutes. Have you decided on a film for this evening?'

She hadn't even thought about it, having been too busy tying herself in knots over the blasted wedding. She said as much as she fetched a bottle of wine and poured herself half a glass before giving a shrug and filling it up. They'd stuck to their 'no booze in the week' rule, but it was Saturday night and the fact she was worrying about her bloody father when he'd proven time and again he couldn't give a stuff about anyone other than himself was enough to drive her to drink. 'It's stupid of me to even think about going, isn't it?'

It wasn't hard for Alex to pick up the thread of her conversation, given she'd been banging on about it all day. 'I told you earlier, you must do whatever is best for you. You don't have to throw confetti and dance at the reception or anything, you could just show your face at the church.'

'The church.' She snorted. 'I bet the last time Kevin set foot in there was when he married Mum.'

Alex shook his head as he collected the empty plates and began filling them with steaming spaghetti and rich beef bolognese. 'He's got more front than Brighton beach, as Pop would say.' After placing her food in front of her, he rested a hand on her shoulder. She looked up to see his brows knitted together in concern. 'Maybe you should skip the church and drop into the reception instead?' he suggested gently. 'It'll be the first time you've been there since the funeral, I'm guessing?'

She turned her head to place a kiss on the back of his hand, touched as ever at his concern for her. 'I've popped in a couple of times when I've been up to put flowers down for Mum.' Not that she was particularly religious or anything, but she'd found a quiet comfort in the solitude of the old stone walls. 'I'll be all right. I shall imagine her sitting next to me and what she'd have to say about it.' Ivy laughed, already knowing the kind of acerbic things Jen would have said if she were around.

Alex squeezed her shoulder gently. 'I'll come with you if you like and whisper horrible things about Wendy's dress and your dad's cheap suit.'

It hadn't occurred to her to ask him. They hadn't kept the romance between them a state secret or anything, but they also hadn't made a show of it around the village either. The couple of nights they'd been out to the pub, they'd sat in a group with Laurie, Jake and a few other friends, and no one who didn't already know would've noticed anything between them. If they walked into the church together it would be making a statement, especially given the way he'd supported her at her mum's funeral. 'I'll be okay on my own. Besides, there's the small matter of someone having to look after the shop.'

'We can stick a note in the window saying we'll be back in an hour. It's not like we'd be closed all day and Monday's tend to be quiet.' Alex took his seat opposite her and twirled up a forkful of spaghetti before meeting her gaze. 'Is it a bit too couple-y for you?'

Ivy bit her lip, not quite sure how to answer. 'I'm not sure I'm ready to discuss our arrangement.' Not that Ivy was embarrassed about sleeping with Alex, she'd just been the subject of enough gossip already that year.

He shrugged, the food an inch from his lips. 'So, we don't talk about it. We go, we wish the happy couple well, we come home and put our feet up and forget about them and everyone else. It's not like I'm going to start ravishing you in the back of the pews – unless, you know, that's a kink you haven't told me about.'

Ivy burst out laughing, amazed and grateful that he always managed to find a way to make her feel better. 'It's not on my bucket list of locations.'

'You really do have a list for everything, don't you?'

She twirled up her own spaghetti, letting a cheeky smile play on her lips. 'Maybe I'll share it with you one day. If you're lucky.'

'Paint me green and call me a leprechaun because I intend to be very lucky.' And so he was when she suggested they skip the movie and enjoy an early night together.

Monday morning dawned with a clear sky that promised sunshine and the kind of hot temperature that gave hope of a long summer to come. Ivy accepted a kiss from Alex before he slid from the bed to take first go in the shower, giving her five extra minutes to luxuriate in the warm spot he'd left beside her. In spite of her worries over the wedding, she'd slept like a log. Though she refused to give in to the temptation to spend every night with him, Ivy always slept better in Alex's bed. Perhaps she should use some of her proceeds from the cottage and treat herself to a new mattress, although she doubted it had anything to do with the quality or otherwise of her current one. Still, she should remain respectful of his space, especially when her room was out of bounds thanks to one very large, very grumpy cat.

On that thought, she scooted from the bed, gathered her scattered clothing from the carpet and was back in her own room before she heard the thud of the shower shutting off. She took a little time to sort out her clothes for the day – a pair of white linen trousers with such wide flares she suspected they were from the seventies, and a peasant blouse with pretty spring flowers embroidered around the neck and hemline. She hung a peach silk blouse on the back of her bedroom door, which she could switch for the peasant top if she decided to go to the wedding, then dug out a pair of wedge-heeled sandals and a straw hat with a neutral band to which she could clip a couple of silk flowers, to dress it up.

By the time Ivy had finished in the shower, Alex was in the kitchen and the smell of fresh-brewed coffee filled the air. When she saw he'd placed a mug just outside her bedroom door, her stomach did a little flip. It wasn't getting addicted to the scent and feel of his body beside her that she needed to worry about, it was the sweet little gestures that always managed to catch her off guard. *There's no rush*, she told herself as she carried the coffee into her room as if the mug were made of precious metal. *Focus on the now and enjoy what you have.* It was hard not to dream of the future sometimes, though, whatever her head cautioned.

The fine weather had brought the shoppers out and they were kept busy for the first couple of hours. It was testament to the good feeling amongst the locals towards Alex that even those who said they'd just popped in for a browse never seemed to leave empty-handed. Everyone knew how hard it was to sustain a business in the Point and it was heartening to see them continuing to show their support. Alex and Ivy's next big test would be the start of the school holidays when they could expect an influx of day and weekend trippers. The bank holiday had been a success, but the coming months would prove whether the shop had a long-term future. Ivy had designed a few posters, which Laurie and several other of the business owners along the front had agreed to put up in their windows. There wasn't much more they could do other than cross their fingers that the weather gods would continue to smile on the Point, because everyone could do with a financial boost.

Ivy hadn't realised the time until Alex made his way to the centre of the shop and clapped his hands together. 'Just a heads up,' he called out in a clear, authoritative tone. 'Due to a prior engagement we need to close the shop in about quarter of an hour. We'll be open again by one p.m. at the latest. Thank you for your attention.' When their eyes met, she gave him a hard stare because she still hadn't decided if she was going to the wedding, and she wasn't at all sure she liked this high-handed approach of his. It had been welcome enough when she'd needed someone to lean on at her mum's funeral, but whatever was going on between them in the privacy of their flat upstairs didn't give him the right to make decisions on her behalf.

'Nothing wrong, I hope.' Ivy startled at the voice behind her and turned to find Tracy, the receptionist from Harry's office, watching her with the kind of avid curiosity that made some people slow down when passing a traffic accident. Ivy wondered how she managed to keep her job at the solicitor's without bursting at the seams with all the personal stuff she must be privy to.

'Everything's fine,' Ivy assured her. 'Was there something in particular you were looking for?' *Other than a bit of gossip.*

Caught on the hop, Tracy flushed as she reached blindly towards the mannequin clad in a handkerchief-style sundress next to Ivy's counter. It was a new design Ivy had found a pattern for and she'd put it on display to gauge people's reactions before she committed to making more than the half a dozen samples she'd run up on her sewing machine. 'I was wondering if you did this in any other colours?' Tracy asked, fingering the pale-pink cotton with little purple paisley swirls.

'If you like the design, I can make you one in whatever material takes your fancy.' Ivy reached for the swatch book she'd made up and opened it on the counter in front of Tracy. 'Same goes for anything else you see on display. I'm still doing individual commissions, alterations and repairs.' She grinned as she slid her pattern book next to the material swatches. 'If it's within my capabilities to make it, you can have it, basically.'

'Oh, that's great to know. I'll make sure I spread the word for you. My sister is having a baby in a couple of months so I could do with something for the christening, actually. I don't get much time to go into town to look around and most of my online shopping attempts end in disaster.' Tracy rolled her eyes. 'And then it's a faff to try and send back anything that doesn't fit so it just ends up in the back of the wardrobe.'

'It's hard to buy off the peg when we're all different shapes and sizes, too,' Ivy sympathised. 'If you've got stuff you don't want that you haven't worn then you can bring it in. I'm not guaranteeing I'll take it, but I might be able to alter some of it for you, or repurpose the items.'

'If you could, that would get me back in Ben's good books. He's always moaning at me for buying clothes I never wear.'

'Well, we can't have that, can we?' Ivy gave her a conspiratorial smile. 'Let's fix up a time that works for you and I can come around to yours. If you do decide you want something for the christening, I can take a proper set of measurements at the same time. I've got a changing area here we can use.' Ivy pointed to the back corner of her section of the shop, where she'd hung some curtains that could be pulled across to create a dressing room. 'But things like that are always a bit more comfortable in the privacy of your own home, I find.'

Tracy was positively beaming now. 'That sounds wonderful.' She checked her watch. 'Look, I'm on my coffee break, so I need to get back, but I have a half-day every other Wednesday afternoon. Are you free next week?'

'Let's get it in the diary now.'

With a well and truly distracted Tracy dispatched with an appointment for two o'clock the following Wednesday afternoon, and the other handful of customers gently ushered out by Alex, Ivy waited until he'd locked the door and flipped the sign to 'closed' before she rounded upon him. 'You have no right to take over like this.'

'Like what?' Alex held up his hands in surrender. 'All I've done is given you a bit of breathing space. Even if you choose not to go to the wedding, I thought you might like to avoid anyone who does go and might be tempted to pop in on their way back and tell you all about it.'

'Oh.' Ivy felt her indignation leak away like air from an old party balloon. 'Umm, thank you?'

'You're welcome,' he said, sounding a bit put out. 'Look, it was something that occurred to me at the last minute, and I was going to sound you out before I did it, but then I got caught up in a discussion about the relative merits of half a dozen different picture books suitable for a six-month-old. I was tempted to point out that if the kid was anything like Max was at that age, she should try and work out which one tasted the best as he shoved everything he could get his hands on straight into his mouth.'

'Maybe you should just design a range of flavour-infused books for infants,' Ivy said with a laugh, glad he always found a way to smooth over the misunderstandings between them. 'You'd make a fortune.'

Alex grinned. 'I could enter the next season of *Dragon's Den*.' He held out his hand to her. 'So, what's it going to be, Ms Fisher? The wedding of the year or a little mid-morning delight courtesy of your favourite man?'

'Well, when you put it like that,' she said as she placed her palm in his and let him lead her through the shop, 'there's really only one choice.' She waited until he'd turned an eager grin on her to land the teasing blow. 'Get your suit on, we're off to church.'

She was still giggling to herself over Alex's abject disappointment when she met him on the landing, she in her peach silk blouse and trousers combo and him in a dark-grey suit with a pale-blue shirt and a pink tie. He lifted a finger to touch one of the half-dozen silk flowers she'd pinned to her hat. 'These are pretty. Did you make them?'

'Too fiddly. We could look for a wholesaler that does them though,' she mused, her mind already picturing a large wicker basket filled with different blooms on the corner of her counter and tall vases with long-stemmed ones dotted here and there around the shop floor. They'd bring some extra colour to the place, especially in the winter when the flower troughs and pots out the front would be bare.

'Not everything has to be a business opportunity,' he said, with a wry shake of his head.

'Maybe not, but it's a good idea all the same.' She heaved a sigh, knowing the topic of conversation was nothing more than a delaying tactic on her part. 'Let's get this over and done with, shall we?'

Alex took her hand and squeezed. 'If it's a short service we might still get back in time for a quickie.'

'Not everything has to be an opportunity to get naked,' she said, turning his earlier words back on him.

'Maybe not, but it's a good idea all the same.'

* * *

The walk to the church didn't take more than a few minutes. Thankfully, due to the location of the shop they were able to take a different route from the one they'd made together in January. When they reached the squat, sturdy stone church with its small clock tower there were one or two people standing around on the pavement. 'Here we go,' Alex murmured under his breath as he reached for her hand. 'Morning, Doc,' he said, approaching Malcolm Gadd, who had been the Point's doctor prior to his brother.

'Hello, Alex, hello, Ivy. How are you both?' He gave Ivy the merest ghost of a wink before touching the arm of his... girlfriend? Partner? Ivy wasn't sure what term people of Doc and Barbara's age used to define their relationship. 'Barbara, love, look who's here,' Doc said.

Barbara Mitchell, clad in a floral day dress with a powder-blue jacket over it and a matching hat, turned around and almost managed to hide her double-take when she saw Ivy. She covered her surprise with a beaming smile as she came over to kiss Ivy's cheek. 'Hello, darling. How's that dratted cat?'

'He's fine,' Ivy said, accepting the embrace with a smile. 'Shedding fur all over my bedding as we speak, no doubt.'

Barbara tsked and shook her head. 'I hope he's not making too much of a nuisance of himself. How are things between...?' She tilted her head towards Alex.

'Not much better, I'm afraid,' Ivy said, lowering her voice. 'Lucifer peed on a basket of Alex's washing last week.' Ivy pulled a face. 'Luckily it hadn't been in the machine, so I was able to get everything clean.'

'He's a bloody menace,' Alex grumbled. 'I wouldn't mind so much if it was men in general he was wary of, but he positively adores Nick and Jake. Won't stay away from either of them when they drop around.'

'Oh, he's just trying to show you who's boss,' Barbara said, giving Alex a sympathetic pat on the arm. 'He'll come around eventually.'

'If you say so.' Alex's tone said he rather doubted it.

'Right, then, shall we go on?' Barbara said, sliding her arm through Doc's. 'I want to get a seat on the aisle so I can properly enjoy the view.'

Ivy managed to turn her laugh into a cough. God love Barbara, at least she wasn't ever subtle about things.

On entering the church, it soon became apparent that Barbara had no need to worry about her view being blocked because other than their little group there were maybe ten other people scattered around the pews on the left-hand side, including Bev, Kitty and a couple of the other knitting-circle ladies. Ivy pretended not to see Bev's wide-eyed look of amazement as she returned Kitty's wave.

'Where do you want to sit?' Alex asked, drawing her attention away from the older women.

Ivy eyed the empty side of the church, which was traditionally reserved for the groom's family. Though her grandparents had passed, her dad had a few cousins still living in the Point. And he'd been working at the warehouse a long time, surely one or two of his mates would've taken the trouble to drive over to attend, even on a work day? Something didn't feel right at all. 'Somewhere here, I guess, but not too close to the front.' They were just sliding into the row, third from the front, when Reverend Steele came hurrying out of his little vestry, white cassock billowing. 'Ivy, hello. Can I have a quick word?'

'Um, okay,' Ivy agreed, exchanging a quick look with Alex before she followed the vicar back towards the vestry.

When they entered the small room, Ivy came face to face with Pete Bray, the landlord of The Sailor's Rest. Pete was looking distinctly uncomfortable in a neat navy-blue suit with a huge lily stuffed in the buttonhole. 'Hello, lovey,' he said. 'Can't say I was expecting to see you today.'

Appreciating his blunt honesty, Ivy gave him a rueful smile. 'Can't say I was expecting to be here, but there we are. At least it'll give Bev something to talk about.' They exchanged a knowing grin while the vicar pretended to look elsewhere. *Oops.* 'Where's Kevin?'

The vicar chafed his hands together, something akin to distress on his round face. 'That's rather the issue I wanted to talk to you about. We can't seem to get hold of him.'

A sick feeling of dread soured Ivy's stomach. 'You've checked the flat?'

Pete nodded, his expression grim. 'I just got back from there. We had a few drinks in the pub last night, not a stag do as such, just a couple of beers. I can't say I was all that keen when he asked me to stand up with him, but I didn't know how to refuse without being rude.' He gave Ivy an apologetic look, as though she might hold him being her father's best man against him.

'It was good of you to do it,' she reassured him. 'So, last night was the last time you saw him?'

Pete nodded again. 'I'd offered to meet him at the flat and walk up with him, but he said he'd make his own way. Wendy stayed with her folks last night. I guess she wanted to preserve that "not seeing the bride on the morning of the wedding" malarkey. Seems a bit bloody daft to me when they've been shacked up together all these years.'

'When there was no sign of your father, Peter tried calling him and he's just got back from checking the flat,' the vicar interjected, trying to keep the conversation on course. He lifted the flowing sleeve of his robes to check his watch. 'I do hope nothing untoward has happened.' He cast a worried look out of the door towards where the small congregation waited.

'Perhaps we should check outside?' Ivy suggested, though the queasy feeling in the pit of her stomach was growing worse by the second. 'With any luck we'll see him coming up the street.'

Alex rose as they approached and fell into step beside her. The four of them made an awkward procession up the aisle and Ivy did her best to keep her eyes focused straight ahead. The whispers and mutterings that had started grew louder as they passed the other guests.

Come on, Kevin, prove me wrong for once in your miserable life.

It was a vain thought because the street was deserted when they got outside. Holding Alex back, Ivy let the vicar and Pete get far enough ahead so she couldn't be overheard. 'Kevin hasn't shown up yet, and I've got a bad feeling.'

Alex steered her over to a shady spot beneath the clock tower and braced a hand on the wall beside her head as he stared down at her in concern. 'You think he's done a bunk, don't you?'

Ivy nodded. 'I'm afraid so.' She couldn't explain why she was so certain, other than from her own past experience. One minute her dad had been sitting in his usual spot at the kitchen table while they ate supper and chatted about her day at school, and the next morning he'd been gone. 'When he left Mum, it was like he'd vanished into thin air. It took us three days to track him down to Wendy's flat.' She shivered at the awful memory of those days when they'd feared the very worst. 'He'd packed up all his clothes without Mum noticing somehow – she always thought he'd come home early and hidden his case in the car. He waited until we were asleep and snuck out of the cottage.'

'What an absolute bastard.' Alex's voice was cold with a kind of rage she hadn't thought him capable of. He wasn't a saint, and she'd heard him rant and swear more than once during the refurbishment of the shop when something or other had gone wrong, but it was as if she were looking at a stranger.

Realising his anger came from some need to protect her, Ivy reached out and took his hands. 'It was a long time ago. A memory of an old hurt, nothing more,' she told him.

He released a shuddering breath and the flinty look eased from his eyes. 'I'd still like five minutes with him in a dark alley.'

She managed a small smile. 'He's not worth the bruised knuckles, or the trouble that would come with it. He can't touch me or my life any more, Alex. I won't let him. My decision to come today was for Wendy's sake, not for his. Kevin "can get in the sea" – that's what Mum said about him before Christmas.'

'Umm, Ivy?' Reverend Steele's slightly panicked call drew their attention towards a shiny black Jaguar saloon, the bonnet festooned with white ribbons, that was pulling up outside the church.

'Oh, bloody hell.' Until that moment she'd been too preoccupied with her father's absence and the old memories it had stirred up to think much about Wendy. She glanced up at Alex, in panic. 'What are we going to say to her?'

He put an arm around her shoulders and drew her against him. 'We're not going to say anything to her. Leave that up to the vicar. If Kevin's really done the dirty on her, then there's nothing you can say that's going to make it any better.'

She knew he was right, but still, it felt wrong to just stand there and watch as Wendy got out of the car, Wendy's father looking smart in a grey morning suit waiting on the pavement to take her arm. At Wendy's first shriek, Ivy turned her face into Alex's chest, not wanting to witness the terrible truth. 'Here's trouble,' he muttered into her hair before she felt him step away.

Turning to look, she saw him hurrying towards the open door of the church where one or two of the other guests had appeared. With the same calm tone of authority he'd used in the shop earlier, Alex shooed them back inside. Wendy was crying now, huge racking sobs that all but broke Ivy's heart to hear. Wishing she knew what to do for the best, she followed Alex back into the church and pushed the door shut behind her.

'What's going on?' Bev demanded, looking as though she was ready to push Alex out of the way.

'Sit down, Bev,' Kitty said, pulling on her arm. 'Please.'

Ivy wished the ground would open and swallow her up as she stared at the small cluster of people twisted around in their seats all looking at her. She could've been cuddled up with Alex in his nice big bed, but no, she'd felt the need to try and do the right thing and once again her bloody father had made a spectacle of her. 'We're not sure at the moment,' she said, trying to emulate the firm tone Alex had used. 'All I know is that Kevin isn't here.' A collective gasp rose, and she paused until everyone had settled down again. 'The vicar is talking to Wendy and her parents and letting them know. We—' she shot Bev a warning glance '—are going to wait in here and give her some privacy.'

Bev spun around in her seat to face Kitty. 'I told you there was something fishy going on. It didn't sit right the way they were rushing into things.'

Ivy walked away at that point because Bev was never going to change and she didn't have the strength to deal with it right then. She peeked out of the door and saw the car had disappeared, leaving the vicar and Pete huddled together on the pavement. Trusting Alex to hold the fort, Ivy let herself out and walked towards them. 'She's gone to the flat,' Reverend Steele said as soon as she was within earshot. 'Her parents tried to persuade her to go back to their house, but she was having none of it.'

'Kev better not be there, or she'll be up on a murder charge,' Pete muttered, scuffing his shoe on the pavement.

'You'd better go and say something,' she said to the vicar. 'I'm not sure Alex can keep them penned in much longer.'

'Oh yes, of course.' He hurried off towards the church, leaving Ivy alone with Pete.

'A right bloody mess,' he grumbled as he checked his watch.

'If you need to get off, Pete, just go.' She sighed. 'They'll all be in for a drink and a gossip, so you'd better brace yourself.'

'At least the bloody buffet will get eaten, I suppose.' He shook his head. 'I'm ever so sorry, lovey.'

'Not your fault, Pete. It's not anyone's fault but his.'

Ivy waited until he'd started trudging down the street before she whipped her phone out of her bag and dialled Sylvia Morgan's number.

'What a rotten bastard,' she said, echoing Ivy's own feelings after she'd blurted out the whole sorry tale. 'Right, well, I'd better get up there and see what's what. Andrew can look after things here.'

'Do you want me to meet you there?' Ivy asked, though it was the last thing she wanted to do.

'No, darling. Leave it with me for now. If you could give Nerissa a bell, she can give Tom the heads up. If Wendy was in as much of a state as you said, then it might be worth him popping to the flat in case she needs something to help calm her down.'

'Okay, I'll call her now.' Ivy sighed. 'Thank you, Sylvia. I didn't know who else to call.'

'I know I'm not your mum, darling, and I'd never try to replace her, but that's why Andrew and I are here. We think of you as one of our own so, of course, you should always call me when you need to.'

Ivy had to swallow around a huge lump in her throat. 'Thank you. I love you both.'

'We love you, too. Now you leave everything to me, and I'll message you an update once I find out what's going on.'

They were just saying goodbye when Alex appeared. 'Ready to go?' he asked.

Ivy shot a quick glance behind him at the rest of the guests exiting the church. 'Yes, let's get out of here.'

17

Alex made the decision to keep the shop closed for the rest of the day as they were walking home from church. Regardless of how well Ivy appeared to be coping, it was clear her father's behaviour had stirred up some bad feelings from the past. She would need a bit of time and space to process that. He also had a feeling that once word got out of Kevin's no-show there would be some who wouldn't be able to resist popping into the shop to try and get Ivy's reaction to it. If he could shield her from that for even the rest of the day, then it seemed a small price to pay. He told her his plan as he unlocked the front door. 'No one's going to be interested in buying anything, anyway, are they?'

Ivy tugged off her straw hat and ruffled a hand through her curls. 'You're probably right.'

The lack of push-back worried him because she'd been all fire and fury earlier when she'd thought he was making decisions on her behalf. This time, though, he knew he wasn't just trying to protect Ivy. He didn't think he had it in him to be polite if the likes of Bev came sniffing around. Better to lose half a quiet afternoon's takings than lose his customers altogether because he couldn't hold his temper with them.

'Why don't you go up and have a soak in the bath and I'll cash up for the day and make sure we're all prepped to reopen in the morning?'

'I can stay and give you a hand?' It was a listless offer, as though it had taken all of Ivy's strength to face everyone at the church and now she had nothing left to give.

He shook his head. 'It won't take me long. Come on, let's get you upstairs and into the tub.'

When they reached the top of the stairs Ivy turned into him, curling her arms around his waist. 'You're always taking care of me. It seems a bit unfair.'

Alex returned the hug. 'Life isn't always a perfect balance of give and take. You need to take a bit more at the moment, and I'm very happy to give you whatever it is you need. I'm sure there'll come a time when I'll need your support.'

She lifted her head to look at him. 'When you need me, I'll be here, I promise.' The wedge heels she was wearing put her mouth at just the perfect height for him to claim a kiss and he took full advantage, revelling in the way she always melted into him. He was tempted for a moment to forget the cashing up and just sweep her into his arms and carry her off to his bed for the rest of the afternoon, but he resisted. It might help her to forget everything else for a while, but all the muddled-up emotions she must be wrestling with would still be waiting for her to deal with. He'd not forgotten the terrible sight of her on the beach after her mother's funeral when she'd become too overwhelmed by a grief held back for too long. He never wanted to see her like that again, so he eased the intensity of the kiss until their heartbeats were something close to normal. When they finally broke apart there was a sparkle back in her eyes and a hint of colour on her pale cheeks. 'I'd better go and have my bath,' she said, giving him a dreamy smile that made him wish he'd got the plumbers to install a larger tub so he could slip into the warm water with her.

'And I'd better go and get changed and sort things out downstairs.'

Neither of them moved for a long moment and Alex felt something shift and settle inside him. He might not have been in the right headspace for something serious with her in the beginning, but he was getting closer to it every day. For all she thought she was taking too much at the moment, he knew she'd given him something far more precious. Being around her was helping to shape him into the man he wanted to be.

* * *

Alex took his time closing things up, putting stray books back on the right shelves, straightening the stuffed bears and other knick-knacks Ivy had dotted around the place, and giving all the surfaces a wipe down with the antibacterial spray they kept under the counter. As he climbed the stairs, the smell of frying meat and spices wafted down to greet him. Entering the kitchen, he found a barefoot Ivy standing at the cooker, stirring a big pot of something. She was dressed in a pair of those yoga pants she loved so much – these ones a delightful pink and white candy stripe that made her legs look like sticks of rock. When she turned to greet him, he saw she'd pinched one of his T-shirts to wear and he was surprised at the depth of possessiveness he felt towards her. He *liked* her in his clothes, as though she needed a physical connection to him even though he'd only been a shout away. 'I thought it was my turn to cook,' he said, for want of something to say that didn't betray his feelings too much.

'I felt so much better after my bath and I wanted to do a little something for you,' she said, giving him that sweet, shy smile of hers. 'It's beef bourguignon, if that's okay?'

His stomach gave a little rumble of appreciative anticipation and he patted it with a grin. 'Sounds fabulous. Is there anything I can do to help?'

She shook her head. 'No, I'm just about there. Another few minutes and I can shove it in the oven on low and we can forget about it for a couple of hours.' She turned back to the pot. 'Did you get everything sorted downstairs?'

'Yup.' Alex dropped into one of the kitchen chairs, content to watch her potter around while she finished up. 'And I don't think we have to worry about missing out on any customers. I didn't see a soul pass in all the time I was down there.'

Ivy placed a lid on the cast-iron pot and put it in the oven before she came and joined him at the table. 'Laurie called just before you came up. The café is buzzing, and Jake said there are so many people at the pub they're having to stand out on the pavement.'

Alex shook his head. 'Poor Wendy, she's never going to live it down, is she? Has anyone worked out exactly what happened?'

Ivy took his hand and squeezed it as her eyes grew shadowed. 'Kevin's gone. From what Sylvia told Laurie it's almost a carbon copy of when he walked out on me and Mum. He's locked Wendy out of his bank account. She used to do all their household stuff, apparently, but he's changed all his passwords.'

'Well, that can't be good,' Alex said, thinking about how much money Kevin had made from his share of the cottage sale.

'It gets worse.' Ivy heaved a sigh. 'Wendy managed to get hold of Kevin's supervisor at work and he was surprised to hear from her. He didn't think they were still together any more. Kevin's been seeing the woman who does the wages for the past couple of months. Word is they've gone on holiday together.'

'A couple of months? Jesus Christ, what a bastard!'

Ivy nodded. 'He must've already been seeing her when he proposed to Wendy. What kind of a monster does something like that?'

'The kind who needed to keep her sweet long enough to force you out of the cottage and pocket the cash from selling it. What a fucking coward.'

'I can't stop thinking about Wendy.' Ivy pressed a finger to the corner of her eye and Alex could see a tear glistening there. 'How could he do this to her?'

'You tried to warn her,' Alex pointed out as he tugged Ivy out of her chair and across into his lap so he could hold her.

'I didn't try hard enough.'

No. He would not let her shoulder responsibility for any of this. Placing a firm finger under her chin, he tilted her head up so he could look her in the eye. 'None of this is your fault, do you hear me?'

There was a long pause before she acquiesced with a reluctant nod. 'I know, but still I can't help worrying about the fact that he's a part of me. No matter how hard I try to pretend otherwise, he's still my father.'

'Genetically, perhaps, but he hasn't done anything to earn the title other than that. You are the woman your mother made you. The woman I—' he caught himself almost saying the woman I love and quickly changed it to '—am proud to call my best friend as well as the one I am lucky enough to have as my lover. You are sweet and generous and infinitely kind and caring. I watch you every day in the shop and I see how you are with people, how they always come away smiling after they've spent time with you even if it's just a few minutes. You are all that is good and right in this world, and I won't let you believe for one minute that you carry any taint of association from that man.'

Ivy cupped his face and kissed him. 'You should hire yourself out as a motivational coach.'

He gave her a frustrated squeeze because this was too serious a moment to brush off with a joke. 'I mean it.'

'I know you do, and thank you.' She kissed him again then rested her head against his chest, and they sat quietly for a moment. 'I still think I should try and do something for Wendy, though I've no idea what.'

Alex gave it some thought, because anything was better than dealing with the dawning realisation of just how much the woman in his arms had come to mean to him. 'You could ask her to lunch sometime, once the dust has settled a bit, I mean. Let people see the two of you out and about, present a united front and make it clear the only person who should be ashamed to show their face is Kevin.'

'She might not want to see me,' Ivy said, with a sigh. 'I probably wouldn't in her shoes, but I suppose I could give it a try. Maybe I'll rope in Sylvia and Laurie and a couple of others so it's not just the two of us.' She lifted her head to look up at him. 'What do you think?'

'I think you're wonderful.' It was as close as he dared get to speak the truth in his heart.

For now.

* * *

Alex was up early again the next morning. It had been a month since his conversation with his editor about cancelling the rest of his 'Heartbreak Kid' contract and his inbox remained ominously silent. He'd composed half a dozen ultra-casual, just-wanting-to-check-in emails and deleted them all. They could either accept his decision, or, what, sue him for breach of contract? It still wouldn't get them any more books, and he didn't think the publishers would want the negative publicity a conflict was bound to attract. All he could do was hope they came around and let the 'Kid' sink into eventual obscurity. Alex tried to pull himself out of the doom spiral of worry and focus on the precious bit of quiet and work on his other project. Yesterday's sunshine had given way to a band of low pressure, bringing leaden skies and a damp chill to the region. They'd had a grand total of three customers all morning, which didn't require both of them to be on the shop floor, so Ivy was out the back, the whir of her sewing machine filling the occasional silence when the ever-present radio had a quiet moment.

He stared at his hands hovering over the keys of his laptop and willed them to start moving but they remained resolutely still. His protagonist had finally cornered a pretty Russian thief who just happened to have a bob of shiny red curls and a set of very distracting curves. He'd tried telling himself he'd based the character on Scarlett Johansson's portrayal of the Black Widow in the hugely successful Marvel movie franchise, because he was a fan of the films. And he might even have started off picturing Natasha Romanoff as his inspiration for Irina, but somewhere along the way his description on the page had morphed into the face he woke up to most mornings. He was supposed to be writing a thriller, but if he carried on mooning like this he was in danger of veering off into something more akin to a romantic suspense. Ten minutes later, he was still trying to decide if Irina was going to kiss his hero or stab him when his mobile rang and he shoved his laptop aside with relief.

'Hello, Mum,' he said, pleasantly surprised as she didn't tend to call him during the week. 'Everything okay?'

'Hello, darling. I'm sorry to bother you when you're working but your father had an accident. I'm sitting in A & E at St Mary's and no one will tell me what's going on!' She sounded frantic, on the edge of tears, and Alex felt his world tilt on its axis.

'What happened? Are you okay?' The radio on his desk started blaring out some inane jingle and he yanked the power cord out of the back to shut the damn thing up.

'I'm fine. He was up on a ladder trimming back the wisteria because it's gone absolutely crazy this year and was blocking the light into the bedroom. I told him to get someone in to do it, but you know how stubborn he is.'

Alex did indeed know. He pictured the climbing plant that had adorned the back wall of his parents' home for as long as he could remember and he shuddered at the drop from the upper-floor windows to the ground below. It was mostly grass beneath, but if his father had fallen to the side then he might have landed on the edge of the patio. A sick churning started in his stomach. 'How badly is he hurt?'

'I don't know! They're not telling me anything,' she repeated. 'The ambulance crew said he's definitely broken his leg, but they strapped him to a backboard with this huge collar in case he'd done something else. He said he wasn't knocked out, but there's a nasty cut on the back of his head. What if he's done something awful to his brain?'

There was a shrill edge to her voice now, and Alex knew he couldn't leave her to deal with it on her own. 'I'm coming,' he said, cutting into her stream of panicked words. 'Right now.'

'But, no, you can't. What about the shop?' Philippa wailed.

'Ivy can handle it.' He was already out of his seat and heading into her workroom as he said it.

She looked up at the mention of her name, her foot going still on the pedal of her sewing machine. 'What's wrong?'

Alex put his hand over his phone. 'Dad's come off a ladder. I need to get up there.'

'Of course, you do. Let me go upstairs and throw some things in a bag for you.'

By the time he'd assured his mother he would call her back once he was in the car and on his way, Ivy had returned with a holdall with enough clean clothes for a week and his wash kit. 'I hate to leave you in the lurch like this,' Alex said.

'It's fine.' She put her arms around him. 'Promise me you'll drive safely.'

'I promise.' He held her tight for a few seconds as he tried to clear his head for the journey ahead. 'I'll give you a call when I get there. Speaking of which, I need to call Tom.'

Ivy took his phone from his hand and tucked it in his shirt pocket. 'I'll call him and let him know and you can speak to him when you've had an update from your mum.'

'Good idea.' Alex picked up the bag, looking around as he tried to remember if he had everything he needed. He spotted his laptop still open on the counter, wondered if he should take it with him then decided he probably wouldn't have time to even think about writing, and everything else he needed to do could be done with his phone. 'Will you shut my laptop down for me?' He gave her his password when she agreed and had to laugh as she began shooing him towards the back door.

'Just go, will you? I'll handle everything here.'

'You're the best,' he said, grabbing one last quick kiss before he turned his attention to the drive ahead of him.

It took him several attempts to get hold of his mum, because every time he instructed the hands-free to dial her number he got the engaged tone. Deciding she was probably doing a ring around he concentrated on negotiating the winding back roads that would take him away from the Point and onto the motorway. Twenty minutes later he was just clearing the slipway when his phone rang.

It was Tom on the other end. 'I've just spoken to the A & E

doctor that admitted Pop,' he said by way of introduction. 'I was on the phone with Mimi when the doctor came to see her and she just shoved the phone into his hand.' Tom laughed, which immediately made Alex feel better. 'Pop's gone into surgery for his leg. It's a clean break so should be okay. They're a bit worried about the bump on his head but there's no sign of a bleed on the X-ray and he was coherent all the time.'

'Oh, thank god,' Alex said, the icy grip of fear that had settled around his heart melting a little. 'We can't lose him.'

'No,' Tom said, in a flat, serious voice. 'We can't.' A sigh gusted in Alex's ear. 'What the bloody hell was he doing up a ladder in the first place, stupid fool?'

'Being Pop.' They laughed, but there was an edge of grimness to it. 'We need to have a chat with him when he's recovered a bit. The house is going to be too much for them to manage in a few years, especially if he carries on doing jobs he shouldn't.'

'He's going to hate that.'

It was true, but that didn't mean it wasn't going to happen anyway. 'Mum was already making noises about relocating to the Point. If we make a concerted effort maybe we can persuade him to think about it.'

'I know the kids would love to see more of them again,' Tom agreed.

'So get Max on the case. I'm all for a bit of emotional blackmail if it makes Pop see sense.'

'I've already suggested to Mimi that they come here while Pop recuperates. He'll run her ragged otherwise, and we've got plenty of space downstairs. I'll get Andrew and the lads over and we can move the stuff out of the spare room into the dining room. There's a downstairs toilet and a shower in the surgery. He'll have more freedom to move around rather than being stuck upstairs at home.'

Thank god for Tom and his ever-practical brain. 'That's a great idea. I'll talk him into it, persuade him it's for Mum's sake rather than his.'

'And I'll set the kids to work on him while he's here.' Tom laughed. 'Poor Pop isn't going to know what's hit him. Give me a call when you get to the hospital, okay? And don't worry about Ivy or the shop, Linda's already on her way over there to see if she needs a hand. She's been rattling around the place since she got back from her cruise, so she was more than glad to be able to feel useful. You know how much she enjoyed herself when she stepped in so Ivy could sort the cottage out. If the business stretches to it, you might have a part-time assistant on your hands. Don't worry about rushing back, we'll see to everything this end.'

'Cheers, Tommy, I knew I could rely on you.' With a plan of action agreed, Alex began to breathe easier.

'Always. Call me when you get there, yeah?'

18

The break in Archie's leg was a bit more complicated to deal with than the doctors had anticipated so they were keeping him in hospital for a few days. Though she missed having Alex around, especially in the evenings, Ivy had been inundated with offers of help so she'd told him to stay there and take care of his mum until he could bring both of them back to the Point. The staff at the hospital had supported their plan for Archie to recuperate at Tom's and Alex said he'd capitulated with a surprising lack of argument.

'Maybe he gave himself more of a fright than he's willing to admit,' Ivy said when she talked to Alex on his second night at his parents' house.

'Maybe. He certainly scared Mum half to death. She's ready to sell up and move them into a bungalow tomorrow.' He sighed. 'I just hope he hasn't done any lasting damage to his mobility. If he can't get back out on the golf course, he'll be unbearable.'

'Let's look on the bright side until we know otherwise, hey?' Ivy knew all too well what it was like to always expect the worst, and even when her mum had been in remission, she'd had to fight not to wrap her up in cotton wool. 'We'll all make sure he does his rehab exercises and he'll be back on his feet in no time.' She crossed her fingers while she said it, but she did it out of sight of the screen so Alex wouldn't notice.

'How's things at the shop?' he asked, obviously ready to change the subject.

'All good. Linda's been in every day between ten and two so I'm able to have a break for lunch. She's coming in all day on Saturday and Jake said he'll pop in for a bit as well in case I need a hand shifting stock around. Word's got around that you are away because Kitty and Barbara dropped in this afternoon to make sure I didn't need anything.' They'd ended up staying for an hour and by the time they'd gone they were full of plans for starting a book club.

'Any word on Wendy?'

Ivy shook her head. 'She's taken a couple of weeks off from her job at the grocer's. She had them booked anyway because they were supposed to be going to Spain on honeymoon. She's staying with her parents, according to Barbara – and she'd be the one to know,' she added wryly.

'The knitting-circle mafia strikes again,' Alex said with a laugh. 'I don't blame Wendy for keeping her head down.'

'Me neither. I know the address so I'll pop a note through the door in the next couple of days and let her know I'd be happy to meet up when she feels up to it.'

'And what's your plan for the rest of the evening?'

'I'm having an early night with the other man in my life,' Ivy teased.

'That bloody cat. Tell him not to get used to having you around because when I get home I'm keeping you all to myself for at least a week.' He settled back against the pillows with a sigh. 'I can't sleep without you, Ivy. I even miss you sticking your cold feet on me in the middle of the night, what's that all about?'

She'd been missing him too and had taken to sleeping in one of his T-shirts as well as cuddling up to the pillow she'd taken off his bed because it held faint traces of his aftershave, and that other scent that was quintessentially Alex. 'Do you know when you'll be back?'

He shook his head. 'Not before the middle of next week, I don't think.'

'Okay.' She tried to keep the disappointment out of her voice. 'Well, don't worry about a thing here. I'll hold the fort until you're home.'

'Thanks, sweetheart. Knowing I have you to come home to makes all the difference in the world.'

When the front door opened the next morning, Ivy looked up wondering why Linda was back already. It had been so quiet, she'd decided to take a walk around to Laurie's café and pick them up a treat for lunch. 'Did you forget your purse...oh, sorry,' she said to a blonde woman she didn't recognise. 'I thought you were someone else.'

'Is Alex here?' the woman asked as she began prowling around the shop. And *prowling* was the exact word that immediately came to mind to describe the way the woman was scanning the place as though searching for something, or someone perhaps, given her question.

Ivy got up from behind the counter and moved to intercept the woman, who was making a beeline towards the back of the shop. 'He's away for a few days. Is there something I can help you with?'

The woman all but sneered as she eyed Ivy up and down. 'I hardly think so.'

Ivy clenched her fist so she wouldn't smooth a hand over the front of the painter's smock she was wearing over a pair of old jeans. She'd been working on an old chest of drawers out in the yard and was dressed for that, rather than looking like something off the catwalk as this stranger did. 'I'll leave you to browse, then,' Ivy said stiffly, taking up post behind what was usually Alex's counter as it was nearest to the back of the shop. That way she'd be able to keep a close eye on this unwelcome visitor.

The woman headed over to the nearest set of bookshelves, but there was something about her manner that gave Ivy the impression she was watching her out of the corner of her eye rather than browsing for something to read. Ivy took a stack of receipts from beneath the counter and pretended to check them, though she'd already been through them the day before when she'd reconciled the till. An uncomfortable silence settled between them as the woman moved to the next set of shelves and scanned the titles. 'Do you know when he'll be back?'

Ivy stiffened. Who was she, and what did she want with Alex? 'I'm afraid not. You can leave a message with me if you like, and I'll make sure he gets it.'

The woman laughed, a brittle snap of noise that made Ivy want to wince. 'Oh, I've got a message for him all right, but I don't need you to pass it on. He'll find out for himself soon enough.'

Okay, she'd had just about enough of this cryptic bullshit. 'Are you going to buy something or just hang around making a nuisance of yourself?'

The woman raised a snooty eyebrow at her. 'Well, your customer service leaves a lot to be desired, I must say. I'll be sure to add it to my Trustpilot review.' The woman drew a book from the shelf and carried it over to the counter. 'I'll take this.' She tossed a copy of *The Marriage Roller Coaster* in front of Ivy.

She'd heard of it, of course. It had been one of those smash-hit bestsellers that featured in all the magazines. She hadn't been interested in reading it herself, but there'd been a lot of speculation about who the anonymous author was. Ivy eyed the overdressed woman in front of her. Up close, Ivy could see how heavy her make-up was, almost mask-like, and it made her own foundation-free skin itch at the thought of it. Come to think of it, she didn't strike Ivy as a reader of angsty male heartache either, but there was no accounting for other people's taste. She rang up the sale, accepted the ten-pound note the woman offered and turned back to the till.

'Oh, you can keep the change,' the woman said. 'And you can keep the book, too.'

Confused, Ivy turned back to her, still clutching the money between thumb and forefinger. 'I'm sorry?'

'I've no doubt you will be when you find out just what kind of man you've got yourself mixed up with.' The woman took what looked like a notepad out of her bag, placed it on top of the book and pushed them both towards Ivy. 'I learned the hard way. Do yourself a favour and have a read and then maybe you'll be able to get out before it's too late.'

'Who the hell are you?' Ivy said, with a horrible feeling of dread.

'Jo.' The woman's red lips stretched in a terrible imitation of a smile. 'Ah, I can see you know who I am. Well, there's two sides to every story, as dear, darling Alex is about to find out.' She patted the book once more then spun on her perfectly spiked heel and walked out, all but banging into Linda, who was just coming in carrying a couple of takeaway cups in a cardboard tray and a large paper bag in her other hand.

'Well, excuse me,' Linda huffed at Jo's departing back before turning to Ivy with a shake of her head. 'Who on earth was that?'

'That,' Ivy said, with a growing sense of dismay, 'was trouble.'

* * *

As soon as she could get away from Linda, Ivy escaped into the back yard saying she needed to finish the chest of drawers. Closing the door behind her, she settled onto the bench she'd placed in the corner that was a perfect suntrap on lovely days like today. Drawing out the book Jo had given her from the big pocket in the front of her smock, Ivy stared at it for a long moment. Not quite sure what was going on, she opened the cover and started to read. Within the first couple of pages she knew what she was holding and the sick feeling in her stomach grew. She recognised the voice speaking to her from the page, though there was a hardness to the humour, an edge to the tone she didn't like. Alex had written this, she was sure of it.

Time stood still as she lost herself in the terrible disaster of a marriage gone horribly wrong, the author making no attempt to hide his contempt for the woman he'd claimed to be madly in love with in the opening few chapters. It was an uncomfortable read, as if she'd picked up someone's diary and was prying into the darkest heart of them, but she couldn't bring herself to put it down. It was ugly and painful, and the narrator was so unlike the Alex she knew and cared about, she struggled to reconcile her doubts with the phrases that jumped out her. Those were Alex's words, but it was a twisted version, as if she'd gone through the looking glass and stumbled across the mirror opposite of *her* Alex. Remembering the notebook Jo had given her, she took it out and began to leaf through. The writing was unmistakably his as she scanned over several pages of notes of ideas about social media and how to get back into the dating game. The word 'game' made her feel slightly sick.

Ivy had to abandon her reading when Linda called for her assistance and was then kept busy for the rest of the day. She tried not to think about the book, but it lurked in the back of her mind all afternoon, like a malignant toad slowly poisoning her thoughts until she couldn't stand it any longer. With half an hour to go until closing, Ivy said goodbye to her last customer of the day and locked the door behind them, flipping the sign to closed and walking off the shop floor without even bothering to turn out the lights. She retrieved the book from where she'd left it at the bottom of the stairs and carried it straight off to her room, where she crawled under the covers and picked up where she'd left off.

She lost track of time and her eyes were burning by the time she finally tossed it aside. She'd read the book from cover to cover, gone back over several of the worst chapters and still didn't know what to think. Her phone rang, and she saw Alex's name come up on the display. She ignored it because she had no idea what to say to him. Her eyes strayed to the deepening light beyond her window and she wondered what time it was. Surprised to see it was past 8 p.m., Ivy rose and closed the curtains. Her mouth was dry, her head aching from too much reading and a lack of food. Dragging herself towards the kitchen, she flicked on the kettle and shoved a couple of slices of bread into the toaster and tried to make sense of the last few hours.

When she couldn't remember locking the shop door, she hurried down to check. Relief flooded her as she saw that, not only was it locked, but she'd remembered to slide the top and bottom bolts in place. She was on her way to check the back door when she spotted Alex's laptop sitting on the counter where he'd left it. It had locked itself by the time she'd thought to check on it so she'd decided not to touch it. She stared at it now, recalling the times she'd seen Alex pecking away at it, the way he'd always shut the lid when she'd asked him how his writing was going. A spy novel, that was what he'd told her he was working on, but what had Jo said? '*I learned the hard way.*'

Feeling sick for snooping, Ivy still couldn't stop herself from waking up the laptop and inputting the password Alex had given her. The screen opened on a Word document, which must've been what Alex had been working on when his mum had called about Archie's accident. *What was she doing?* Ivy slammed the lid down on the laptop and spun away. She couldn't invade Alex's privacy like this. She needed a cup of tea and a decent night's sleep and then she would talk to him about it in the morning. There had to be a reasonable explanation for everything; she'd just let Jo spook her.

She made it halfway up the stairs before turning around.

With a shaking hand, she opened the laptop lid and stared at the handful of lines showing at the top of the page. Red curls. Pale skin. Eyes the colour of a spring morning. Covering her mouth with one hand to block a sob, she slammed the laptop closed and fled back upstairs to her room.

Lucifer jumped up on the bed and she was vaguely aware of him licking her hand, but she didn't move to stroke him. She felt numb, as if her body didn't belong to her. Her stomach rumbled at some point, but she ignored that too. Eventually, she dropped off to sleep still wearing her paint-spattered smock and jeans and, though she'd lain there for hours, she was still no nearer to finding an answer to the question that was churning around in her brain like a demented hamster on a wheel.

What if all this really was just a game to him?

19

Alex woke the next morning and immediately reached for his phone. He'd tried to call Ivy several times but there'd been no answer. A wave of relief washed over him as he saw the WhatsApp notification on his front screen.

Sorry, I fell asleep early and missed your calls.

He was just about to ring her when his mum knocked on his door. 'Are you up?'

'Yes, come in.' It was weird being back in his old bedroom, though it looked nothing like it had when he'd been living at home, his mother having long ago got rid of his posters and sports trophies and repainted the walls a tasteful shade of mocha.

Philippa came in already dressed, carrying a steaming mug of coffee. She looked better than she had when he'd first arrived, but there were still very dark shadows beneath her eyes. 'I brought you a coffee,' she said.

'I can see that.' When she didn't smile at his attempt at teasing,

Alex sat up straighter and patted the edge of his bed, inviting her to sit down. 'What's the matter?'

His mother placed his coffee on the coaster – because, of course, there was a coaster – on the cabinet and took a seat. 'Oh, nothing, really. I'm just not sure we're going to be able to persuade your father about the move. He's too settled here, and we've got so many friends we'd be leaving behind.'

'It sounds like he's not the only one who might not want to move,' Alex said gently, reaching to take her hand. 'I thought it was what you wanted.'

She smiled. 'Oh, it is. I miss you all, especially the children. If we don't take the chance to spend quality time with them now they'll be off and away on their own adventures.'

'So what is it, then?'

She patted the back of his hand. 'I'm just not ready to think about us being old, I suppose.'

'You're not old, Mum,' Alex protested. 'And Pop's not exactly in his dotage.' There was something of an age gap between them, but nothing Alex had ever noticed growing up as his father had always been such a fit and active person, even if he'd had a few years on his friends' fathers.

'I shouldn't be saying this to you, but his fall really shook me up.' When she looked up at him, tears shimmered on her lashes. 'I can't be without him, Alex. He's my everything.'

'Oh, Mum, don't,' Alex said, drawing her into his arms. 'Pop has got years and years left in him yet. Don't think about moving to the Point as giving up, think about it as a new chapter.' He pulled back to look at her. 'But if you're not ready to make the move, then don't let me and Tom railroad you into anything. From a purely selfish point of view, I'd love to have all of you as close as possible, the same way the Morgans all live on top of each other.'

She nodded. 'And I'd like that too. Especially in a few years' time when I hope you'll give me lots of grandbabies to dote on.'

Alex laughed. 'Don't get ahead of yourself, Mother.' As ready as he was to make a permanent commitment to Ivy, there was way too much he wanted to do with her before they even got to thinking about babies. At least now his mum was smiling again.

They were on their way out of the door to visit Pop when Alex's mobile rang. Seeing it was his editor, Alex sent his mother on ahead to the car and closed the front door so he'd have some privacy. 'Hi, Immy. I've been hoping to hear from you, but I have to say I didn't expect you to be calling on a Saturday. Is everything okay?

'Have you seen *The Sun* today?' she said, dispensing with any pleasantries.

'I haven't seen the news at all.' And that tabloid had never been his particular paper of choice. 'I'm just on the way to visit my father in hospital. He had an accident a few days ago.'

'Oh, I'm sorry to hear that.' Immy's sharp tone softened. 'Is he all right?'

'A bit banged up and feeling sorry for himself, but he'll make a good recovery. What's going on? This is clearly about more than my contract.'

'It appears your ex-wife has blown your cover.'

'I'm sorry? What does that mean?'

Immy sighed. 'You need to get hold of a copy of the paper. She's sold an exposé to them claiming to have the real story of *The Marriage Roller Coaster*.'

Alex sat on the bottom of the stairs with a thud, not quite comprehending what he was hearing. 'But how could she possibly know it was me? I've never told anyone other than Tom and my parents. How the hell did she work it out?'

'I have no idea. We've done our best to keep your identity confidential at our end, it's just my close team and the contracts department who know. And royalties, of course, but none of them would know who your ex-wife is or have any reason to contact her. Look, I'm sorry to ask given how things are with your father, but is there any way you can get into the office for a meeting today? This is blowing up on social media and we need to get a handle on things. Fast.'

'I'm already in Richmond, actually. I need to get Mum over to the hospital to see Dad, and then I can get a train in.' Alex scrubbed at his forehead as he tried to make sense of it all. 'How bad is it?'

'It's pretty bad, Alex. We've already locked 'The Heartbreak Kid' Twitter account, but that doesn't help much given the number of followers it already has. Your alter-ego is trending, and not in a good way.'

'Shit.'

'Exactly. Look, I'll call down a pass for you at Reception. Get here as soon as you can, and we'll work on something from this end.' She gave him a grim laugh. 'Well, I suppose there's one silver lining: you won't have to worry about the other two books on your contract now.'

Alex was ushered into a boardroom by Immy's assistant, who immediately disappeared to fetch him a coffee. Though they were dressed in an array of casual jeans and T-shirts that spoke of inter-rupted weekend plans, their grim expressions were all business. The only people Alex recognised were Immy and a woman from the marketing team whose name had completely escaped him for the moment. The man sitting closest to him rose and offered his hand, introducing himself as Danny.

'I'm part of the company PR team,' he said, giving Alex a sympathetic pat on the back as he steered him towards an empty chair. 'Don't worry, it could be a lot worse.'

Tossing a crumpled copy of *The Sun* on the table, Alex slumped into the seat. 'I'm not sure how. Jo's done a right hatchet job on me.'

Danny picked up a pen and began to tap it on the table in a way Alex immediately found irritating. 'You didn't run over a dog while drink-driving, or get caught shagging under-age schoolgirls, or shagging a dog—'

'Yes, thank you, Danny,' Immy said, cutting him off. 'How's your dad?' she asked Alex.

'I didn't get a chance to find out. He was stable last night, so hopefully he's fine. Mum's going to text me an update when she can.'

'Well, if you need to speak to her at any time, then that has to be your priority.'

Alex acknowledged the comment with an appreciative nod. 'Where do things stand?'

Immy sighed. 'Twitter is a hot mess, but that's to be expected. Fingers crossed, it'll blow itself out as quickly as it started. The masses never have much attention span for these things.'

'There's a heavy-weight boxing fight tonight. Sports always trend so that'll knock you down the list a bit. And with any luck someone far more famous will do something far more embarrassing before the end of the day,' Danny chipped in. 'We just need to put out a statement and hope it dies down.'

'I think we need to do a bit more than that,' the marketing woman – *Lindsey!* – said. 'Some of the conversations are veering into dangerous territory so we need to demonstrate we are listening to the concerns women are expressing as part of the discussion.'

Alex didn't like the sound of that at all. '*What* are they saying?' He scrambled for the phone in his pocket.

'Don't,' Lindsey said. 'There's a lot of hyperbole and people drawing the wrong conclusion because they've not read beyond a salacious headline.'

Alex glanced down at the paper. Next to a photo of Jo that was all wide-eyed vulnerability, the banner across the front page screamed:

Heartbreak Kid Made My Life a Living Hell!

He wondered who'd styled her, because the lack of make-up and the baggy jumper wasn't her thing at all. 'They don't think I hurt Jo, do they?' She hadn't accused him of anything like that, just a load of guff about neglecting her and forcing her to look elsewhere for her emotional needs to be met, but if, as Lindsey was suggesting, people weren't looking past the headline then god only knew what they were speculating.

'There's one or two trolls saying stuff like that, but mostly it's about emotional abuse.' Lindsey, at least, had the good grace to wince as she said it.

'Jesus.' Feeling as if he'd been punched in the gut, Alex could only stare helplessly at Immy. 'It was nothing like that. You know that. We can release the original draft to show them how far the book veered away from the truth.'

'I think that's a very bad idea,' Danny put in. 'Wouldn't do to make it look like we punched the story up for sensationalist reasons.' Even if that was exactly what they'd done.

'Enough,' Immy said, folding her hands in front of her. 'I've spoken to the department head and drawn up a plan. Subject to your approval, of course, Alex,' she added, almost as an afterthought.

'I'm sure you know better than me. What have you come up with?'

* * *

By 2 p.m., a statement had been issued refuting the article and pointing out that both the publisher and Alex had been at pains to protect his identity – and in doing so had protected Jo's. A personal paragraph had been added by Alex stating that he regretted the difficult ending of his marriage and that, although it had been the original source of inspiration, the characters and incidents in *The Marriage Roller Coaster* were fictional. Though it stuck in his throat to do so, Alex had extended an apology to Jo for any hurt caused to her and he wished her only happiness for the future. The statement concluded with a commitment to donate all profits to date, and any ongoing from the sale of the title, to Relate and other charities that provided assistance to couples experiencing marital difficulties. Contact numbers and website addresses for support were listed at the end.

'So what should I do now?' Alex asked as Immy walked him towards the elevators.

'Nothing. Concentrate on your dad's recovery. You might get a bit of press interest and it's up to you whether you speak to them or not, but I'd strongly advise against it. You can refer any enquiries to the statement already made and, if they persist, give them Danny's details. I know he comes off a bit brash, but he's very good at his job. He gets paid to deal with this sort of thing so let him get on with it.'

'I don't plan on speaking to anyone about it.' Other than Ivy. He had to get out of there and try and reach her. Was it too much to hope she'd not seen the paper yet? Though he'd never seen her reading *The Sun*, there was a newsagent's on the seafront so there was no way the story hadn't got halfway round the Point and back again. Bev, or one of the other gossipmongers, would've no doubt made a point of carrying the bad news to Ivy as soon as possible. He offered his hand to Immy. 'I can't tell you how sorry I am that things ended this way.'

Taking his hand, she shook it then drew him in for a quick hug. 'I'm sorry too. I hope you find what you're looking for, Alex, and if you ever decide to write something else then you have my details. Just make sure it's a proper work of fiction next time, okay?'

He managed a laugh. 'You can count on it.'

Exiting onto the busy street, he allowed the crowd to carry him along until he found a quiet side road where he could escape the hustle and bustle of central London. Ducking into the doorway of what looked like a delivery access for one of the shops, Alex retrieved his phone and immediately dialled Ivy's number. It rang and rang before eventually switching to voicemail. 'It's me,' he said with a sinking feeling in his gut. 'We need to talk.'

After a dozen different messages, all variations on the same theme, Alex called his brother.

'I can't get hold of Ivy,' he blurted as soon as Tom picked up.

'I'm not surprised she's not answering the phone,' Tom said, sounding bone-tired. 'She couldn't open the shop because a local reporter was waiting on the doorstep this morning. Nick managed to sneak her out through the back, and she's holed up at Laurie and Jake's place at the farm.'

'Shit.' That possibility had never even occurred to him. 'How the hell did they find out where I live?'

'Same way they found out we're related, because the bloody phone at the surgery hasn't stopped ringing. Just as well it's a Saturday, and we only had the men's health clinic scheduled because after that reporter got bored hanging round outside the bookshop, he tried to get into the surgery to interview me. Luckily it was only a local stringer chancing their arm and Jake came down and saw him off. Malcolm moved the clinic to the back room at the pub to be on the safe side, though.' Tom gave a rueful laugh. 'Which will probably double the numbers who show up.'

'Damn it. I need to get back.' Alex banged the back of his head none too gently against the wall behind him as he remembered why he was in London in the first place. 'I spoke to Mum earlier and they're not letting Dad out until Tuesday. I can't leave her to deal with that.'

'Stay until then, and you can bring them both down with you,' Tom suggested. 'There's nothing you can do here and with any luck the reporter will get bored and give up.'

'I don't understand what the hell is happening, Tommy,' Alex said. 'Why would Jo do this?'

'Spite? Jealousy? Bit of both, probably,' Tom suggested. 'What I don't understand is why she's crawled out of the woodwork now. When was the last time you even bloody spoke to her?'

'Not since before Christmas.' Alex recalled how he'd come home after his meeting with Immy to find a rather drunk Jo on his doorstep. *Oh.* 'Damn.'

'What is it?'

Alex sighed. 'She tried to get back with me.'

'She did what?' Tom's voice rose a couple of octaves on the last word.

'I didn't take it seriously. She was half-cut and feeling sorry for herself. It was all a bit embarrassing really. She knocked over a bottle of wine then sent my bags flying. I'd done some Christmas shopping after a meeting with my editor in Soho. Remember that hoodie I bought for Emily, the one with the star on it?'

'She loves it. Nerissa has to practically pry it off her to get it in the wash. Why?'

'Jo made some bitchy remark about it. I think she thought I'd bought it for a new girlfriend or something. Anyway, she scattered half the stuff out of my bags and then was screwing everything up trying to stuff it back...' If he'd been a cartoon character a light bulb would've appeared above his head. 'That's how she found out.'

'Found out what? Stop talking in riddles and half-sentences,' Tom grumbled.

'I've been racking my brain trying to work out how Jo put the pieces together and worked out I was behind 'The Heartbreak Kid'. After my meeting with Immy and buying all those presents I stopped in a pub near the Tube for a drink. I made a load of notes about ideas we'd discussed for the next book and I did some research online at the same time.' He closed his eyes as the memory of getting up from the table ran through his brain. 'I stuffed my notebook into the top of one of the shopping bags and that's the last time I can remember seeing it.'

'You think Jo took it?' Tom sounded sceptical.

'She certainly had the opportunity. I was trying to keep her out of the house so I was pretty distracted. She could've easily shoved it in her pocket when my back was turned.' An image of Jo patting the front of her coat just before he'd managed to finally turf her out flashed back to him. 'I'm almost positive that's what she did. It's the only thing that makes sense.'

'I didn't want to mention it earlier, when you've got enough on your plate, but I think Jo might have shown up here looking for you yesterday,' Tom said, sounding weary.

'Are you serious?' Alex dropped his head back against the wall, feeling as if he was living in some kind of nightmare. 'She didn't go to the shop, did she?'

'I'm afraid so,' Tom said heavily, confirming his worst fears. 'I haven't spoken to Ivy directly, but Linda said she was upset about something yesterday. She also mentioned a customer she didn't recognise who almost knocked Linda flying, and the description sounded an awful lot like Jo. I didn't put two and two together at the time, but, if she's really out to cause you this much trouble, it makes sense she'd want to see your reaction first hand.'

Alex pushed away from the wall and started walking, his feet carrying him towards the nearby Underground station without conscious volition. 'I need to talk to her, find out what the hell she's playing at!' And find out what on earth she'd said to Ivy. He'd seen Jo at her very worst and she didn't pull her punches.

'No!' Tom's voice was as stern and sharp as he'd ever heard it. 'You DO NOT go anywhere near her, do you understand me?'

'But I can't just let her get away with this!' Alex protested. 'She's trying to ruin my reputation and what if she's the reason Ivy won't answer any of my messages? God only knows what she might have said to her!'

'You need to stop and think for a minute instead of jumping feet first into things. That's what got you into this mess in the first place.'

'How is any of this *my* fault?' Alex protested.

'Oh, come off it,' Tom scoffed. 'If you hadn't thrown yourself the world's biggest pity party and written that self-indulgent piece of crap in the first place, none of this would've happened.'

'I was in a bad way! I'd just lost my wife!' The moment the words left his mouth Alex regretted them. Look who he was speaking to. Tom had lost his wife to cancer less than a year before Alex's marriage had blown up. His world had been devastated in the worst way possible and he'd just shouldered it and got on with things. 'Tom—'

'It's fine.' Tom sighed. 'Look, Ally. There's nothing to be gained from speaking to Jo, not when you're this upset. What if she takes whatever you say to her and runs straight back to the press with it? All that would do is fan the flames and drag this out even longer. She's obviously done all this just to get a reaction from you. Don't give her the satisfaction.'

That stopped Alex in his tracks just a few feet from the stairs leading down into the Underground station. Shit. He was right. 'I hate it when you're right,' Alex grumbled.

'I know you do,' Tom replied without an ounce of sympathy. 'Focus on Dad and Mimi and leave Ivy to us. Tuesday night will be soon enough to sort everything out between you two.'

'I hope so.' Even as Alex said it, he thought about the dozens of unanswered messages and wondered if perhaps it was already too late. Maybe Jo had won the final battle before Alex had even known they were still at war.

20

'It's only me!' Ivy heard Laurie call out as she let herself into the cottage. 'Ivy?'

'In here,' Ivy replied, forcing herself to get up from the corner of the sofa where she'd been huddled for most of the day.

'Oh, you poor thing.' Laurie pulled her into a fierce hug. 'What a horrible bloody day. I haven't stopped for a minute, because, of course, the whole village is having a field day over this. Just as well you've stayed out of the way. How's Alex? Have you spoken to him?'

'After what he's done?' Ivy retorted, stepping away from Laurie and slumping back onto the sofa. 'Why would I?'

Laurie frowned. 'Because he's had his name splashed all over the paper by that horrid ex-wife of his, for one. And then there's the small matter of him being your boyfriend to consider. He's probably beside himself with worry over everything, as well as trying to sort out his parents.'

A faint flash of guilt stole over Ivy, but she shoved it away. 'He lied to me.'

'About what?' Laurie perched on the opposite arm of the sofa, her head cocked to the side as she gave Ivy a funny look. 'You knew about him and Jo, right?'

'He told me about their break-up, yes, but he didn't tell me he'd published some tawdry account of it.' She grabbed the copy of Alex's book from the coffee table and tossed it towards Laurie. 'Read it, and then you'll see the kind of person you're feeling so sorry for.'

Laurie pushed the copy of the book onto the floor and kicked it away. 'I don't want to read it, and neither should you. It's a load of old nonsense anyway, he said as much in the statement he released via his publisher.' Sliding from the arm onto the cushion beside Ivy, Laurie took her hand and held it. 'You know Alex, he'd never do anything to hurt anyone. Not intentionally.'

'You don't understand!' Ivy burst out. 'It's not just Jo he's betrayed. He's been writing about me!' The tears she'd been holding off all day flooded her eyes and spilled down over her cheeks. 'He's been using me, Laurie. All this time I thought we had something special going and he's been using me as fodder for his next book.' Not wanting to talk about it any more, Ivy muttered an excuse about needing a shower and all but fled from the room.

By the time Ivy had calmed down enough to emerge from the bathroom, she knew she owed Laurie an apology for lashing out. Raised voices from the kitchen stopped Ivy in her tracks. Jake must've come home while she was in the shower. She couldn't catch what they were saying but there was a sharp edge to Jake's voice that had her creeping closer to listen.

'I know she's your friend, but Alex is *my* friend, and I don't believe for a minute that he'd do something like that. Hell, you've seen the way they look at each other! They're madly in love whatever they might say about taking things slow. Why on earth would he risk everything over a bloody book?'

Madly in love? Ivy thought with an exasperated huff. Jake had no idea what he was talking about.

'I know, I know,' Laurie said in a placating tone. 'But she swears she's seen evidence of it with her own eyes. And if he's so madly in love with her, why wouldn't he tell Ivy about writing a bestseller? She said there was a copy of his book on the shelf in the shop and he never so much as breathed a word to her about it.'

'Maybe if she talked to him, she could ask him.' Jake's tone was acid. 'Poor bloke was beside himself when I spoke to him just now. He can't get back until Tuesday night because Archie's still in the hospital, and Ivy's ignoring his messages. I promised I'd get her to ring him. Where is she?'

Ivy scuttled away from the door and made it into the guest bedroom before she heard Jake calling her name.

'Leave her alone!' she heard Laurie tell him just before a knock sounded on the door.

Ivy ignored it. When Jake spoke, his voice was much quieter than it had been in the kitchen. 'Just talk to him, Ivy. Let him know you're okay.'

Ivy bit her lip to stifle another round of tears. How could she when she wasn't okay? First Alex had lied and now her best friend was fighting with her boyfriend because of it. Ivy sank down on the bed, wondering what the hell she was going to do. She couldn't stay here and cause a rift in Laurie and Jake's relationship and she couldn't go back to the flat. It was too late to do anything about it now, but first thing on Monday morning she was going to have to find herself somewhere to live. It wouldn't be easy with the holiday season about to start, but she had to try.

* * *

Sunday was awful. Ivy stayed in her room as much as possible, only coming out to eat. Jake didn't speak beyond the odd grunt of agreement during Laurie's painful attempts to smooth things over and keep a conversation going. She hadn't mentioned Alex's name, but there was no mistaking the gentle reproof in her eyes whenever she'd looked at Ivy. Unable to face another stilted meal, Ivy snuck out just before sunrise on Monday morning. Hiding away wasn't doing any good, and she couldn't leave the shop closed another day. It was the only security she had, though god only knew how she would find a way to forgive Alex enough to carry on working with him.

A chill hung in the air and the grass to either side of the path that led down from the top of the Point to the village below was heavy with dew. Though the sun was barely a pale streak on the horizon, the dawn chorus was in full swing. Chirps and trills seemed to come from every tree and bush she passed, and she wanted to tell them to shut up because they sounded so cheerful. By the time she'd made it to the seafront, the sky had shifted from deep-grey to a fiery river of oranges, reds and pinks and was now softening to a misty blue that would deepen as the early morning haze burnt off. There was already some activity in the parade of shops along the seafront. The newsagent was rolling up his shutter and she could see a van parked outside the greengrocer's being unloaded. As she drew level, Wendy stepped out of the grocer's doorway dressed in a baggy jumper and a pair of jeans. Her face was pale and unmade, the heavy dye in her hair faded to show several inches of lighter brown roots.

They stopped and stared at each other. Ivy was about to open her mouth when Wendy spoke. 'I got your note.'

Ivy had dropped her a little card saying she hoped everything was okay and suggesting they get together sometime for a coffee.

She'd meant to follow it up with a proper invitation, but hadn't got around to it. 'How's things?'

Wendy laughed. 'Shouldn't I be the one asking you that?'

Ivy scrubbed a hand over her tired face. 'You've heard, then?'

'Come on, this is the Point we're talking about.' She had, well, a point. 'I suppose I should thank you for taking the heat off me for a bit.' Wendy sighed. 'Sorry, that was meant to be a joke but my sense of humour is a bit off at the moment.'

'You haven't had a lot to laugh about,' Ivy conceded. 'Have you heard from him?'

Wendy's features hardened. 'Not a bloody peep.' She scowled at Ivy. 'I know, I know – I should've listened to you.'

Ivy held her hands up. 'That thought didn't even cross my mind. What's done is done. I just wanted to make sure you were all right.'

Wendy shrugged. 'I'll survive.' She narrowed her eyes as though just noticing the direction Ivy had come from. 'I thought I heard you'd moved in above the bookshop.'

'I had. Looks like I'll have to find somewhere else to stay.'

Wendy looked confused. 'Over a bit of fuss in the papers? It'll die down in a day or two and people will forget all about it. I don't know him, as such, but Alex strikes me as a good sort. If he's anything like that brother of his, then he's a treasure. You want to hang onto someone like that. Take it from me, a good man is hard to find.'

'And what if he's not a good man? What if he's a liar and fraud?'

'Then I'd say you'd been unlucky enough to find a bloke just like that bloody father of yours.' Wendy cocked her head. 'You're not serious, are you?'

Ivy thought about what Jake had said the previous evening, then shook it off. 'I don't know the full story yet, but I know enough that I can't trust him.'

'Well, if that's the way of it, then I'm very sorry.' Wendy glanced behind her towards the interior of the shop. 'Look, I've got to get on and finish unloading the van, but if that offer of a coffee stands, maybe I can take you up on it sometime?'

'I'd like that.' With the way things were going, Ivy was going to need all the friends she could get, even if they came from the most unlikely of places. 'Give me a few days to sort things out and I'll call you, okay?'

'I'm not going anywhere,' Wendy said with that cynical laugh Ivy was beginning to realise the other woman used as a shield. 'Take care of yourself, now, Ivy.'

'You too.'

Ivy had made it maybe half a dozen paces away before Wendy called her name. When she turned it was to see the other woman standing next to the van with a thoughtful expression on her face. 'Is it that you can't trust him, or are you just looking for an excuse not to trust him? Not all men are cut from the same cloth as your father, you know?'

21

Though he'd half expected it, it was still a blow to Alex to find both the shop and the flat empty when he finally got back to the Point the following evening. His father's release from the hospital had been delayed by a mix-up with the paperwork so by the time they got on the road it was after lunch, meaning they hit the rush-hour traffic around Bristol and crawled for hours. Archie had become increasingly grumpy as his discomfort grew and by the time Alex had deposited him and his mother in Tom's capable hands he'd been ready to scream, or drive his car up to the Point and straight over the end of it. Only the thought of Ivy had kept him going, and the sight of what he'd come to think of as their home in darkness had almost pushed him to tears.

Entering the kitchen, he tossed his keys on the table and picked up the note lying in the middle of it.

I've cashed up and left everything in the safe. I have an appointment to look at a room tomorrow so I'll be in late. Linda is available to come in if you need her.

I

Alex slumped in the nearest chair and buried his face in his hands. What the hell had he done?

A knock echoed from downstairs, and Alex was out of his chair and bounding down the steps two at a time. 'Did you forget your keys?' he said, fumbling with the lock because he'd forgotten to flip on the lights in his haste to answer it. 'I'm so sor—'

'—oh, it's you.' Alex grumbled.

'What kind of a greeting is that?' Nick asked, shoving a four-pack of beer at him.

'I thought you were... someone else.' Alex trailed off.

'She's up at our place, again,' Jake said from behind Nick. 'Come on, let us in, the food's getting cold.'

Alex stood back and the pair trooped past him, Jake clutching two large pizza boxes. 'You didn't have to come,' he said, grateful down to the tips of his toes that they had.

'Like we'd leave you to wallow alone, you moron.' Nick punched him lightly in the arm. 'Come on, let's crack those beers and you can tell us what the fuck's been going on.'

They'd drunk the beers Nick had brought with him and several more from Alex's stash in the fridge and only a couple of crusts remained in the grease-stained boxes by the time Alex had caught them up on everything. He told them all about Jo and her affair, about why he'd written the book and how the publisher had encouraged him to exaggerate what had happened.

'"The Heartbreak Bloody Kid", I still can't believe it,' Nick said, shaking his head. 'If I'd written a bestseller, you can be sure it's the first thing I told people about me, not the last.'

Alex gave him a wonky smile; he hadn't meant to, but his mouth didn't seem to be working quite right. As a result he enunciated his next words with care. 'If you want to tell people you wrote it, be my guest because I don't want anything to do with it.' He eyed his beer and decided he'd had more than enough so set it down half drunk on the coffee table. 'I'm not that guy, any more, you know? I didn't want people to know about it and judge me for my past. I just want to move forward with my future.' He slumped back in his chair. What future? Without Ivy, what was the point of any of this? Everything he'd told himself about moving to the Point to be part of a community was only half the truth. He'd done it because he wanted to be a part of *her* community. Part of *her* life.

A rustle of sound came from near the door and the next minute, Lucifer had jumped onto Alex's lap and settled down with his head resting on Alex's arm. 'Well, I never thought I'd see the bloody day,' Nick muttered. 'I thought that cat hated your guts.'

'So did I,' Alex replied, reaching out a tentative hand to stroke the big black cat between the ears. When Lucifer started to purr, Alex sighed and slumped deeper into his seat. If even Lucifer was feeling sorry for him, things were pretty bloody dire.

'What I don't understand,' Jake said, with just a hint of a slur in his voice, 'is why Ivy thinks you've been writing about her.'

Alex bolted upright, almost spilling Lucifer off his lap. The cat gave him a half-hearted swipe with his claws before sprawling across his legs once more. 'What the hell are you talking about?' Alex demanded. 'I've never written a word about Ivy.'

Jake shrugged. 'I'm only telling you what she told Laurie. Says she's seen it with her own eyes.'

Alex tried to get his beer-soaked brain to function. How could she have seen something when he'd never written about her? Oh hell. 'Irina!' he all but shouted, startling Lucifer, who bristled and jumped down off his lap.

'Who the hell's Irina?' Nick asked with a confused frown. 'I thought your ex was called Jo.'

Frustrated at his friend's lack of understanding, Alex rolled his eyes. 'Irina's a Russian spy,' he said, stating the obvious.

Jake sat forward in his seat. 'Perhaps you need to start from the beginning. And use very small words because I think I'm a bit drunk.'

* * *

Alex woke the next morning to the insistent beeping of his alarm and a small army of elves jack-hammering the inside of his skull. As he tried to think his way past his hangover he became aware of a heavy weight on his arm and forced his head off the pillow. Lucifer was curled up beside him, pinning Alex's arm down with his heavy body. 'I think I liked it better when we weren't friends,' Alex grumbled as he pulled his arm free.

After a shower and a very strong coffee, he was feeling human enough to steel himself into opening Ivy's bedroom door to retrieve Lucifer's food and water bowls. The scent of her perfume lingered, and it was all he could do not to throw himself on the bed and bury his face into her pillow. Pitiful. Having retrieved the cat's dishes, he closed the door behind him and carried them into the kitchen, where he caught Lucifer trying to lick up the dregs of his coffee. 'Get off the damn table,' he ordered the cat, who to both their surprise, actually did what he was told for a change.

With the cat fed and watered and his dirty mug swapped for a fresh one, Alex carried his coffee downstairs and went through the process of opening the shop for the day. He'd wanted to call Ivy last night as soon as he'd realised why she was so mad at him, but Nick and Jake had talked him out of it. Given how bad his head was even after a couple of paracetamol, it was just as well. He'd have to wait until she came in later and they could talk face to face.

The shop was quiet, and his headache had receded enough that

Alex could've worked on his novel, but he didn't have the heart. He was seriously considering jacking in the whole writing malarkey because, honestly, it was nothing but trouble. Bored and restless, Alex glanced at the front door, willing it to open.

Nothing. Not even a passer-by on the street he could accost. Looked as if his only company was the radio. With a sigh he retrieved a feather duster from under his counter and started running it over the books on the shelves.

'And now,' said the familiar voice of one of the local DJs, 'we have a very special dedication for one of our friends over at Mermaid Tales and Treasures. Alex, this one's for you.'

As the opening bars of 'This Year's Love' by David Gray began to play, the front door opened and Ivy was there. She looked pale, and a little red-eyed, but she was smiling that same sweet smile that never failed to lift his heart. She took a couple of steps inside and held out her hand to him. 'Dance with me?'

Swallowing the lump in his throat, Alex dropped the feather duster and gathered her in his arms. Where she belonged. Where she would always belong. 'I'm sorry,' he whispered against her hair.

'Shh, just dance with me,' she said, smoothing her hands up and down his back as they swayed together.

The song ended, but they remained locked together. 'Jake told me about Irina,' Ivy said into his chest. 'I'm sorry I jumped to the worst possible conclusion.'

'I should've told you,' Alex replied, pressing kiss after kiss against her cheek, her temple, her hair. 'I wanted you to know me as I am now, not who I was back then.'

Ivy tilted her head back so she could meet his gaze. 'I know you, Alex. It wasn't you I had doubts about, it was myself. I was looking for a reason for us to fail. Waiting for you to let me down because that's what Kevin taught me to expect.'

'I'm not him, Ivy. I'm nothing like him, I can promise you that.

And you're not your mum, or Wendy, or any other woman you've watched have their heart broken.'

She nodded but he could see a tear glistening on her lashes. 'I'm scared.'

He tightened his arms around her. 'Me too. But I want to try.' Brushing the tear from her lashes, he bent to kiss her. 'I love you.'

'I love you too,' she said, more tears spilling though she was smiling that sweet, sweet smile. 'And I don't just want to try, I want to succeed. I've written your name on my to-do list and you know how much of a completionist I am.'

Alex grinned. 'Is there anything else on your to-do list?'

'Lots of things.' The way she said it made his head spin and his body tighten. 'But,' she continued, her smile morphing into a cheeky grin, 'unfortunately for you, none of them involve me wearing my red wellies.'

ACKNOWLEDGMENTS

Welcome back to Mermaids Point!

Here we are again! I'm so pleased with how much the Mermaids Point stories have resonated with readers. I hope you enjoy Alex and Ivy's story just as much.

Thanks as always to my wonderful editor, Sarah Ritherdon, who always has my back x.

Thanks to Sue Smith (Copy Editor) and Camilla Lloyd (Proof Reader) for catching my mistakes. Apologies to Sue for the hot mess I got into with my timeline and for your help in untangling it!

To the entire Boldwood team who are the ones who make sure this book finds its way into your hands (or on your e-reader, or into your ears via your favourite audio app!) – thank you.

I'm hugely grateful to Alice Moore for yet another gorgeous cover.

#TeamBoldwood! You are the best and I adore working with you all x.

Shout out to the wonderful members of the Heidi Swain and Friends Facebook group. Thank you, Heidi for your generous welcome to all the authors who are part of the group. And a special mention must go to Fiona Jenkins and Sue Baker who are an absolute dream team when it comes to organising release day celebrations x.

Special mention to Marie Harris for coming up with the name Lucifer for the cat, it's perfect! Thanks also to Victoria Davies who won a competition to name the bookshop. I took a slight liberty with her suggestion, but I loved the gentle pun of a mermaid tail/tale.

And finally, very special thanks to a group of very special friends – Jules Wake, Bella Osborne, Rachel Griffiths, Phillipa Ashley. I love you all xx.

MORE FROM SARAH BENNETT

We hope you enjoyed reading *Love Bloom at Mermaids Point*. If you did, please leave a review.

If you'd like to gift a copy, this book is also available as an ebook, digital audio download and audiobook CD.

Sign up to Sarah Bennett's mailing list for news, competitions and updates on future books.

https://bit.ly/SarahBennettNewsletter

Summer Kisses at Mermaids Point, another warm, escapist, feel-good story from Sarah Bennett, is available now.

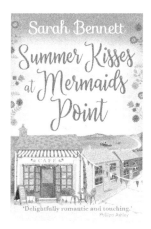

ABOUT THE AUTHOR

Sarah Bennett is the bestselling author of several romantic fiction trilogies including those set in *Butterfly Cove* and *Lavender Bay*. Born and raised in a military family she is happily married to her own Officer and when not reading or writing enjoys sailing the high seas.

Visit Sarah's website: https://sarahbennettauthor.wordpress.com/

Follow Sarah on social media:

- facebook.com/SarahBennettAuthor
- twitter.com/Sarahlou_writes
- bookbub.com/authors/sarah-bennett-b4a48ebb-a5c3-4c39-b59a-09aa9Idc7cfa
- instagram.com/sarahlbennettauthor

ABOUT BOLDWOOD BOOKS

Boldwood Books is a fiction publishing company seeking out the best stories from around the world.

Find out more at www.boldwoodbooks.com

Sign up to the Book and Tonic newsletter for news, offers and competitions from Boldwood Books!

http://www.bit.ly/bookandtonic

We'd love to hear from you, follow us on social media:

facebook.com/BookandTonic

twitter.com/BoldwoodBooks

instagram.com/BookandTonic

Printed in Great Britain
by Amazon